Bodies On the Bridge

by

Richard Albion

Bodies On the Bridge

Cover Art by *Diana Carlile*

The Wild Rose Press, Inc.
PO Box 708
Adams Basin, NY 14410-0708
Visit us at www.thewildrosepress.com

Publishing History
First Edition, 2023
Trade Paperback ISBN 978-1-5092-4455-3
Digital ISBN 978-1-5092-4456-0

Published in the United States of America

"Mas, that's no way to treat a client," McCarrigan said.

"You aren't a client and probably won't be."

"Please, hear me out. It's Tara, I think she's in trouble. She's received strange e-mails, and her office was bugged."

"Call the police department."

"Mas, they're useless with this stuff, and you know it."

The fact that I hadn't hung up on him attracted Sophie's attention. She looked up with a questioning expression on her face.

Covering the mouthpiece, I mouthed "McCarrigan." Then I said, "I am putting you on speaker so Sophie can hear me decline your business."

"Please, hear me out. I'd like to retain you. I really think she's in trouble."

Something in his voice made me pause, not fear, more like concern. Coming from him about another person…that wasn't what I expected…

"…Tara and I are in a relationship, which for obvious business reasons, we want to keep confidential."

"Why us?" I asked, "You don't like us anymore than we like you."

He laughed out loud, a laugh without any humor in it. "True Mas, but I know you get results. More importantly, I know you can keep a confidence."

Sophie shrugged. "Okay, we will meet you on the proviso you tell us everything you know. Then we'll tell you if we're interested. When can you come to our office?"

Dedication

To the Mistress of all, she knows who she is.

Frances, Editor Extraordinaire. Still working on making me a better writer

Diana Carlile. Cover illustrator maestro

Chapter One

I was beat. We'd had a late night, and my first impression was the alarm blaring off like a siren I didn't want to hear. Then sounds of the new day percolated like the scent of coffee, and I suspected Sophie was already up making breakfast. The fragrance of brewing coffee confirmed my suspicions, but what I needed was a wake-up shower. The cold water quickly brought me round and to instant life. While I was under the cold deluge, a cup appeared on the vanity. The aroma of coffee wafted around the room as I dried off and inhaled.

Before I had time to enjoy the perfect moment, Sophie, half-dressed with her coffee in hand, called me with a note of urgency in her voice. "Quick, get in here."

The local news channel signaled, "Breaking News." My attention turned into focus, and I followed the report as best I could.

"The bodies of two men, as yet unidentified, have been found on the Golden Gate Bridge. The police are treating it as a homicide. Reports indicate the bodies have been mutilated making identification difficult. Police are withholding details until further investigations are completed. The bodies were found attached by their necks to a post on the San Francisco side of the bridge. There is speculation that it is gang

1

related, but no confirmation. Authorities are playing this down as they don't want to give out misleading information. We will be following this story closely and bring you any updates as we have them. This is Gina Chang for KQEG news handing you back to the studio."

Great way to start the day—a grisly murder. Not that San Francisco didn't have its share of them. The way the bodies were displayed so publicly made me think the perpetrator was sending a message. We didn't usually have that level of gang warfare in SF. *Not my problem* was my first response. Not my job anymore.

Sophie looked over to me, waiting. "Drugs, gangs, or…?"

"I don't know. This one's guaranteed to be a mess. It's going to be a publicity nightmare for whoever's desks these files land on."

"Kenzo?"

"Different district. Did I tell you Kenzo got promoted to lieutenant?"

Sophie nodded approvingly. "Well deserved. Assisting us with the Bay murders put his career on the line."

"What's for breakfast?"

"Coffee and something healthy for a change." She laughed and left me thinking about the consequences of the gruesome public display. It was a message to someone.

Breakfast came and went, and we made our way to the private investigation office of Hammett-Chandler and associates. That sounded pretty good, although the only associate was Marie the office manager. She had been there for us when we needed her, and due to the large finders-fee coming our way, Sophie and I agreed Marie should become a partner in the company, as much as a reward for her loyalty as for tax reasons, a long story.

With a fresh coffee, I settled in to check e-mail when Marie called out, "Mas, it's McCarrigan for you."

"The McCarrigan?"

"Yes."

"What does he want?" We had a history with McCarrigan, and not a particularly cordial one. Which is why I was surprised at his call.

"Take the call. I'm sure he'll tell you." So much for respect from the "associate." We couldn't function without her as the office manager and, soon to be, third partner.

"Put him through." The line went live. "McCarrigan, what do you want?"

"Mas, that's no way to treat a client."

"You aren't a client and probably won't be."

"Please hear me out. It's Tara, I think she's in trouble. She's received strange e-mails, and her office was bugged."

"Call the police department."

"They're useless with this stuff, and you know it."

The fact that I hadn't hung up on him attracted Sophie's attention. She looked up with a questioning expression on her face. Covering the mouthpiece, I mouthed "McCarrigan" and said, "I am putting you on speaker so Sophie can hear me decline your business."

"Please, hear me out. I'd like to retain you. I really think she's in trouble."

Something in his voice made me pause, not fear, more like concern. Coming from him, about another person…that wasn't what I expected.

Sophie blurted out, "He's fucking her."

I looked at Sophie in surprise and heard McCarrigan say, "Not very subtle or polite way of describing it. Tara and I are in a relationship, which for obvious business reasons, we want to keep confidential."

"Why us?" I asked, "You don't like us anymore than we like you."

He laughed out loud, a laugh without any humor in it. "True Mas, but I know you get results. More importantly, I know you can keep a confidence."

Sophie shrugged. "Okay, we will meet you on the proviso you tell us everything you know. Then we'll tell you if we're interested. When can you come to our office?"

"I prefer to meet on neutral territory. How about the Ferry Building, Blue Bottle coffee…my treat, in an hour?"

I looked at Sophie and she nodded. "Ok. We'll see you in an hour." I added, "Don't be late."

"Thank you, I appreciate it, and I'll pay whatever your rate is."

"We haven't agreed to take you as a client, and yes you will." I hung up.

"Did you hear the relief in his voice?" Sophie asked. "He's concerned. It's not like him to get rattled like that. He must believe it's serious."

"I'm more surprised he actually cares about someone, other than himself. She must really be good in bed."

"Mas don't be an asshole. We know she enjoys sex from the dildo episodes."

"Did they ever find the bugs you put in her home?"

"No. They never checked her home because they didn't know we'd been there."

"Are the bugs still live?"

"Probably. I could most likely still get into her computer as well," Sophie said. "I haven't checked since we eliminated her and McCarrigan from involvement in my sister's murder—" Her voice caught at that comment. The loss was still raw.

"Let's see what McCarrigan has to say."

The call from McCarrigan brought back memories, unpleasant memories about how Sophie and I met. It had been a case of serial killings. One victim was her sister. The media dubbed the whole thing "The Bodies in the Bay" killings. We solved it and got justice for all the victims...but it didn't bring them back. Getting some closure for all the families was the best ending we could have hoped for.

A taste of acid rose in my mouth. For some reason, I had a strong suspicion we were going to get pulled into something we shouldn't go near. Still, this was just a meeting. We could walk away.

Chapter Two

Sophie and I left in plenty of time to meet with McCarrigan. We were quiet with our own thoughts. It had only been a few months since we buried her sister, and only a little longer since I'd buried my former partner, who'd been killed in a hit and run. So, we both suffered with recent grief, and struggled with it day by day. Anyone who says "it's life, move on, get over it" hasn't got a fucking clue. Grief is pain, and it continues to hurt even when you deal with it the best you can. It doesn't get easier-it gets different, and we each deal with it in our own way. With me it helped that I had fallen in love with Sophie. Despite that she was my client and my number one big "no-no," it happened anyway. With all that followed, we found each other and leaned on each other, and that helped deepen our relationship.

The Ferry Building is a microcosm of San Francisco's eclectic population, and I love it. The bustle of people using the Ferry's and the farmers market and shops. As we approached the café, I saw McCarrigan arrive from the other entrance, he gestured in acknowledgement. No niceties, no handshakes, just nods, and we waited in line to place out orders.

Blue Bottle coffee always takes time, each drip cup is prepared individually. McCarrigan paid and we waited silently, the three of us in a triad.

Savoring the aroma of the brew, it was almost as good as Blue Mountain coffee…almost, but still worth the wait. We walked as one to the exit and stood together, Alcatraz Island in the background. McCarrigan looked pensive. I said,

"It's your meeting. You start"

McCarrigan looked at both of us and back again, asking, "If you don't take us on as clients, what I am about to say will remain confidential, yes?"

Together, we said, "You have our word, we'll say nothing."

He looked relieved. "I'm not sure where to start."

Before he could continue Sophie asked, "What triggered you?"

"Not sure, just a feeling something wasn't right. At first, I thought it was something I'd said, or done to upset Tara. I'm not very good at this relationship thing. To be honest I'm surprised it's lasted as long as it has."

I said, "Stick to the point."

"Right, about two, maybe three weeks ago. Tara seemed a bit off, not fully there, I thought it was me. When I asked her, she brushed it off saying it was work. You've seen her. She's professional, and very good at what she does. Anyway, she was still out of sorts last weekend, and I pushed. She admitted she thought she was being followed and had received a couple of odd e-mails, plus her office had been bugged."

Sophie asked, "Odd how? Who sent them and what did they say?"

"I don't know. She said she deleted them. The feeling of being followed started about the same time as the first e-mail arrived."

My turn. "Have you noticed anything unusual when you are with her?"

"No, to be honest I concentrate on her, I've never felt like this about anyone before." This was the mean and nasty McCarrigan, who in business dealings would crush you and not think anything of it, being vulnerable. One for the books.

Pressing him I asked, "Well since then, have you noticed anyone out of place?"

"No, not really."

I pressed, "What do you mean 'not really'?"

"We were out to dinner, a business dinner with some potential investors. I thought I had seen someone in the restaurant before, but couldn't place him, then realized I had bumped into him in the elevator in Tara's building. He was tall for an Asian man otherwise I wouldn't have noticed him. A coincidence, I thought. Eventually, Tara came clean with me after I insisted something was up."

Sophie and I looked at each other. Neither of us believed in coincidence, Maybe we should look into this.

"Tara said she had received a couple of odd e-mails." McCarrigan continued, "They were from someone she knew years ago. He mentioned some new business, he shouldn't know about."

Sophie asked, "Did they mention specific people or companies?

"I don't know. You'd have to speak to Tara about that."

My turn, "How come you are contacting us and not her?

"Tara was rather emphatic about not speaking to

you ever again after you bugged her office. She doesn't know I'm talking to you, yet. I wanted to feel you out first. Will you assist?"

I looked at Sophie, she nodded and said, "We will look at this. Only after we all meet and agree on the terms. Tara has to know what's going on. We'll need her cooperation."

McCarrigan was quiet before saying, "Okay, let me get her on board. I think this is more significant than she is letting on. She's kinda blown it off with me, but I'm sure she's concerned. The last sweep of her office came up with four listening devices."

Sophie promptly asked, "Did you keep them?

"No, the man who found them showed them to Tara, and she told him to get rid of them. Was that wrong?"

"Yes, you can tell a lot from the type of device used" I asked, "Can recover at least one of them?"

"That will all have to come from Tara."

Concluding the meeting, I said, "If, Tara agrees to us investigating the issue on her behalf, we will sign contracts with both of you. That makes you our clients, which covers confidentiality, our rates, scope, and anything else we agree to include."

"Fair enough, expect my call sooner than later."

We parted company. Sophie and I hopped a tram up to Fisherman's wharf and had lunch at the Boudin bakery, a tourist trap, but still the best sourdough bread in the city. We kept our own council until we were seated where no one could overhear us.

Sophie asked, "What do you think?"

"McCarrigan is no fool, or easily put off. Something has him worried, and if he's worried, I would be too."

"My thought exactly. I'll check on the bugs we left in her place. They should still be active. You never know. We may pick up information that will be helpful. I'll review her computer. Deleted e-mails leave trails. Grabbing them back shouldn't be too difficult, unless she is really good."

"Before we sign contracts?"

"Hell yes, if we know what we are getting into, we have the choice of not taking them on as clients."

We enjoyed the lunch and made our leisurely way back to the office. Losing the coin toss, I was to break the news to Marie. We would be listening to a lot of boring digital recordings of Tara Zosa's home adventures. Imagining Marie's response made me smile. Sophie would be concentrating on Tara's computer and e-mail accounts.

Marie's response to the task was as expected. "Are you fucking kidding me? It's going to be boring business crap, or her doing herself with a vibrator. Neither of which is any fun."

Sophie said, "No, but it may give us a reason to take or not take her on as client. McCarrigan thinks she is being stalked and wants to protect her."

"Why didn't you say so?" Marie bridled and said, "Give me the details and the dates, I'll start listening. Nothing on my desk that can't wait a day or two."

God bless Marie. When she got her teeth into something, whatever it was got done and done well. Sophie set Marie up on a separate laptop and accessed the remote recording bank for the bugs in Tara's home. Input the date parameters and left her to the tedious job of listening to a lot of not much. Marie and I would switch off every hour, so neither of us became completely unhinged. Sophie began digging into Tara's computer.

Sitting waiting for my turn on the listening chore, I began to think about McCarrigan and his ask. If he was in a relationship with Tara, maybe it was about him and not Tara. He would be a more logical target. Possibly someone was using Tara to access him. Hopefully, we would get something useful before we met with McCarrigan and Tara. Time passed quickly, and it was my turn on the headset. I asked, "Marie, anything interesting."

"Nothing relevant, but she sure does like her sex toys. Definitely turn down the volume when the vibrator's going. A couple of calls. I assume it's McCarrigan. Certainly, a male from the way she talks. That's it."

Sitting at my desk, the laptop in front of me, headphones on, I settled in where Marie left off. People think being a Private Investigator is all excitement, guns drawn, and car chases like on TV. Ninety percent of the time it's tedious, boring work, which hopefully pays off down the line.

Marie was right. It was boring. The time stamps were all early morning or evenings. The morning calls were mostly confirming that day's calendar, the evening calls were personal, and I agreed with Marie, they were to a male, and it was probably McCarrigan.

She was also right about the volume when Tara indulged in sex toy, play time. The sounds and my imagination played havoc with my groin. My cock engorged, filling the chastity cage I wore, since I'd asked Sophie's alter ego, Ms. Circe to be my key holder. After we met, it had taken a while before I recognized Sophie as a BDSM Dominant, and that recognition aroused a history I'd suppressed too long. Taking a chance, I embraced my submissive side, and now she was my partner in business and life. Mixing business and pleasure could, and should, have been a mistake. In this instance, it worked out for both of us. For all the shitty stuff that had happened to us, we were making good progress together. By the end of the day, I'd come up with nothing useful. We would be digging in again tomorrow.

****

In the morning, it was back to the boring stuff. Thankfully, there were only three weeks of it to trudge through. Concentrated listening is tiring and more difficult than people realize, draining in fact. The hour over, I handed it back to Marie. She was on the phone and gave me the thumbs up, she would get back on the chore after the call. I needed to cleanse my ears and lose the erection.

Wearing a chastity device is physically not an issue. Between the ears is a different matter. It's where the trouble starts. The pleasure and frustration of not being able to touch your own penis, or more importantly being able do anything about it, not knowing when you would get a release, and of what nature it would be? I loved it. It was my mental release…a catharsis if you will.

When I was a police department inspector, it was my way of dealing with pressure and stress. Resistance to falling into the usual traps of gambling, drugs, excessive alcohol, or screwing around required a release valve. Mine was giving up control, being someone else's responsibility for a while. It kept me sane, got me in trouble, and saved my ass. It was also the cause of my resignation from the only job I ever wanted, a San Francisco Police Inspector. Later, becoming a private investigator was merely a substitution for my former career. I came to terms with my decision because I was doing well enough to be able to pick and choose my clients.

Sophie interrupted my train of thought, "Mas, I still have access to Tara's digital life. She is pretty thorough with her protocols and keeps everything cleaner than most. I'm resurrecting the deleted e-mails, but it's taking longer than I expected due to the volume. Should have them by the end of the day. Anything on the listening front?"

"Nothing so far," I said. "We have only done an hour each so far. Calls to a male, probably McCarrigan. Usual day to day stuff, and of course, her own entertainment. Which is disconcerting."

Sophie looked directly at my groin and grinned, reaching inside her silk shirt she pulled out a gold chain with a key attached. She twirled it. "Wondering when this particular key will be used?"

Shit this is what I mean, the pleasure of frustration and not knowing. This was exciting, wonderful, and terrible, all at once. "Of course. However, this is all business...for now." Deflecting, I asked, "When is your target practice?"

She caught me and laughed. "That's called changing the subject. Maybe we can discuss your issue tonight. Practice is tomorrow, usual time and place."

When we became partners, I insisted she get trained in self-defense and become familiar with firearms. She resisted at first, saying she was the tech side of the partnership, and she was…is, but I wanted her to at least survive an altercation. Competency with a firearm would increase her chances of survival. You never knew when it would be needed. Hopefully never—but it's better to know how and not need it, than need it and not know how.

Sophie's weapons lessons were given by a San Francisco police officer who was also a member of the BDSM community, who went by the moniker of *Big Boots*. He always wore his uniform knee-high motorcycle boots. His first assessment confirmed what I suspected about Sophie—she was not a natural, but worked hard, listened, and was always in control. His comment about her control made me laugh. Sophie always wanted to be in control.

She tried various pistols and settled on a CZ sub compact. Big Boots put her through her paces, and after several months of regular practice, he said he'd be comfortable with her having his back. That was praise indeed. The self-defense classes were run at the Shotokan Karate Dojo, where Lt. Kenzo trained and taught. Although, he didn't teach the street survival, self-defense class.

****

Marie reported in. Nada for us, so we switched again. Sophie still buried her computer screens, Marie to whatever she'd been doing, and I clamped on the head set to listen to more of the same. Feeling myself start to drift off, I rubbed my eyes. Sophie looked up, and then straight back to her screen.

Later, I'd picked up nothing at all useful. Damn it. We decided to get out of the office for lunch. It was a break we all needed. We walked to the local sandwich shop, sat at the back booth, and discussed the current case while we ate. Sophie would write up the tech side about how the fraud was committed. I'd do the overview and the make suggestions on improving procedures going forward with the recommendation of getting the Feds and local police involved. With the information and evidence we were providing, they'd have no trouble bringing criminal charges against a former employee and her partner, a current employee. Marie would do the financials, billing etc., and put the whole package together. Great teamwork.

After lunch, it was Marie's turn to listen. She'd only been on for a few minutes when she shouted, "Jackpot! Guys listen to this. Two males invading her place. They are speaking Chinese."

Sophie and I both went over to Marie's desk. Sophie took the timeline back and replayed it for us. All three of us were silent and intent on listening to the sounds coming out of the speaker. Sounds of the door opening and closing, footsteps on the hardwood floor, then nothing as they walked on the carpeted area of the living room.

One spoke, definitely a man—definitely not Japanese. I knew enough to recognize that. Certainly, an Asian language, probably Chinese.

Marie asked Sophie, "Would you make me a copy to take home? If Chung can't translate it, I am sure his parents will be able to, depending on the dialect."

I asked, "He's not travelling?"

"Not this week." Marie snickered saying, "We are having some fun until he travels again."

I wasn't going to ask what that entailed, but after

Marie had seen my chastity cage when I was in hospital, she persuaded Chung to wear one. Chung travelled a lot on business, so he was only caged when he was home. Sophie and I had the feeling, Marie was working on a long-term plan to change that.

Sophie pointed to the machine. "How soon can we get a translation?"

"If Chung can do it, probably tomorrow. If not a couple of days, max. His parents are transitioning out of their business and have more flexible schedules now."

Sophie continued, "Was this all they said?"

"I don't know. I stopped as soon as I caught it and called you guys."

"Okay, if you discover there is any more to copy, let me know."

Marie looked pensive before speaking, "We had better keep this in the family, just in case they are a threat to Tara and McCarrigan. We don't know what they're saying."

"Good thinking." I said, "We should probably warn them all that the information could be sensitive and make sure they let us know ASAP if anything suspicious happens. We need to keep them out of it."

With that settled, we each went back to our allotted tasks. Sophie marked the section to copy, and Marie went back to listening for any further conversation. Despite Tara's Asian heritage, if it was Chinese, I thought it could still be about McCarrigan. He did a lot of business in Asia. Mostly tech related, although he had fingers in many pies and previously admitted he wasn't averse to bending or even breaking rules. *Food for thought.*

Marie called out that she had more conversation in

the foreign language. Bits and pieces, sounding more like questions and answers than conversation. She'd noted each of them on the timeline.

Sophie said, "When you're done, I'll copy all of them in one shot."

Marie nodded and went back to listening, but she found nothing more by the time she finished her shift. Taking over, I doubted there would be anything else. I was right. In my hour, all I heard was Tara's voice, and that covered three days. We were coming up to date.

Whatever the intruders were doing, or looking for, it did not raise any suspicions with Tara. She would have noticed a break in, especially if anything had been taken. Maybe they were putting something in. We had bugged her home, why wouldn't someone else. Damn it, we needed more information, but I was still leaning toward McCarrigan as the primary target, and Tara secondary, due to her proximity to McCarrigan. Like her or not, we would protect her.

Now we waited for Sophie to retrieve Tara's e-mails, and the translation from Chung or his family. The rest of the day was spent doing the day-to-day crap which I hated, and Marie was so good at. Close of business we said our good nights.

Chapter Three

Sophie retrieved the two relevant e-mails, taking more effort than she had anticipated. Reviewing them as we ate a take-out dinner. At first scan, they looked innocuous. The attachment on the first one seemed to belong with the text in the e-mail.

"Tomorrow I will back track on the sender." She said, "I don't think this is as simple as it seems. There is something off about them."

"What do you mean?"

"Not sure, just a feeling. I will know more tomorrow when I can really get into it." While she was saying that, she pulled out the key chain and twirled it.

My eyes followed the spinning key that never failed to get my attention. Sophie did it when she was thinking absent mindedly, and when she wanted to tease and frustrate me. Now I could tell which it was, and tonight it was definitely absent minded, until she saw my expression.

A sensual smile spread across her face. "Mas, something got your attention? Sorry, it was a thinking twirl. I'm too tired to play tonight. You can help me get ready for bed if you choose.

"Of course, I would be delighted."

"Then please lay out the sheer white baby-doll…there's a doll." She laughed at her own joke. My cock was rapidly filling, she turned, walking toward the bedroom. As she reached the doorway, she looked back and crooked a finger for me to follow. I followed. The baby-doll was hanging in the closet. Taking it off the hanger, I lay it on top of her pillow.

"I am going to tease you. No release tonight, you still have to earn that, and your frustration level isn't quite where I want it to be, yet."

"It's there, believe me."

She chuckled. "I will be the judge of that, and unsolicited comments could delay your release. Let's sleep on it."

Sophie undressed slowly and sensuously, not a striptease. This was way more intimate. To tease me, and display her control, and for me to enjoy the sight of her body, and the frustration of not being able to do anything about it. Button by button her shirt loosened from her body, finally slipping down her arms landing in a pile on the floor. Picking it up, her warm fragrance enveloped me. With her back to me, she reached the zipper of her skirt and slowly dragged it downward, the skirt fell in a pool at her feet. Stepping out so I could retrieve it, she turned to face me.

A groan escaped my lips, which brought a smile. Right leg stocking released and rolled down. Lifting her leg, she gently placed her foot on my knee, knowing I would gently remove it, I did, repeating the process on her left leg.

The garter belt landed in my lap, hanging on my erection filled metal cage. A feeling of wanting her, and the impossible action of getting inside her engulfed me. My face flushed. When Sophie saw the effect she was having on me, she leaned in and kissed me deeply.

Silently, she continued to disrobe. The bra released

modestly held in front of her. I was fixated on her as the straps slid down her arms, and she pulled each arm out one at a time. Her bra landed on top of the garter belt. It weighed nothing and felt heavy on my cage. Freed, her breasts swung free. Her nipples quickly hardened with the change in temperature, pebbles in a crinkled sea. Could I ever tire of seeing her? Never. Her panties followed.

As my eyes enveloped her. She instructed, "My baby doll Mas."

Laying her garments to one side, holding the baby-doll as she raised her arms, it slipped easily over her outstretched arms and head. The diaphanous silk floated down around her, her nipples making pointed tents in the fabric, her darker aureole clearly visible.

Hugging her to me, I kissed her. She kissed me back.

"Let's get to sleep. I am sure tomorrow will be busy."

Lying next to her always felt like we were meant to be. We spooned, and soon she was breathing slowly and evenly. Sleep evaded me. The frustration of her teasing me, but mostly the case McCarrigan had dropped on us. I had the same bad feeling as when Sophie came to me about her missing sister. Nothing I could put my finger on, just a gut feeling.

Sleep finally took me, but it was not a restful slumber.

Rising early, I put on the coffee without disturbing Sophie. Sleepily Sophie came in the kitchen and asked, "Why are you up so early?"

"A bad night. Something is bugging me. Just a feeling."

"The last time that happened all hell broke loose. Gimme a hug." As we hugged, she said, "I hope you are wrong."

"Me too."

Separating, Sophie went to get dressed and I finished making breakfast. I have never tired of that first hit of good coffee. Savoring the flavor and the warmth, it had a calming effect on me. Whatever the day would bring, it would bring. Together we walked to the office expecting to beat Marie who was not known for being an early bird. Today I was wrong! Marie was in. The office coffee pot was ready, and there was a disapproving look on her face.

"I was just about to call you. We got a translation of what we recorded in Tara's place. Don't think you are going to like it. Chung could do most of it, but he gave it to his father who completed it and checked it. It is Chinese. One of them has a dialect. There are some words from him that neither could make out. They were planting bugs. That part was clear. They had already done Tara's office and were finishing with her home. They were also looking for something that was never mentioned, but it was clear they were working on instructions from someone. Between them, they wrote a transcript. The gaps are the words they couldn't make out or understand. I re-did the translations to make it a smoother read. It's in your inboxes."

She stopped. That was the most we had heard from Marie in one go for a long time. We both looked at her. She looked at us, "What?"

"Nothing, great job," I said. "Please thank Chung and his dad."

"You mean father, he is old school."

"Fine, just thank them. I need to call McCarrigan and let him know we will take them on. He needs to get his sweeper into Tara's office ASAP for another sweep to make sure they got everything."

"Mas, wait on her home. We have bugs in there. It may be useful to leave them in place. Just warn Tara not to say anything compromising in her home.

"Good thought, we'll have to be careful how we put that to them. McCarrigan will convince her if we convince him."

"That's on you Mas." Continuing, she asked the question, "Do we wait to inform them until they are clients, or be proactive and let them know first?

"I would rather wait, but I don't see how we can if she is in danger."

"My thought exactly. Call McCarrigan."

Interacting with McCarrigan was not something I liked to do, didn't like or trust him. This was different, someone could be in jeopardy. His PA answered and was going to put me off. I said to tell him who was calling. On hold, I smiled imagined the conversation on the other end. Click, McCarrigan was on.

"Mas what couldn't wait?"

"We were doing some background digging and came across an interesting tidbit. When was Tara's office swept for devices?"

He said, "A couple of weeks ago. That's when they found the bugs, I told you about. They're not due for a week, why?"

"Get him in again, just to be on the safe side. We have a different proposition for her home if you become clients. How's that going by the way?"

"Working on it, she is stubborn as hell."

Laughing I said, "Like finds like."

He laughed, the first genuinely open laugh I'd heard from him.

"Yes, and no complaints."

"Persuade her fast. Just a gut feeling, but Sophie and I agree something is off."

"Mas, you will hear from me today. After I get her office checked out."

"You still don't trust us?"

"If I didn't, I wouldn't have contacted you. Doesn't hurt to confirm."

He clicked off the call.

Sophie said, "I'm getting into those e-mails."

"Okay." There was nothing for me to do, so I took the opportunity to get to the gun range for regular practice. It was a quiet this early, and I had one side of the alleys to myself. Ninety minutes later, I was covered in GSR and satisfied with the results. Going home, first I'd clean my weapon, an ingrained habit, then shower and dress in clean clothes.

Picking up lunch for us on the way back to the office. Another beautiful day that makes you thankful you live in San Francisco. That tickle was still there, like the calm before the storm. Trying to shake it off I looked up the calendar for the Cauldron, the BDSM club both Sophie and I felt at home in. Nothing going on that night, check Sorcerers another established club, nothing. Last attempt a new club, Specter. That space specialized in bondage, specifically rope bondage, but was still open to lots of other play. Nothing, what the hell, this was San Francisco, there was always something going on, apparently not tonight. Lunch was welcomed by Sophie with a grunt, and Marie with a thank you.

Asking, "What's up with Sophie?"

"She started cursing up a storm, about twenty minutes ago. I think it's to do with the e-mails she is working on."

Knowing better than to disturb Sophie when she was in that mood. Leaving her to surface when she did, Marie and I ate lunch together at her desk.

"Please thank Chung and his 'Father' for their translation."

"They were happy to oblige."

"Well, it helped us out big time. By the way how is Chung adapting to his chastity cage?" Marie chuckled and blushed. A little color hit her cheek, and that was a first.

"He wasn't sure about it at first, but I can be very persuasive. Anyway, we started slowly. Sophie gave me some good tips. Starting out very light and making sure the cage fit properly, he started wearing it for an hour or so, then longer. As he became more used to it, we left it on overnight. Initially, he had access to the keys, now he doesn't. He doesn't even realize he's lost access."

"As long as he doesn't blame me, for his situation."

"Oh, he doesn't know about you. He thinks I came up with this on my own, by being involved in the Bodies in the Bay killings. The kink aspects were all in the media."

Curiously, I asked, "Where do you keep the key?

"Why? You aren't going to tell him, are you?"

"God no, that's your affair, just nosey that's all."

"One's in a safe place at home, in case of emergencies, the other." Smiling she pulled out a chain from her top and there it was a long stainless-steel key, similar to the one for my cage.

"That, is a key!"

"Yes, it's a special laser cut key. His cage has a built-in lock, it's neat and very secure. Sophie's recommended it. Don't be surprised if she makes some changes for you."

Before I went down that rabbit hole, we heard a shout from Sophie,

"Gottcha, you bastard."

We both went into the inner office and stood behind Sophie, looking over her shoulder at three screens full of data. Before we could open our mouths.

Sophie launched into the sender of the 'Tara' e-mails,

"Son of a bitch was sneaky. Whoever sent the e-mails teased Tara, so she would open them, and the attachment. As soon as she opened the e-mail attachment, open access to her computer."

I asked, "Like what you did with the Police Dept?

"The same idea. Everything on her computer is an open secret. I caught it, so we are not compromised like her. We have to get this information to her. From here it looks like industrial espionage, and strangely I don't think it's the Chinese. I have hit some fire walls and distractions. It looks more like eastern European shenanigans."

I asked, "Russia?"

"Maybe. Probably. It's not China. They are clever. I'm thinking Russia or one of their associated hacking operations."

"Good enough for now." I said, "We should be hearing from McCarrigan by end of the day, if Tara agrees to meet."

Now we had information that would be of interest, and hopefully lead to protecting Tara, if she was the primary target. If it had been the Chinese, I would have suspected McCarrigan as the primary target, now it could be either, Tara or McCarrigan as targets. It would be interesting to see how they took the information. Then more waiting while Sophie carried on doing her tech thing.

Puttering and putzing about, I needed something specific to do. Marie asked, "Would you go to the post office for me, rather than wait until the end of the day?"

"Sure." Anything was better than nothing, and the walk would do me good. Walking helped me think. Mulling over the conversation the Chinese break-in artists had, as well as planting the bugs, I noted they had been instructed to find something. Their limited conversation confirmed they hadn't found it, therefore it was well hidden, or they didn't recognize it.

No that didn't fly; they'd have been told exactly what to look for. Tara didn't have it, or maybe she didn't know she had it. Too many variables. I...we needed more data.

The trip to the post office didn't take long, no line for a change, and the time was well spent thinking. We would have to wait for McCarrigan to call.

He called as we were about to close-up. Curtly I asked, "What took you so long?

"Talking Tara into meeting with you. Had the sweeper go through her office, twice, and found a new bug one in her PA's land line. Yes, we kept it. When the new device was found, it shook Tara. That's twice someone has broken into her office without anyone noticing. This has finally made her nervous. I persuaded her to meet with you. She wants the authorities kept out of this. I told her you could guarantee that. You can, right?"

"Sure. We'll explain everything when we meet, and you become clients. Can we do that tonight?

"Yes, at my place. It's secure and tight. No bugs, and I always have a jammer running when talking about anything remotely sensitive."

"Good thinking. Time?"

He went silent for a moment. "Eight is the earliest I can do. That okay with you?"

"Sophie and I'll be there. Text me your address. I assume you have building security?"

"Yes, and I'll leave notice that I am expecting you."

"Please make sure Tara has her laptop with her. Sophie will need to take a look at it. Oh, and don't forget the listening device. Till tonight."

Cutting the call, I told Sophie about the arrangements. She confirmed they were fine, and she left with Marie saying she would get dinner ready. Thanking her, I went into the filing cabinet to pull out all the required documents to contract a client. Taking out two sets, one for Tara the other for McCarrigan because they were not married or partnered. We wanted them both to be clients to cover all the bases. I reviewed the documents making sure they were correct. This would legally cover everyone.

Dinner was ready when I got home. While we ate, we discussed how to run the upcoming meeting. McCarrigan should be relaxed and comfortable in his own environment. Tara should be at ease, with McCarrigan there and in his surroundings. None of that meant shit to Sophie and me, we were usually out of our environment. We were the ones with the ability to help our clients; if we weren't, we didn't take them on. In this case, we had plenty of information ahead of time, and hopefully it would give us the leverage we needed to convince Tara she needed help—specifically us.

Chapter Four

We took a ride share to McCarrigan's place and were early. The apartment was in one of the expensive downtown towers. We were expected. Security at the front desk called McCarrigan announcing our arrival and directed us to a bank of elevators. While not penthouse level, he would have a good view of the city. Exiting the elevator, we hesitated to orient ourselves. A door opened, and McCarrigan silently waved at us.

The apartment was well appointed, and thick carpet absorbed the sound of our footsteps. The furniture was all modern and angular, as were the abstract paintings decorating the walls. What caught my attention was the view. Big windows looked out toward the Bay bridge, the bridge glittering with the white and red lights of the traffic coming from and going to Oakland and the East Bay.

Tara's voice broke my reverie, "Hammett you aren't here for the view."

"No, we aren't. Sophie and I are here to assist you. Even before you sign a client contract...if you sign, anything you say will remain confidential between the four of us. Unless, and this goes even after we sign contracts, if we know or believe you are going to harm yourself or someone else, we will take appropriate action. Is that clear?"

They both nodded in agreement. Tara and

McCarrigan sat together, closer than friends, but not as close as I expected lovers to sit. They looked on edge. Sophie and I sat opposite.

I glanced at McCarrigan and asked, "Your jammer is running I assume?"

"Yes," was his terse response.

We had agreed that Sophie would start with the tech stuff, while I observed the two of them and their interactions with us.

Sophie began, "We have info that you had been bugged, office and home. McCarrigan has confirmed that your office was bugged. Tara, may I see an example?"

Tara handed over a small, clear plastic container which rattled with the listening device. "This was the one found in the land line phone. We have requested the other ones from the previous sweep. Haven't heard back yet."

Sophie said, "The devices in your home, Mas and I would like you to leave them in place for now. You never know when they may be useful in giving misinformation."

McCarrigan seemed to take that as a positive. Tara was still looking apprehensive and uncomfortable.

Sophie continued, "We also believe your computer may have been compromised."

That got a reaction from Tara. "What, that's my business. Without my computer, I may as well not get up in the morning. It can't have been compromised. I am very careful and have all sorts of anti-virus stuff on it."

"It doesn't have to be a virus. There are other nasties, not as obvious, but just as dangerous. We need to look at your computer to confirm that, one way or the other."

Tara skeptically and emphatically stated, "Not a chance. You two are messing with me You don't actually know anything. You're fishing." Under her animosity, she looked worried.

Jumping in I said, "Tara, we are very good at what we do. We believe we can assist you in whatever is going on. To do that most effectively, we need your assistance. We look into your computer. If you're right and we find nothing, we walk away no harm no foul. If we are right. You sign on as clients, and we will be working for you and do everything in our power to protect you physically and technologically. Ask your boyfriend."

She shot daggers at me with her eyes. McCarrigan smiled and moved closer to Tara saying, "Tara, I think it's a no-lose situation for you. If they find nothing, you're good. If they do, we sign the contracts. They sorted out the encryption app issue, way before I could have. We will both be covered as clients."

She looked at him, not scared, but not the same confident woman we had first met. Reluctantly, she said, "Alright, alright. If you think they are what they say they are, I'll sign *IF* they find anything. Either of you use any of my information, clients, or contacts for your own benefit. I will sue your collective asses out of existence. Promise."

Sophie bridled at her comment. "You have nothing we want."

Before Tara could answer, McCarrigan interrupted, "Tara, I trust them regarding tech issues as much as I trust anyone. They'll do as they say, and the contract covers us, as well as them. Go ahead give Sophie your computer."

Cautiously, Tara handed over her computer to Sophie, who got up and went to the dining room table, asking Tara for her password. Tara snorted and without Sophie being able to see, entered her password. The screen blazed to life. Sophie's fingers started to fly over the keyboard. While Sophie was doing that, I asked Tara questions about the e-mails.

"Tara did you recognize the sender?

"Kind of. I was suspicious."

"Then why open them?"

Sheepishly she said, "I believed they were from someone I knew well, when I was married."

Tara was being evasive. We could let that slide for now. My immediate responsibility was to buy time for Sophie. She had to make the questioning look good and not too easy. After using our back door to Tara's laptop and discovering what we already had found. She continued to question Tara, and I threw in the odd question now and then, so it didn't seem connected. When I asked if she did any business with Eastern Europe. That one caught both of them off guard. Both answered "no".

Sophie exclaimed, "Got it. You've been compromised. It's a type of Trojan horse. When you opened the attachment in e-mail, you loaded a Trojan horse. Since then, everything you have on your computer has been visible to the persons who sent you the email. The second e-mail was to confirm they had access. You thought you recognized the original sender's address, but it wasn't actually him, was it?"

Tara looked angry and hurt. She was anxious. "At

first, I thought he'd sent me the e-mail in error. The content didn't make sense. I figured it was a mistake. When I got the second one, I called him. He denied sending anything at all."

I asked, "Is that when you told McCarrigan?"

"Yes. Kevin took it seriously and told me I should report it to the authorities. I can't do that. My clients are sensitive to exposure of any sort. Besides, the police aren't known for being very successful with this type of thing."

Sophie added, "You need to let your friend know his system has also been compromised. We'll start digging and try to find out who is behind this and why. First thing you do is get a new computer. I'll install better protections on that one. In the future, you be careful about what you open. Keep this one and use it, letting them see everything that goes on, the longer I have access, the better chance I'll be able to follow the trail back to its origination. Hopefully, they won't know I'm after them. Any questions?"

"What do they want with me, I am a facilitator, deal maker and connector. I deal more with the accountants and lawyers, than the principals once the deal looks good."

Sophie responded, "You have access to someone, something they want or need to protect. I'll work on the tech end. Mas will investigate everything else. Mas anything to add?"

"Yes, keep everything as normal as possible, same routine. Your office has been deloused." Looking at McCarrigan, he nodded at me in confirmation. "You can speak freely there, at home be aware they are probably listening to everything until Sophie can get in and sweep it to confirm you're bugged."

McCarrigan interrupted and asked, "Why not use the same company that does her office?"

Quickly I answered, "Because the office had been cleaned up. If Tara's being observed, they will see the same company doing the same to her home, we want to cover all our bases and keep them off balance for as long as possible. They won't recognize Sophie."

He shrugged in compliance. "This is a sophisticated attack, there has to be a good reason for it. Let's get the paperwork done and get started resolving this."

The next hour plus, was taken up with reviewing and signing the contracts. Both Tara and McCarrigan asked a lot of good clarifying questions. Dealing with smart people is always good, but never easy. It extends the time everything takes, including all the paperwork signed and sealed, fees agreed, and promises of deposit amounts to be transferred the next day.

We all shook hands and Tara had a parting shot, "Thank you. I still don't like you, but thank you for doing this."

Sophie and I looked at each other, smiled, and together we said, "It's what we do."

We took the elevator down, remaining silent until we exited the building. We both started talking at once. I let her to go first.

"I have been thinking this is a pretty significant attempt on a single person. It's got to be something important."

"Or valuable. She knows more than she is telling us. Let's find out what we can before we go back at her. Would you print me out a list of all the people she has been dealing with over the last six months, I can always work back from there if necessary. With the timeline it's probably more recent."

"Yeah, I got that feeling as well. You will have the printout first thing, and I will keep backtracking the tech stuff."

Smiling to myself, I knew I would have the information I wanted waiting for me tomorrow. Sophie would be up early and be in the office before the early bird.

Chapter Five

When I surfaced, Sophie's side of the bed was cold, and the house was quiet. I figured she'd left early. After a quick shower, I dressed, grabbed a to-go cup of coffee that she'd brewed earlier, and savored the coffee as I headed to the office. I called a breakfast order of focaccia into Liguria's—the best focaccia in the city. Knowing it would be appreciated by all of us, so I made it a double order.

Marie and I arrived together. She noticed what I was carrying and asked, "What's the occasion?"

"Sophie got her teeth into something and has an early start."

"Oh God, she is going to drive us nuts."

Laughing, I agreed. As predicted, the printout I requested was waiting for me. This would be a good start, seeing if anyone or anything popped up as suspicious. The container with the bug from Tara's office had a note on it. *'Don't think it's Chinese. It's an older type. Will search more.'*

Sophie kissed me, grabbed a section of focaccia, and ate, as she immersed herself with her computer screens. I could never figure out how anyone could view three screens and concentrate on all three at once. It was something beyond my technical capabilities.

With breakfast demolished, I settled into reading the printouts. Most PI stuff is dry as dust, but it's what feeds the case. Most people would find it boring, but the "ah ha" moments make it worthwhile.

No "ah ha" moments from the text I read. Tara was busy and tenacious with her deals. Everyone she dealt with seemed to be on the up and up. The stateside contacts all seemed beyond reproach. The big company names were well known in the tech industry. The smaller start-ups would bear a closer look. There was not much personal stuff in the printouts, so far, assuming she would use her phone for that. Needing a break, I called Tara to set a time for Sophie visit her. Her personal assistant answered, and I was put straight through to a frosty Tara.

"Hello, Mr. Hammett."

"Good morning, Tara. I need to confirm you have a new computer and can you let me know when it would be convenient for Sophie to add protections to it?"

"It will be delivered by noon. She can come this afternoon. I have meetings out of the office after two. She can do it then while I'm out, and my PA can keep an eye on her."

"Thank you. You do realize we are working for you?"

"Yes, it docsn't mean I have to like it."

"Sophie also needs to get into your home to confirm there are no devices there."

"Fine. My PA has a key. Get it all done today."

"We'll take care of it."

"Hold on." The line went to music, and when we resumed, Kristen, her PA was on with us. Tara gave her instructions and left me to organize the logistics with Kristen, which didn't take long. After hanging up, I had the feeling we were already down a rabbit hole we shouldn't have approached, but it was too late. Calling out to get Sophie's attention, not always easy when she was in search mode, my voice made her look up.

"What?"

"You have two appointments this afternoon. Tara's office. Post 2:00 pm. She won't be there. You can also sweep her home for the bugs our Chinese friends installed.

"Oh good. I wouldn't want her around anyway...bitch. Installing the protection software shouldn't take too long. Regarding our devices, never know when they'll be useful. I will map out where the new ones are and let Tara know. Who's the PA?"

"Kristen, the same person as when I last visited. Cute and very protective of Tara."

"Cute?"

Smiling, I added, "I appreciate the fine female form. In fact, the day I stop, bury me. I'll be dead."

"Hmmm, we'll see how dead you are tonight. Now let me get back to work."

The balance of the day for me was continuing to read the printout information. Making notes as I went, checking online if a name or a company piqued my curiosity. A take-out lunch, picked up by Marie, went bite by bite as I concentrated on the reading. Sophie tapped away until it was time to leave for her appointments with Tara's PA and waved good-bye to us.

Damn it, there was really nothing to get my teeth into. Nothing seemed suspicious. Tara looked clean from the information we had. Maybe as we had surmised, she didn't know what she had. Bleary eyed, I had a headache and called it a day, leaving Marie to close-up shop. Nothing from Sophie. I assumed there were no problems. She would fill me in when she got home.

Working-out in the spare bedroom, I ran myself into a sweaty mess and felt a lot better. The headache finally dissipated as I luxuriated in a stinging hot shower. Almost human again, I dressed and started dinner. Dinner was a quick and simple, baked fish over fresh pasta, all from the local Italian market. A bottle of California chardonnay chilled, waiting and ready for Sophie to arrive.

Where the hell was she? She should have been home by now. Tempted to call, I resisted. She was a big girl. There must be a good reason she was late. A little more time passed, and I, beginning to get worried, paced the floor. Sophie came in bright and lit up.

She started before I could comment, "Kristen is a gold mine of info, and you're right, she's very protective of Tara, which is why I'm late. She noticed changes in her boss, and she's concerned. I explained who I was and what we were doing, and she wants to help. I also think she wanted to unload, so we went for a couple of drinks after I'd swept the house. Our Chinese friends did a thorough job in every room in the house. Anyway, I marked the location of each one, mapped each room, and gave it to Kristen.

"Okay, then what did Kristen say that can help us?"

"Directly nothing. Tara's business is doing very well, and she is looking to expand the office. Kristen is in on the planning. She is overqualified as a PA. Tara knows it and pays her well to keep her. Tara. as we know, is driven to succeed and has been casting her net a little further afield from the US, Japan, and some other Asian countries, mainly China and Korea. She's been busy marketing herself. There have been connections to Europe as well, via the new contacts. Kristen is concerned Tara is spreading herself a bit thin—not doing her due diligence about who she is dealing with, not as well as she used to. Remember she dropped Kasagawa ASAP when she found out he was under the eye of certain U.S. Government departments and a front for the Yakuza."

"What makes her think Tara is not doing her usual level of checks and balances?"

"A combination of things—the number of contacts to check, and the decreased time they spend on each one."

"Has she any idea of who could be a threat to Tara"

"No idea, but she thinks it has to be fairly recent."

"Probably, but I wouldn't count out an established client, things change and so do clients. Enough, we can chat more after dinner which is ready."

"Good, and I will need to decompress as desert."

That meant Sophie would be in charge as the dominant Ms. Circe. When we went to a BDSM club she was always addressed as her alter ego Ms. Circe. She would be pleasured, and I had a chance to get out of my penis prison.

"Let's get to dinner."

We ate together, savoring the food and each other's company. As Sophie was already a couple of glasses of wine ahead of me, she was circumspect about how much she drank, and I limited my intake, not wanting to mute the upcoming sensations with alcohol.

Anticipation grew as dinner neared its end. My

heartbeat faster, with the thoughts of what would be required of me. My cock cage began to fill as I thought of my upcoming service to the woman I loved. We cleared the remains of our repast with a calm urgency. Both wanting the evening to continue toward our satisfaction, each would be different, yet belong to both of us.

Sophie instructed me to disrobe and put on the hog-tie she left in the middle of the sitting room floor. This hog-tie was a steel ring, with four chains attached, ending in two ankle cuffs and two wrist cuffs. Quickly naked, I had become adept at getting myself into the hog-tie. Locking the four cuffs on and kneeling, I was ready for whatever my Ms. Circe demanded of me. She was inventive and caring, demanding of perfection, knowing we would never reach it. Each time I saw her, she took my breath away.

She had left as partner Sophie and returned as Ms. Circe. Wearing a deep emerald-green satin robe, wrapped tightly against her, and tied at the waist. Looking up at her I knew she was naked under the robe. Tonight, would be one of service, not a scene played out as performance. Her tits swayed as she moved, the satin appeared as water it moved so fluidly. Sophie's hard nipples made sharp points in the fabric, as the light hit the satin sheen.

As she moved toward me, one leg hidden by the waterfall of satin, one leg exposed. The green fabric and the naked leg, played against each other. The naked leg would disappear under the green, and then reappear with her next step. Her walk was slow and deliberate. Stopping directly in front of me she leaned over me, our lips met, and she kissed me. My already filling cock was hardening to full erection.

Rising up, Ms. Circe pulled the golden chain from between her breasts, dangling the key in front of me. "Would Mas like me to remove the cage?

"Yes, Ms. Circe."

"Are you sure?"

"Yes, Ms. Circe."

"Hmmm, be careful what you wish for."

What did she mean? Usually, if I was let out of the cage, a release was allowed. She was teasing me, or did she have something else in mind. My dick was full. Her teasing, and the anticipation of what was to come, was driving me crazy...and I loved it.

"I think I will let it out for a while."

Kneeling in front of me, her robe spread out like a pool, one leg bare, and I could almost see the top of her thigh...almost. The fold of satin refused to slip and give me that delight. With my arms restricted behind me, I could not touch what I desired most in the world. Her fragrance I could enjoy. Breathing her in, I groaned, which caused a low sensual laugh to escape her parted lips.

With every pump of my heart, my captured dick made the cage move. Sophie gently held the cage in one hand and slid the key into the lock with the other. The lock opened with the slightest turn of the key. The cage sprang away from the back retaining ring. Slowly, she eased the cage down and off my cock. With no weight at all, my erection stood proudly out in front of me. In these moments, Ms. Circe did not allow me to talk, unless she required an answer.

Quietly she commented, "A fine specimen of manhood, one I will continue to enjoy, when I choose."

Watching her as she continued to uncage me, she removed the back ring. Free of the metal chastity device, the air felt good against my skin. The restraints prevented me from touching myself. I could do nothing about my jutting hard-on. The pleasure of this frustration was calming. Closing my eyes, I enjoyed the sensation of restriction and freedom.

Nails sliding down the length of my erect penis brought me back to earth. The sensation was soul searing, in my aroused state, pleasure rose to ecstasy. Slowly and deliberately, she raked my cock, making patterns in my flesh. Each stroke, drawn out in a different pattern, never enough pressure to bring me off. Only to tease me with what might be, but I suspected wouldn't be tonight.

Ms. Circe continued her sensual ministrations, all the while talking to me in a low voice, "Mas, does this feel good? I can do this for hours. You wanted out, and now you are. No regrets, I hope."

She continued the whispering and dragging her nails on me, zoning out I was almost in a trance. Ms. Circe's deep, wet kiss brought me back to reality.

"Enough fun for you, I need my desert."

She had moved the chair I had made for this moment, to the other side of the room. Most of the seat had been removed in a large 'U' shape, with just enough left to support her gorgeous ass and thighs, when her legs were spread wide. She turned looking directly at me, flipping wide open the skirts of the robe, bearing her neatly trimmed mount of Venus.

An involuntary groan of pleasure hissed past my lips. Sitting, legs spread wide Sophie pointed at me, and crooked a finger to indicate I should move to her. Her breasts were rising and falling more rapidly, in anticipation of my coming ministrations. Knowing she would be wet for me, moving over to her as quickly as I could, not easy in the hog-tie. On my knees, I struggled to reach her, this was part of her pleasure, each time I moved my dick would wave in front of me, the frustration was intense, and that brought pleasure to both of us.

Finally, I stopped between her legs, I was perspiring from the effort. She bounced my dick up and down with her foot chuckling at my reaction. Aroused at my inability to stop her doing anything she desired she used my knees as a pivot pulling my shoulders forward, my mouth landing exactly on her dripping wet pussy. Burying my face deep in her, I licked. The last thing I heard, was a loud moan of satisfaction as her legs clamped down on my head.

Her fragrance filled all my senses, my tongue lapped at her. Varying my strokes, I worked on my lover. Using her physical reactions to guide me, I played with her, drinking in her juices. She changed her position with her legs over my back. Pressing me onward, I changed the pace and pressure.

My erection had not diminished, and the sensation of it standing out in front of me as I licked my partner, lover, and mistress, to orgasm, increased my feeling of submission and calmness. This is where I wanted to be, needed to be, and Ms. Circe was the other side of the same coin. Her thighs began to tremble, as she tried to hold off the inevitable for as long as possible. Nothing was going to stop me from bringing her to nirvana. Focusing my efforts on her clit, manipulating it like a tiny penis. Pushing her toward the abyss of pleasure, she was getting to the point of no return.

Sophie's legs gripped me in a spasm of rictus. Everything stopped, including her breathing. I sensed no motion at all. It couldn't last. Suddenly she released an explosive shuddering moan, and her whole body trembled. She rubbed my face up and down her slit and covered me in her liquid orgasm, then descended gradually into relaxed stillness. The wetness ran down my face and off my chin. I loved this moment, the feeling we were not two separate entities, but one, joined. I remained still and silent until she was ready to move.

Pleasure given and received, what could be better than that, and it really didn't matter how that was achieved as along as it was consensual. Still hard, I doubted I'd be lucky and get my own release. Coming around, she kissed me again,

"Mas, I love you, all of you. I wish we had met a long time ago."

She eased me back on my knees so my feet were on the ground, and I could relax my arms and shoulders.

"Don't go away."

Laughing at her own joke, she stood and left me. Returning, she knelt in front of me, and the cold from an ice pack hit my cock and balls. I violently jerked back. She was going to put me straight back in the chastity cage. Damn it.

"Yes, Mas. This time you go straight back into chastity. Be careful what you wish for. You were out of the cage as you wanted. Don't worry you'll get your release, when and how I decide."

"Ms. Circe I am at your pleasure."

"I know, and I love you for it."

With a practiced hand, Sophie quickly fitted the retaining ring. Lubing up my still chilled and soft cock she slid the tube part of the chastity device on me and locked it in place.

"Done."

Sophie put the keys to my cuffs in front of me. Scooting around I groped for the means of my release. Finding them was only the beginning, I had to get the correct key into the correct lock. For the first time in a long time, the first attempt was a success. Once one lock was undone, the rest followed easily and quickly.

Picking up a Q-tip she left for me, I poked and prodded my dick inside the tube, via the slots, until it felt comfortable. Back to reality. Locked up again until Sophie decided otherwise. Life was good.

"I have been thinking, Mas. If you wanted, you could probably pull out of the cage—not that I think you would." Here it comes, what Marie had hinted at earlier in the day. "A more secure one would give us both more peace of mind. Don't you think?"

"How much more secure were you considering?"

"Oh, I don't know, I have just been thinking about it, I will do some research and see what's out there."

"Do I get any say in this?"

"Of course, this is for both of us. You need to do research as well. We will have a conversation, negotiation, consent, and joint agreement."

"Fair enough, I will my research."

"Damn we are a great couple Mas, two sides of the same coin-right?"

"Right."

Standing we hugged and kissed as equal partners. Feeling her nipples poke into me as the slippery satin robe slid over my bare chest. She felt so good, and I couldn't wait to get to bed and cuddle. The light went out, and I was asleep in seconds.

Chapter Six

Shrouded in fog, the new day arrived. It was one of those days where I didn't want to get out of bed, but I did anyway. Grumpy about the damp veil over the city, I would be irritable until the sun breached the marine layer. There's a reason San Francisco is called Fog City.

Sophie was up and ready to go, blew me a kiss and waved goodbye as I stepped from the shower. She knew I'd be irritable. At least she left me coffee and toast before she escaped my mood. She went to the office, one to work and two to warn Marie I'd be the bear with a sore head. Fuck it. A happy face would show up at the office just to confuse them. The walk was easy, and I actually didn't feel too cranky. The happy face made it through the door.

Sophie gave me a serious look. "Get your coffee then we need to talk."

Returning a few minutes later, armed with a mug of coffee, I asked, "What's so urgent?

"I think we have a situation."

"What are you talking about?"

"Just for jollies, I used our police department back door to look at the case of the two guys found on the Golden Gate Bridge. Kinda wish I hadn't. You remember the two bodies they found the other day?" I nodded, and she continued, "It sounds crazy, but I think

48

they may be the two who bugged Tara's office and home."

"How'd you come up with that connection?"

"Our guys are Chinese. The two men on the bridge are Chinese. One unidentified, and the other an ABC." I hadn't heard that term in a while, American Born Chinese. "His fingerprints were in the system. Department of Defense, Colin Wang Lee, former military. The other is probably offshore. Nothing to ID him so far. They were just muscle. Question is why were they killed?"

Thinking about that, I summed up my thoughts, "You think they were killed after the bugs were found in Tara's office and neutralized. That's a high price to pay for that failure. Are the autopsies on file yet?"

"Mas, only the preliminary."

"Cause of death?"

"The offshore guy was heart failure. Colin Wang Lee's cause of death was gun shot—one in the chest, another to the back of the head—definitely overkill. Either would have done the job. There is something else not in the media."

Her tone of voice made me look up.

"What?"

"They had both been castrated and tongues cut out, mutilated with an Asian symbol carved into their chests."

"Pre or postmortem?" I asked. "The mutilation was sending a message to someone."

"Undetermined as yet. The theory is post."

I considered what I'd heard so far. "Whoever did it, didn't care that the bodies would be identified. They knew for sure one would be, and the other wouldn't be in our systems. The one not in our systems will be hard to trace…Shit."

Sophie looked pale. "Curiosity killed the cat. I regret looking. The photos were pretty ugly."

"No, this is good. It's data I hope will help us figure out who is after Tara."

"Mas, doing that to people…is just so sick, and that means dangerous."

"We know someone is after Tara, but no one knows we are looking out for her…yet. Sophie, do you think the bugs were planted purposely to be found in order to draw someone or something out?"

"That's possible and makes the person orchestrating this smart and devious, if it's true."

Thinking out loud, I added, "Maybe they were killed, not for failing with the bugs, but for not finding what they were sent to retrieve. We need to review all the folks Tara has done or attempted to do business with over the last six months and work back. Especially the ones that didn't pan out. The reason has to be with her somewhere."

"Why are you so sure it's to do with Tara's business?"

"No one kills two people for a sandwich. The whole banquet? Sure. This has to be something of immense value, or a secret big enough it would be a disaster if it came out."

"It would have to be really significant, and I haven't found anything like that, at least not yet. I know keep looking."

"Took the words right out of my mouth."

"Do we tell the authorities?

"Not yet. Maybe never," I said. "Let's see what we

come up with. Our first responsibility is to our client. She definitely needs to upgrade her security, office, home, and personal. You keep doing your computer thing, I'll talk to McCarrigan about it."

"You don't think he's involved with this?"

"Not a chance. You've seen him with her. He's smitten. Besides, he's too smart to bring us in if he's involved."

"Good point."

"Sophie, we'll take care of this."

I got merely a wan smile before her head dropped back behind her computer screen. Seeing the preliminary photos had gotten to her. She was used to the nice clean code of computer language, not the reality of messy real life. Having seen enough in my career, even I wasn't immune. At my first burned corpse, I lost my lunch. The stench seemed to invade my nostrils and taste buds for days. Roast pork was off the menu for months after.

Everything fades or changes with time, even grief. I still often thought about my former partner Simon. The perp had not been apprehended and probably wouldn't be now. Sophie still had weeping sessions over her sister. At least she had some justice, with the actual killers going to jail for life, and knowing the ones who ordered the killings were probably at the bottom of a Japanese harbor. Becoming maudlin with my thoughts and the dreary weather, I had to get out.

Calling McCarrigan, I was put through immediately. Before I could start, he asked, "Any progress?

"Some. Can we meet today?"

"My office?"

"How about the Blue bottle, eleven-thirty."

"Okay, Mas, I maybe a few minutes late."

"Not a problem."

"Sounds serious, is it?"

"Could be. See you at eleven-thirty."

Someone in Tara's camp needed to know what was going on, and I didn't want it to be Tara. Not yet. Perhaps later when we had gained her trust. Until then I would use McCarrigan as a go between. We didn't know enough yet, other than to play defense.

Again, I looked over the transcripts of the Chinese home invaders to see if I had missed anything. Nothing, but it confirmed they were definitely sent to retrieve something as well as plant bugs. They had access to her computer, which meant she was an open book. If it wasn't on that, what and where could it be? Being wrapped up in the transcripts, I was almost late leaving for my meeting with McCarrigan. Now I had more fucking questions than answers.

Grabbing my jacket for the dampness of the day, I made good time getting to the Ferry building. He hadn't arrived, and knowing what his previous coffee choice was, I ordered for both of us.

The order was called just as McCarrigan showed up. Seeing what I'd ordered, he said, "You're observant Mas. Haven't got a clue what you're drinking." I shrugged and continued. "I love San Francisco, but this damp shit, ugh. Let's walk inside today."

We moved out into the main throughway of the Ferry Building. Each sipping and savoring our coffees for a few strides. Thinking of how to broach the subject, McCarrigan beat me too it.

"You have concerns about Tara, don't you?

"Yes. You heard about the two bodies found on the Golden Gate Bridge?"

"Of course, what do they have to do with anything?"

"We have information that potentially links them to the break in of Tara's office and home. If that's so, we think Tara could be in danger. We want her to install, or upgrade her security, office, home, and personal. She's not likely to accept a recommendation from us. You have to persuade her it's a good idea on general principal. In fact, with the security you have in your building, could she stay with you until this is over?"

"I don't know about the staying with me part—we aren't quite there, yet."

"Why not try. It could bring you closer together. Worth a shot. You could even use the need for security for bringing it up. If nothing else, it shows you care."

He looked at me, deciding if I was talking piss, or if I was serious. Serious was all I ever was when it came to client safety.

"I'll think about it, the staying with me part. I agree with all the rest."

"I have a driver for her, sound and very dependable. If he's available."

"Driver?"

"Yes, no more public transport for a while."

"She uses cabs or ride share."

"Not anymore. Does she own a car?"

"Yes. A left over from her divorce. She hardly ever uses it."

"Good, you need to get her to take this seriously, but I don't want to scare her, at least not unless we have to."

"Scare her?"

"Not unless she becomes too stubborn with the preventive measures. If those two murders are connected, Tara is definitely in jeopardy."

"How will you know if she is or isn't?"

"We're working on that."

"Work faster."

"It takes whatever time it takes. Rush and hurry are partners in mistakes."

"Do you need anything from me?"

"We were hoping you would feel that way. Right now, only your persuasion. If that changes, we'll let you know."

"Okay, I'll work on her. Let me know about the driver, yes?"

"ASAP."

As we parted company, I called the prospective driver. Oso was someone I had known from my days in the SFPD. One of the success stories; he had turned his life around. Knowing I could rely on him to do any job given him, and do it well, as long as it was physical. He answered my call sounding sleepy, like I'd woken him.

"Hola."

"Oso, it's me Mas. Wake up. I got a job for you if you are available."

Oso answered, his Hispanic accent thick enough to cut with a knife, "Mas, hey man, what you needs?"

"Still got a clean driving license and a nice suit?"

"Sure. Suit needs a cleaning, that's all. What's the job, and what's it pay?"

"Pay will be a daily rate. Protecting a client if she needs it. Mostly driving her around to meetings and back. Just making sure she's safe. Mostly places here in the city. Then home at the end of the day. Your evenings are free."

"That's cool man. Not much going on during the day."

"Not sure how long it will last. I'll send you details as soon as I get them"

"Gracias, you're a good hombre, Mas."

"Nada, Oso."

Another piece sorted. Now all we needed was Tara to play nice and follow our advice—that might be the hardest part. I didn't like relying on McCarrigan for that aspect. As I made my back to the office, I hoped Sophie had something positive to report, but when I arrived, she wasn't at her desk. Marie reminded me she was at her self-defense class, and then had errands to run.

Shit, my mind was going. I was the one who set up the class for her.

Marie went to pick up lunch while I guarded the home front. We were just finishing our repast when Sophie rolled in, sweaty and disheveled. The sweat made her thin shirt cling to her, distracting me. With the outline of her bra clearly visible and her nipples aroused and pointed, the visual made my dick plump, filling the cage.

"Good class?"

"Fuck, yes… Don't mess with me, or I'll do nasty things to you," she said, smiling.

"You ran errands like that?" My eyes focused on her wet t-shirt. I loved the physical confidence this class had given her.

"I ran an errand before the class. The bugs in Tara's office are of Russian design, so they could have been made anywhere in the Eastern bloc. They're an old design, and have been discontinued for ages, but are still functional and inexpensive."

"Russian! Question. Are Russian or Eastern Europeans behind this, or is it the Chinese using Russian materials? The Chinese and Russian's were once close."

"Don't know? I need to eat, and then go home and shower."

With a grin I said, "Yes, please shower."

"Good one Mas, keep it up, and I may misplace a key."

Picking up her lunch, she joined Marie at her desk. I needed to divert my thoughts away from my groin, reverting back to what Sophie had said about the bug.

Russian? What the hell was going on? Tara ran an international company, dealing almost exclusively with the western U.S. and the Asian markets, it didn't include Russia. Starting a list of stuff, I needed to review, dig into, and get Sophie on as well. The list grew too fast, the answer had to be with Tara. The smallest thing could lead us in the right direction. Sophie went home to clean up and soon returned ready to do her thing.

McCarrigan called mid-afternoon saying he had managed to get Tara to agree to install better security. Tara contacted the same firm he had used for his office and home. I knew them. No issues there. It was a good reputable company. She also reluctantly agreed to have a driver take her to all her meetings.

Good. I passed on Oso's telephone number to McCarrigan, saying Oso could start tomorrow morning. "Tara should expect a very large, Hispanic man. He goes by Oso. That's it. No Mr. and no last name."

McCarrigan thanked me and hung up.

Oso answered on the first ring and took down the details about Tara's home and office. "I'll be ready and waiting for her *la manana. Gracias*, Mas."

"Just be ready. She could be in trouble."

"Trust me bro—she's safe with me." He hung up as if saying I didn't need to remind him, it's taken care of. If I didn't think it was, I wouldn't have suggested him.

One more thing checked off the list.

"Bastards!" Sophie's exclamation brought me up short, and Marie asked, "Is everything alright."

Sophie fist pumped. "They were smart, but I'm still queen bee. The messages were bounced all over the place but guess where they originated. Well…?"

Before we could offer a guess, she continued, "Russia. Saint Petersburg to be exact."

When she stopped for breath, I asked, "You sure?"

"Of course, I'm sure. I said so, didn't I?"

"Yes, my dear, you did. Seems odd it would be Russian. We need a sit down with Tara. The answer has to be with her."

"Good luck with that. You know how she feels about you. Us."

"Yeah, well this concerns her welfare. When you get a chance, please check to see if there's an update on the autopsy for the two vics on the bridge, and find out whose desk that case landed on, and anything else that catches your eye while you're in there. I'll conference McCarrigan and Tara together, that should ease the request for a meeting."

"Good idea. Now leave me alone so I can take care of all your tasks, like I have nothing to do."

Grinning at her attitude, I left her to her tasks. The Russian connection was a new twist, although after the hacking and interference with the last election, it shouldn't be a surprise. That was government sponsored. This didn't have the feel of government backing. Perhaps a subcontract. I wondered could it be freelance or unconnected? Calling McCarrigan was becoming a bad habit, but he took my call and agreed to call Tara, making it a three-way conference.

Tara took McCarrigan's call and reluctantly agreed to speak with me. I took my time and told her what we found so far and explained what we really needed was a face to face. We needed her active participation in reviewing all her business contacts going back as far as we needed to. There had to be a connection—detailed effort had gone into breaching her security. When that failed, they, whoever "they" were, might try something of a more aggressive nature. We agreed to meet at McCarrigan's apartment that evening to go over all her projects, all of them, even the projects that never left the ground.

Tara noted, "This could take some time. I've had a busy year."

"No problem. We are in for as long as it takes."

I relayed the time and place of our project meeting to Sophie via e-mail. She'd be deep in her tasks, and I didn't want to get an earful for disturbing her.

She worked the rest of the day with no outbursts. Later, when Marie called out goodnight, Sophie responded with an absent-minded grunt and I said, "Be safe," and waved goodnight.

The meeting would be early, so I went out to pick up Chinese take-out and returned, the aroma of the hot food wafting in the office finally aroused Sophie's attention.

"That smells good, and I'm so ready for it. What's the time?"

I told her as I popped a couple of beers from the fridge. "Enough time to eat and get to our appointment with Tara at McCarrigan's apartment."

Surprised she asked, "When did that happen?"

"I sent you an e-mail with the details."

"Oh sorry, I didn't check anything posted this morning."

"You complain when I interrupt you, so I sent you an e-mail."

"You listened. Sorry, this one's on me. I should've checked."

"No harm, no foul. We have time. Did you discover anything?"

"The full autopsy on the Chinese vics will be in tomorrow. The PD team, handling this case, is led by a detective named Gomez."

I interrupted, "Inspector."

"Okay, Inspector Gomez. You said Kenzo is a lieutenant. Do you think Kenzo got a promotion due to solving my sister's murder, or was he due?"

"He earned it, but it didn't hurt clearing up that case." We both smiled at that. Some good was coming out of the deaths in that case. "Anything else?"

"Jesus Mas, give me a minute. I'm telling you. About the case, they got nothing. They are following up with the DoD on Colin Wang Lee. You know how slowly government departments work. The part about the mutilations is being kept out of the media, as is their ethnic background. Apparently, they don't want to start rumors of a gang war in Chinatown."

"Make's sense. They don't want anything scaring the tourists."

Sophie continued, "Nothing in the file yet about checking overseas. That will be a chore and a half. They may be waiting for all the forensics to come in.

"Anything on Tara's contacts, now that we've expanded the timeline to a year?"

"No, she has been busy. Not liking her is one thing. I have to respect that she works her ass off. She is non-stop, even on vacation she made contacts."

Laughing, I said, "Just means she could write-off the whole trip."

"God Mas, you are so cynical…but probably right."

Let's finish eating and get going unless there's anything else? I have a feeling it's going to be a long one.

"One more thing, a suicide, two weeks ago. The forensics team finished analyzing all the data, looking at where he landed, etcetera. Looks more like a homicide. That one is Kenzo's. Anyway, when the team loads anything else regarding our Chinese friends, I'll let you know."

"Okay, don't spend too much time on it."

In a way, I was glad it was murder. Suicides were always the worst. I never did understand what could drive someone to do something so desperate and final. God, I hated that part of the Inspectors job—handling that call, and then telling the relatives what had happened. We dug into the food and polished off most of the takeout, holding to just one beer each.

Chapter Seven

We took a cab to McCarrigan's, and only just made the time. The traffic was completely grid locked. McCarrigan had notified the reception of our arrival, and he was again waiting for us to get off the elevator.

He had laid on snacks and a pot of coffee—thoughtful and unexpected. Tara had a glass a wine and McCarrigan a glass filled with amber liquor. He asked if we would like anything stronger than coffee. Together we chorused.

"Coffee's fine, thank you."

He looked at Tara and said, "Let's get this show on the road."

"Before we start," I said. "I want to confirm Oso will be at your home early. You can't miss him. He is a very large man, and he will drive you everywhere, escort you in and out of buildings, door to door. This is probably overkill, but it's better to have too much, than not enough. Please do not try to slip him or dismiss him. This is for your security…Okay?"

Tara looked away from me, and toward McCarrigan, he smiled and nodded. Tara looking subdued, answered, "I understand you are trying to protect me, but you are also making me nervous. Is all this really necessary?"

Sophie answered, seriously and matter of factly, "We do. If we didn't, we wouldn't be suggesting it.

You are very good at what you do. So are we. Each to their own.

"Okay, I get it. Let's start. Where do you want to begin?"

"Sophie and I believe the answer is in your business dealings, probably in the recent past. It could be in something that didn't complete or go forward. Are there any projects that you had issues with?"

She snorted, "Every project has issues, all sorts, financial, accounting, legal, logistical time, gender. You name it, it happens on every project."

"None stand out?"

"No, nothing right now."

Sophie interrupted, "Sorry, Mas. Tara mentioning accounting just reminded me. When we were talking earlier, it was an accountant who was killed. Murder by suicide. Sorry to sidetrack."

Tara looked annoyed and said, "How about we work backwards from just before the bugs were found? Reverse chronology."

We all agreed that made sense. Tara worked her computer, and we all discussed each project as it came up, drilling her on details. She was good, with a memory like a bear trap. She knew her business and had great recall, providing details that many people would not retain. I could tell Sophie was impressed. I certainly was.

After an hour McCarrigan called time. We agreed to a short break. This was almost like an interrogation, without the police station and lousy coffee. We identified six projects in the four months before the bugs were discovered that we felt deserved a deeper dive.

We picked at the snacks. Sophie made it obvious she would like to continue. Compromising, we moved to the dining room table where we could continue discussing the projects and snack.

McCarrigan played office boy picking up anything Tara printed. We all made notes, comments, and wrote questions on the hard copy. Four brains are better than two, especially when one of them knew the material from scratch. We decided that six projects were enough to deal with as a start. They broke down into one completed project, a complicated one that had a lot of issues getting to completion. Three were started, two of which had stalled for varied reasons, and one was nearing completion. The last two didn't even get off the ground. We left them for last to look at.

Tara chose the completed project with issues to start on. With the four of us tearing at them, breaking down all the components and looking at everyone involved, who they were and what part they played. Tara answered every question quickly and succinctly. Sophie used her laptop to investigate things as Tara spoke or McCarrigan and I had questions. We could find nothing suspicious with anything or anyone involved. Pass. Next one.

Next was a failure from day one. Looking at it, I was surprised Tara went anywhere near it. Even I could see it was cluster-fuck from the start, no one agreeing on anything, under-capitalized, and on a stupid timeline. Even she seemed a bit embarrassed about this one, and it was soon cast aside.

Working as efficiently as we were, the process was still tiring. Focusing so intently was mentally exhausting. On a lot of the technicalities, I was out of my depth, but Sophie more than compensated for me. McCarrigan and Tara were sharp as tacks looking at it as a business exercise, rather than anything personal. More coffee, drinks, and snacks. The second one crashed. Nothing there. On to the third one.

This was another one that did not really get off the ground. A merger-acquisition of a small U.S. company, with a healthy outlook and doing well. The buyers were a Chinese company looking to get a foot hold in the U.S. communications field.

A frown crossed Tara's face as she said, "This one was odd. Everything looked good, very good. We all thought it was going to be an easy one. The buyer offered to pay a premium for the company. This one is definitely worth a look."

We all agreed and began tearing the package apart, looking at the individuals involved on both sides, starting with the U.S. side. Tara read off the team she had put together to act on behalf of the U.S. company. She read off the law firm and the attorneys assigned to her, then the accounting firm and the accountants who would be crunching the numbers.

That was when Sophie exclaimed, "Robert Clegg. Shit, are you sure?"

Tara bridled saying, "Of course, I am. Why?"

Sophie continued, "He committed suicide, or rather was supposed to have. That's going to be changed to homicide real soon. That probably will not be released to the media, until they have a suspect."

Tara looked stricken and asked, "When did this happen. How do you know all this?"

I quickly said, "It was on the news. His name came out later."

Tara repeated the second part, "How do you know this?"

Sophie answered, "We have sources and resources that are not available to other people."

This was a connection, we needed to drill Tara on this one. I asked, "What do you know about Robert Clegg? How well did you know him? Circumstances, anything and everything.

Tara was silent for a minute before asking again, "Are you sure it's Robert?

Sophie responded, "The police are."

She collected herself before she answered, "Robert is-was a very clever guy. He was a freelance accounting consultant. His specialty was forensic accounting." She gave a small laugh. "He was a strange man and very smart, almost genius level. He did the mergers and acquisitions, financials, and accounting work, worked tax season, etcetera to pay the bills until something came along that caught his interest. Originally, I met Robert through Kasagawa. He liked to use him because he was so thorough in his work. Finding things 'not kosher,' Robert's phrase, I don't know how Kasagawa found him. Robert liked Kasagawa because he treated him and his work with formal respect."

Sophie and I looked at each other and gave a slight nod. We knew Kasagawa had been in the BDSM community, and I wondered if Robert was also in the BDSM community. Another avenue to follow. I encouraged Tara to keep talking.

"Well, however they met, I'm glad they did. Robert was awesome. He is the reason this one didn't fly. He couldn't pin down exactly what wasn't right about the deal with the information we had. He requested more files and filings. Both companies were very slow in responding—if they did at all. Robert's suspicions increased. The buyers were not as forth coming as they should have been, even for an offshore company. He researched them and kept hitting walls. He reported to me and the attorneys that there was nothing he could prove, but he would not recommend moving forward with the deal, not until he was sure all was kosher. He never got back to me after delivering that report, and since then I haven't required his services. The U.S. company was approached by another offshore entity, and as our negotiations had not gone well, they decided to use someone other than me. That deal, will probably close soon."

I asked, "Was that a disappointment for you?"

Tara responded indignantly, "Of course it was. I hate to lose any deal. It happens. You brush it off, and on to the next one. That's life in this business."

I continued, "Do you think Robert would have kept working on that project, after it had crashed?"

"Maybe. If it interested him. Like I said, he was a genius and strange. The oddest things set him off."

"Such as?"

"Coffee…his own sixteen-ounce mug without a handle. Three sugars had to go in first, then milk, never cream, topped up to exactly half an inch of the rim. There was a mark inside. He would start drinking when it was almost boiling and sip it until it was gone, however cold it got."

Sophie commented, "Sounds like it could have been genetic."

Tara shook her head saying, "Not sure what it was. He said he'd been tested and wasn't on the spectrum.

He didn't talk about it, and nothing about his family, if he had any. We left it alone, and that was fine with him.

Thinking out loud, I said, "Tara, if he did continue to look into the conglomerate, that could be a reason you were in their sights. You employed him. Perhaps the principals thought you were behind his continued investigations."

"Why would I be interested? The deal fell through."

"As far as you know. What if a different division of the same corporation made the new offer to the buy U.S. company without anyone knowing? It would roll up to the same principals. By the way, what type of company is the U.S. target?"

"A digital media company, called 3DMedia. They are small, flexible, and very good. Most of their work is done in house. It's a one stop shop for design, creation, production, marketing, and advertising. Does that matter?"

"Don't know. What records do you have on them? I would like for Sophie and me to take a look at everything you have."

"Sure, it's all been digitized and archived, I keep everything for the correct period and then I dump it."

Sophie asked, "So it's not on your computer?"

"No, I move everything once I'm finished with it. Everything is put on external hard drives. If it's small on a flash drive or two. That way my computer is clean and doesn't get cluttered."

Sophie commented, "Smart way to do it. This one couldn't have been too big if it never got off the ground?"

"Probably not, I will get Kristen to check

tomorrow, and get you a copy."

Sophie thanked Tara, and I could see she was growing on her.

"This could be the reason you were bugged, home and office, and your computer hacked," I said. "They didn't find what they were looking for on your computer, because you had already moved it. Where do you store the back-up hard drives?"

"A couple are in the office safe, most are in the safe deposit box at the bank, no reason to keep them close, and the bank is safe, fire and hopefully earthquake proof."

I asked, "The archive record for this project is in the bank-right?"

"Of course."

"You label everything right?"

"Naturally."

"So, the intruders who planted the bugs didn't find what they were sent to find, I would put money on that your office safe was breached. You have been in the safe since, right?"

"Yes, nothing is missing, I would have noticed."

Continuing I said, "This makes sense as to why you were targeted. There is something you have, or they think you have. That flash drive connects you to Robert and to the project itself."

Sophie continued, "They probably thought that you would initially be an easier target than Robert, when that failed, they went after him directly.

That didn't sound right, so I asked, "What's the timeline for Robert's apparent suicide and then the two bodies turning up on the Golden Gate?"

Sophie thought for a minute before saying, "Damn-it, Mas. You're thinking "they" were after Robert first. He's killed, and then the bugs are found in Tara's office, and they didn't find the back-up records there, or on Tara's computer."

I loved the way Sophie quickly put things together.

"Yes, except I don't think they were supposed to kill Robert. Something must have gone wrong. He came in and disturbed them. They may have been planting bugs in his place, panicked, and sent him flying off the balcony. Then they must perform and get the necessary from Tara. They fucked-up and paid the price."

McCarrigan chimed in, "I have a question. Why leave the bodies in such a public place? Isn't that counter intuitive for covering up the killings?"

Everyone looked at me.

"That's two questions. First, this is not a one-man operation there will be a hierarchy, whom ever it is, is sending a message, don't screw up or you pay the price, and letting his bosses know he is taking care of business. Second, they don't want the killings covered up, part of the message. One body was easily identified through the DoD, but probably impossible to connect with whom actually ordered the killing. The other man will be impossible to identify, if he is not in any of our systems. They are both way-down in the organization, not on anyone's radar. The display causes a stir, rumors of a Chinatown gang war, gets the Police chasing that one, to make sure it's actually a rumor."

Sophie asked, "Is that why they were Mutilated?

Tara reacted saying, "Mutilated, that's sick."

"But smart, it gets attention, gruesome sells news."

McCarrigan jumped on that comment, "I thought you said they didn't care about the bodies being identified?"

"They don't really, it's deflection and distraction, sending a message to those who know, and sending the authorities in the wrong direction."

He looked thoughtful and said, "That does make sense."

Looking at the other three, we were all tired.

I suggested, "Look these are good leads, but I think we need to call it a night." Everyone nodded in agreement. "Great, Tara we would like to review the archive data that Robert sent you, along with anything else you have pertaining to that project. Is that okay?"

She looked exhausted but said, "Sure, I'll get Kristen to retrieve it from the bank and deliver it to you tomorrow. Unless…you want to pick it up?"

"Kristen knows me. I'll meet her inside the bank just in case anyone is observing you and your office. Would going to the bank be out of the ordinary for her?"

"No, she often comes and goes. It's a company safety deposit box. We are the only ones with access. I'll text you the bank details."

"Get her there early. Tell her I'll be waiting for her inside and check for surveillance."

With the next steps set. We thanked Tara for her help, and McCarrigan for his hospitality. As we left, he offered his hand and thanked us for taking the case. Surprised, I took it. Sophie hugged McCarrigan and we left.

On the ride down Sophie commented, "Once you get to know them, they aren't as bad as I thought they were. I think we had a bad start."

Laughing I said, "Yeah, you could say that, but a

Tiger is just a big cat until it eats you. I don't trust either of them."

When arrived home we went straight to bed. We cuddled together, both of us too tired for anything but sleep. Today had been a long day, but hopefully a profitable one, with new leads and a possible motive for all the activities around our client.

Chapter Eight

For once I was up early and looked forward to the day. Sophie groaned at my cheerfulness saying she preferred me grumpy in the morning. She had to be tired if I was up first. Yesterday had been tiring, physically and mentally. Coffee on, coffee ready, coffee poured into a go cup. I blew Sophie a kiss, and I was out the door.

The office was dark when I opened the door, first in. I smiled to myself. The day had started out all right. However, this was not going to be a habit. I switched on all the lights in the place that Sophie called home, and then I warmed up the computer array.

My cell went off. No one called this early unless it was a problem. Looking at the number, I recognized it as Oso's. This had to be a problem.

"Hello, Oso?"

"Hola, Mas. Got here early an' hung around, then I sees someone parked a few cars back from this lady's house. Not doing nothing. Just parked. Keep me eye on it and go to the front door, she let me in. So, I wait in the house for her to finish getting ready."

"Get on with it, Oso."

"Sorry, Mas. Anyway, I gets the car—nice wheels man—classic. Pull the car out of the garage and double park it—open the door for her. We get going, and she tells me the address. The car waitin' was still doing nothing, then pulls out and follows us. So, I drive real careful like. He's still there, couple cars back. Then I do some evasive stuff, like last minute turns. This guy's like glue. Traffic's too busy for me to really lose him, so I figure, if I can get a picture of him or the plates that would be good, right?"

"Right."

"Thanks. So, I get my phone ready, pull into a spot for deliveries, and hop out as if to open her door. I get a good one of the front and the driver as he passes, then I took one of the back, too. I did good, right?"

"Perfect, Oso. Text me the photos and make sure you keep those eyes peeled for trouble. Call if you need me, anytime. Got it?"

"Got it, Mas."

"Thanks, Oso. Good job. Real clever work." Never underestimate the value of what a few good words will do.

Bing, my cell went off. Oso's text appeared, a black SUV, California plates, the driver was visible, not a great shot through the windshield, but it was a start. The driver didn't look Chinese. Hopefully, Sophie would be able to use her tech wizardry to get a better image. I saved the images and sent them to Sophie's e-mail, requesting that she get info on the license plate and improve the image of the driver.

Checking the time, I noted if I left now for the bank, I'd get there on opening and that would let me get settled to wait for Kristen.

Walking San Francisco is always…well mostly, a pleasure. The number of people on the sidewalk increased the closer I got to Market Street. Slowing my walk, I loved the hustle and bustle of the city. It vibrated with an addictive energy.

The bank was opening just as I arrived. I walked straight in, picked a seat where I could see both entrances, and then waited for Kristen. Ten minutes later, she entered and went directly to the safe deposit entrance. They checked her in and disappeared.

Keeping an eye on both doors, I studied every person who entered after her. None looked suspicious or seemed to be looking for her. A few minutes later, Kristen re-appeared and thanked the bank employee for his help. It didn't appear that she'd picked up anything, and her bag didn't seem any fuller, but then again, a flash drive isn't a large item.

She looked over at me and pretended to be surprised to see me. She made a show of coming over and greeting me as an old friend while I carefully scanned the lobby and teller areas. Nothing seemed out of order.

Standing to greet her, I linked arms with her and said, "Let's get out of here."

We left together, chatting about nothing. As the door closed behind us, she asked, "Was I followed?"

"Not that I'm aware of. Did you get the flash drive from Mr. Clegg?"

"It's not singular. There are five. Tara's archive of the project and four more from Mr. Clegg."

"What! Do you have time for a coffee?"

"Sure, if it's a quick one. Tara is out at meetings until lunch, and the office is fairly quiet."

We walked briskly to the next block and found a café that was busy but not packed. We ordered, waited without chatting and then, once we had our drinks, we found an open booth at the back of the café.

As soon as we were seated, I started talking. "I was told there was only one flash drive for the whole project because it never got off the ground."

"Right. I remember this one. It was a disaster. I always felt there was something off about the deal. It was all too rushed. Tara is usually methodical and careful with everything, and this was a mess—not so much from our end—more from the acquisition side. Getting anything from them was like pulling teeth. They were a pain in my butt. The calls and e-mails were insane, and they were very unresponsive. I don't know what happened, but Tara eventually pulled the plug on it. I for one was glad. We deal with a lot of Asian companies, and they can be a bit difficult, but it's usually a communications issue. This one was just off. Thinking back, 3DMedia were not as forthcoming as I would have expected."

"When did Tara receive the other flash drives?"

"Tara didn't. I did. I open all the mail. So when the first flash drive arrived, it had a note saying it was notes on the project that needed archiving. Mr. Clegg was a strange man, not in a creepy way, just odd. Did Tara tell you about his coffee?

"Yes, she did mention that."

"That, and he always had to have the first coat peg on the left, for his coat, and his hat had to have its own peg never on top of his coat. He was always nice and courteous to me—old fashioned in some ways but spot on with technology. Anyway, he always followed up after a project with final notes and summaries. I wasn't surprised to get the first one. No point telling Tara, I knew the drill, archive it away with everything else dealing with the project. The second one after the project…that was surprising. His handwritten note accompanying it said, 'Additional information.' Then the third and fourth said the same thing. I assumed he had stuff left over, and since the company was so bad at responding, I thought they were just sending stuff very late. Is there a problem with them?"

"Don't know for sure, which is why we wanted to review the data. Based on what you just told me, we need them reviewed ASAP. When did you get the last one?"

Kristen thought for a moment. "I'm not sure— three, four weeks ago. I put it in the bank with the rest of them." She reached into her bag. I stopped her as she was going to pass them to me over the table.

"No, pass them to me under the table if you can get them out of your bag without being seen."

"I can't. Is this really necessary?"

"Just a precaution."

"Okay, I'll go to the rest room. Then I'll be able to pass them to you easily."

"Fine." Kristen went off to the rest room with a puzzled look on her face. I figured she was going to call Tara and ask what was going on. Returning from the restroom she looked more relaxed.

As soon as she sat down, I asked, "Did Tara say everything was okay and to give me the drives?"

"How did you know?"

"You were agitated when you left, more relaxed when you came back. Who else would you call?"

"Well, Mr. Smarty Pants, she was surprised about the extra flash drives. She said to give them to you, to copy them, and get them back to me in time to return them to the bank-today."

"No problem. They will be done, and back with you today."

"Put your left hand under the table palm up."

Casually I leaned on the table with my right elbow and slid my left hand under the table. Feeling her hand, actually her fist, palm down brush mine, we stopped, our hands moved back, and I felt her fingers open. The five flash drives landed in my palm and fit comfortably in my hand. I closed my fingers over them.

She leaned back against the padded seat back. I mirrored her and pulled back from the table. Then I put both hands in my jacket pockets, released the flash drives, and kept my hands in my pockets.

We ended the meeting with our goodbyes, and my promise to have the copies to her in good time to return them to the bank.

We separated. She took off on foot, being close to her office. Deciding I needed to get back to the office quickly, I picked up a cab. Sophie would be wondering what was taking so long. I knew she wanted to get at the information on the original archives.

Well, she would to be as surprised as I was with the additional drives. This could be the reason why Robert Clegg had been killed and why Tara had been targeted.

Digging into other people's business can be a dangerous occupation. We would soon know one way or the other.

Walking in the door I was verbally assaulted by Sophie with, "Did you get it?"

Not being able to resist teasing her, I said, "Oh you mean them."

"What do you mean them?"

"Apparently, Mr. Clegg followed up with four additional flash drives. Kristen just put them in the bank without telling Tara. It was normal procedure, other than there were more follow up drives than usual. Kristen reiterated that Clegg was a little strange in an old-fashioned courteous way."

Sophie chuckled. "Odd balls. Gotta love 'em. While I was waiting…" Was a not so subtle a jab at my tardiness. "I got to thinking…if Kasagawa knew him and trusted Clegg, maybe he was in the kink community as well."

"I saw the look you gave me when Tara mentioned she met him through Kasagawa. That thought had crossed my mind as well. Question is, do we know if he was into kink? We don't have access to his computer. I don't recognize him from the clubs, but that is not a surprise. He could have played more in private parties, rather than the general public parties. There is the Black Rose over in Berkeley…God, I haven't been there in years."

Sophie's tone was questioning, "How come you haven't mentioned that one to me?"

"Over the bridge, it's a pain to get to, and it drags up some memories I would rather not think about."

"Got it, Mas. No problem. I understand better than you think."

"Wouldn't surprise me. Want the flash drives?"

"Stupid question, give 'em up partner."

I handed her the flash drives and told her she needed to copy each, because I agreed to get them back to Tara early in the afternoon. Sophie immediately looked at the identity markings.

Tara's was easy. It had a number and archive

written on it. The others from Mr. Clegg were identified by the same number as Tara's, but which order was anyone's guess. Knowing Sophie, she would want to dive into them straight away. She would also get cranky at any interruption, so I left her to it.

Clearing up odds and ends on my desk made the morning go fast. I decided to take Marie to an early lunch, but she put me off for half an hour, saying she had to complete something official for the business. Better her than me. I left her alone and sat pondering where we were with this case. Some odd links and coincidences—coincidences none of us believed in. The Russia thing was odd, being on the west coast, we dealt with an array of Asian countries and cultures, not all of them nice and legitimate, but never Russia.

Crime has no nationality, no race or gender, or religion for that matter, unless you count love of money as a religion. "Follow the money" was usually a truism that had proven its accuracy throughout time. It certainly had for us.

Sophie and I were waiting on the final documents for the new partnership. In the course Sophie's sister's murder case, a side benefit provided us with several million dollars in finder's fees, not to mention other "not quite so legal" numbers of dollars. All was safely stashed offshore, until we could access it without raising too many IRS eyebrows. We were going to bring the money in through the business, and as an LLC business, pay less tax on it than if it went directly to each of us. Marie was unaware of the windfall about to land in her lap, and we couldn't wait to tell her.

It was going to make her and Chung's life a little easier. As much as I love San Francisco, the cost of real estate is fucking insane. Anyway, they would now be able to buy a place of their own and start the family they were putting off.

Thinking of Marie and Chung, recently I had started to notice the way Marie had been dressing, in lower neck lines and tighter tops, sometimes shirts in sheer-ish fabrics. Ever since I'd known her, she'd worn pants. Now she was into shorter skirts and dresses. The change was recent, and I think that it coincided with putting Chung in a chastity device. I wondered how much Sophie had to do with Marie's changes in her wardrobe. If she was, I would bet lingerie and stockings would be part of the wardrobe overhaul.

Marie was lighter and more flirtatious, provocative without being obvious or trashy. Her mouth was still as sarcastic and caustic as ever. She also carried herself with more confidence. Coincidence? Nah, I didn't believe in them. Well, whatever worked. You have to grab happiness when and wherever you can, it could be snatched away at any second.

Finally, Marie was ready, and it wasn't so early a lunch. Still, I was ready and going to enjoy it, wherever she chose. She picked a local favorite of ours, a bar-restaurant. It was close, and they knew us as regulars. Serving a California fusion menu, which meant the chef made whatever he liked, with whatever was good at the market. No printed menus—only a chalk board that changed daily. We were early, not early enough. They were just started to bustle. We were seated and quickly ordered.

As we waited for our drinks. Marie asked, "How are you doing, Mas?"

The question surprised me. "Why do you ask."

"Just checking. You seem happy with Sophie. More content than you have been in a long time. I don't know…you still seem to have a shadow, or dark cloud hanging around. Hey, don't mind me, just asking?"

"Nice to know you care. I'm doing okay. Finally working through some stuff about Simon. His death was such a waste. Grieving sucks."

"I miss Simon. Chung says no one can really die, not as long as someone has a good memory of them, I kinda like that."

"I like that too, and I have a load of good memories of Simon. His death, going on without him…it hurt so bad before I met Sophie. Somedays it was hard to get out of bed."

"I know. I had to call you, remember." We both laughed at that, and that broke the spell.

"Thanks for asking. I know I wasn't fun to be around."

"Neither was I. Isn't it strange, how a tragedy like Sophie's brought us out of the gloom?"

"I'm just thankful and, to answer your question properly, yes, I am happier than I have been in years. And mostly due to Sophie. As she puts it 'we are two sides of the same coin'."

"All I can say is, you two are weirdly good together, and I am happy for you both. Cheers."

"I think that's a compliment, and I'll take it."

Our drinks had arrived. The meal went quickly, we laughed a lot, and it felt good. While we were walking back to the office, a thought popped into my head from nowhere.

Sophie was still buried in her screens. Marie left a sandwich by her cold coffee and received a grunt of thanks. Smiling to myself I sat down and saw the five flash drives sitting in a baggy, labelled and ready to deliver back to Kristen. That chore would be taken care of, sooner than later.

I knew the number I dialed would be answered. It was—just before it went to voice mail. My ask was going to be a big favor, and I was not sure if I was going too far. This was not something I would discuss over the phone, this had to be a face to face ask. Cautiously I asked if it was okay to talk. He said it was. Saying I needed a meeting, and that it was a sensitive matter, we agreed to meet at the restaurant-coffee shop near the karate Dojo where Sophie trained. Couldn't be today, lunch tomorrow was the soonest.

I took the meeting and said, "Upstairs, tea and bites are on me." He laughed and agreed it was on my dime.

Satisfied with the call, I sat back and thought about the history between us, and how it had gotten better recently. Looking forward to seeing him, I blocked my calendar. Nothing for the rest of the day meant I could use the time to drop off the copied flash drives and get in some target practice. Leaving a note on Sophie's cup, I told Marie where I was going, picked up the flash drives, and wondered what could be so important that it got Clegg killed.

Walking to where I rented a parking spot I called Oso, just to check in.

He answered on the first ring. "Hola Mas."

"Hola Oso, anything happening?"

"Nada since I called you. Easy job, but this Senorita is a busy bitch. She never stops. First this place then that, next on and on. She's on the phone all the time she's in the car. We only stop for lunch. She buys and makes sure we sit together, not like a boss. I like her, Mas. She treats me okay."

"Good to hear, Oso. Make sure you keep an eye out, we aren't sure, but someone maybe targeting her."

"Figured with the tail this morning, ain't seen that car since. Keeping a look out for it, an anyone else. Hey gotta go, she's coming now."

He hung up and was doing what he was paid for, looking out for the client. Wondering what he could have been, if not for a few poor choices when he was young. He'd paid the price and seemed to be doing okay now.

The drive to Tara's office was uneventful, and parking was a goddam nightmare. Finally, I found a meter as a car pulled out, and I pulled in. As luck would have it, there was enough time on it for me to get to Tara's office and back.

Kristen looked up as I walked in. "The originals?"

"Yes, as promised. I have my car would you like a ride to the bank?"

"No, thank you. Never mind. Yes. Actually, I will walk back, Tara is out, and it'll be quicker if you take me."

"Only the two of you here?"

"Usually there is a third, but he's off today—family issue. Okay, let's go. I'll meet you at the elevator. I have to lock up and set the alarm."

Leaving the building, I guided her to the car, and opened it for her. She smiled her thanks. Looking around, I saw nothing untoward, got in, and drove to the bank. Dropping Kristen off, I waited until she entered the bank, which annoyed the driver behind me. Tough.

Next stop? A quick visit home to collect my weapon, then on to the gun range.

It was amazing how therapeutic shooting at paper targets could be—including the ritual of putting on eye and ear protection. Taking my time to go through the process of loading the magazine and the two spares, and then inserting one magazine into the weapon, I followed by pulling back the slide and slipping off the safety. I placed the pistol on the bench facing down range and sent the target down to twenty feet, then picked up the pistol. Breath in—breath out. Bang! A hole appeared in the center ring, slightly off to the right of the cross, but still center.

Before I met Sophie, I had let myself get rusty, shooting wise. Now that Sophie was shooting, I needed to practice. She may not be a natural, but she was dedicated. Going back to her control issues, she just had to be in control. It surprised me we worked so well together in business. It came down to mutual respect for each other's areas of expertise.

Out of work was a different matter. The kink aspect was part of us, not all of us. It wasn't a matter of choice, it was who we were, and what we needed to be fulfilled as human beings. Sophie's earlier quote of "two sides of the same coin" rang true to me.

Banging my way through a hundred rounds, I felt better even if I was covered in gunshot residue, known to fans of TV detective stories as GSR. I went home and dropped all my clothes in the dirty hamper. After I showered off all the day's grime, I felt refreshed, and since the time had slipped away, there was no point going back to the office.

I figured we'd eaten out enough—it was time for a

homemade dinner. Something simple and tasty. Chili and rice sounded good. Prepping for the chili, I didn't hear Sophie come in. It must have been a sixth sense that made me spin around, knife in hand, ready for anything.

The look of surprise on her face was priceless. "How the hell do you do that, I was silent. I wanted to surprise you."

Sheepishly, I put the knife down and hugged her. "Sorry, I don't know. It's just some sense I've always had."

"Well, you scared the shit out of me."

As I kissed her deeply, I enjoyed the way she responded, and my hand strayed to her breast. She felt so good.

"Did I say you could fondle me?" Her hand went to her hip. "Well?"

"No, you didn't."

"You were gentle, and it did feel good after a day of staring at screens. I'll forgive you this time."

"Thank you."

"What's for dinner?"

"Chili and rice."

"Spicy?"

"Oh yes."

"Good. After dinner we need to talk, I have gone over the flash drives. Some of the info was easy to decipher and understand. Some of it will take time to unravel, and I think we'll need a forensic accountant ourselves. Looks like a money laundering scheme and probably something else. I am thinking someone wanted access to a media company, and that is why the 3DMedia was a target for purchase. Anyway, diner first. I am starving."

Going back to prepping the food, it was like meditation. I knew what I was doing so my mind started to wander. Money laundering, and media, Russian interference, both the Russian government and mob had fingers in both those pies. With sanctions on the government, they had to get hard currency somehow, and the criminals needed to clean their money. Still, we had to find out why target Tara, the only way she would be safe is find out who had targeted her and why. From what Sophie said it sounded like Mr. Clegg had found something. I hoped it was on the flash drives, we could find it, and understand it.

Even though I say so myself, dinner was exactly as promised-simple and good. We killed a couple of beers each while we ate and talked through what Sophie had viewed on the flash drives.

She had opened all the flash drives to ascertain the order in which she should review them. The first one was the Tara project archive to get an overview of the entire project. At first look it seemed a straightforward deal. Sophie made a list of all the emails to and from and who was copied on them. Next, she reviewed the four additional drives Mr. Clegg had sent checking the order in which he had sent them.

Mr. Clegg had found something that intrigued him, followed up of his own volition and sent it to Tara, not knowing she had never seen it, or did he? He'd worked with her before. He knew her process and used her as a safe drop for the additional information. Each flash drive contained details of his research, each one had pieces of information, and built on information contained in the others. The last one was the most valuable one, having most of the information collated, but not all. Sophie thought the next he would have sent, would have put everything together as a complete picture.

Sophie said there were charts and flow diagrams. A lot of accounting terms Sophie didn't understand, and a few accounting concepts that were hard to grasp. I was not looking forward to reading through it, and I knew I would have to. Even if we didn't understand it all, it would give us leads and when needed, get experts to break it down for us, in words of one syllable if necessary.

Tired from the day Sophie didn't feel like playing a D/s scene and I was happy to go along.

"Would you like a massage and an early night. "

"Massage sounds wonderful, please."

We moved into the bedroom; I did have an ulterior motive. Getting to see her naked and getting to lay my hands on her, even if I didn't get a release, it was worth the visuals. Just thinking about it got me hard, feeling the cock cage constrict my rigid member. My thoughts went to the pleasure of frustration, and the frustration of pleasure. Taking my time with the massage, I think it relaxed me as much as Sophie. When I had finished, I quickly undressed and climbed in beside Sophie and was also out like a light

Chapter Nine

With a start, I awoke and realized I was alone in bed. Sounds from the kitchen must have woken me. Sophie was usually more a morning person, I was not. The clock mocked me, and I groaned as I gathered the energy to get up.

Sophie came into the room with a tray. "Last night was just what I needed, and you get a reward for such a great massage. Breakfast in bed for once. Don't get used to it. Coffee and Huevos rancheros. Enjoy I am off to the office. Love you."

Speechless, I waved as she closed the door. I sat up to enjoy the feast before me. How the hell did an East Coast girl learn how to cook Mexican food this well. I wasn't going to argue, just savor it. This was a good start to the day. I could see more massages in the near future if this was the result.

Getting to the office in a good frame of mind. Marie looked up and sarcastically said, "Hola, Jefe." Obviously, Sophie had told her about my Mexican breakfast.

Very funny, but nothing was going to spoil this start to the day. Coffee in hand, Sophie and I went over all the information we had so far. She was going to do a deeper dive on the flash drives and get some references on a forensic accountant if we got to that point. My job was to review the flash drives myself, starting with

Tara's archived project for an overview. This was certainly not my favorite pastime, and it would be a trial for me. At least, I had my meeting set for late morning, and that would be a better use of my time, and hopefully more profitable.

Tara's archived information of the project was interesting. Giving an insight to how she thought and worked her processes. As an overview it was a big picture, and there was no way this deal should have folded. This was a simple deal. Most of the issues came from the buyer. Tara said the problems usually got sorted out in a mutually beneficial way, and the deals got done.

The pushback came when Mr. Clegg got involved and started his financial analysis. Up until then everything went smoothly. Understanding why the deal folded would be a good starting point. Something Mr. Clegg had discovered or uncovered triggered the buyer. Tara herself terminated the agreement, cutting her losses. In my humble opinion, she had made the right decision.

Interesting though, according to the e-mails in the file, 3DMedia didn't seem to upset about the collapse of a very good deal for them. It made me wonder if they'd already been approached by some other interested party or a different division of the original buyer. Food for thought.

Mr. Clegg's flash drives were a very different matter. These flash drives were torture to go through, mainly because I didn't understand a lot of what was going on, or the depth of the financial and accounting detail. Balancing a checkbook is one thing. This was not on a different level; it was on another planet. All the words were English, but still, I didn't understand them. Our office books and financials were handled by Marie, I just signed the checks.

I came up for air just in time to get ready for my meeting. Telling Sophie that I was going, she waved but kept working.

"Marie, please, make sure Sophie has lunch, will you?" She promised she would.

Parking wouldn't be an issue. The traffic was going to suck, even though I left with plenty of time which was a good idea. On the drive, I thought about the man I was meeting. We went far back, and I'd trusted him with my life more than once. He had never failed me, but that was when I was an Inspector. Remembering how he had taken a significant risk in helping us solve Sophie's sisters' murder. That could have tanked his career, and that gave me reason to be positive. I arrived with a few minutes to spare, and as expected, parking was easy. I entered the Café Wanatabe, where San was in his usual place behind the counter. He smiled and nodded a bow.

I returned the bow and asked, "Is the upper floor available?" There were always "Go" games set up, and people came and went at all hours.

"Yes, Mr. Hammett. Will anyone be joining you?"

"Hopefully, Mr. Otake."

As I finished speaking a voice answered, "He's here." I turned to meet the voice.

It was Kenzo Otake, recently promoted SFPD Inspector to Lieutenant. It was good to see him. We hugged and went up the narrow stairs to one of the rooms above the café.

We sat opposite each other at one of the small

tables, and Kenzo got the conversation started, "So why the clandestine meeting, you haven't gotten yourself into something you shouldn't have?"

The look on my face told him all he needed to know. "Oh, shit Mas, what is it."

"Off the clock and off the record?"

The look on his face was somber, "Yes, off the clock and off the record. What do you need?"

"Information. Information that may have something to do with two different case's that are currently active in the police department."

"If they are police cases, how are you involved?"

"A client was referred to us. They thought they were being targeted on business matters. Turns out, they'd been bugged, home and office, their computer had a nasty planted and was an open book. Well, that one still is. We managed to find out that the two men who planted the bugs were Chinese. Then two corpses show up on the Golden Gate Bridge...Chinese corpses."

Kenzo interrupted, "How do you know they are the same two?"

"We don't, for sure. Coincidence? You don't believe in them anymore than we do. Anyway, our client also had dealings with a Mr. Robert Clegg, a suicide turned homicide."

"That's not public knowledge, how do you know this. Do we have a leak?"

"I can't say how we know. You do not have a leak, at least not that we know of. Two men target and bug our client and end up dead. Then someone our client worked with, apparently on several projects, ends up dead. Suicide? Or really a homicide? We think it's all connected, and the timing is very suspect."

"How so?"

"We are working on the premise that Clegg may have been killed by mistake. Whatever the killers were after they didn't get. The culprits then bug and try to get it from our client. Fail again, and they pay the ultimate price. Mutilated bodies left in a very public place to get a lot of media attention."

"They sure do…unfortunately."

"It also serves as a warning to others and distracts the authorities. A gang war rumor has to be investigated. Right?"

Kenzo was thoughtful and took his time before commenting. Wanatabe brought up a pot of tea and mixed pot stickers, serving us silently, he then quickly left us to our business.

"Mas, your theory is flimsy, circumstantial, and not really connected. You wouldn't go on this little evidence, not on the worst day you ever had. You're keeping something back."

He put me in a bad spot. I needed his help, but I didn't want to tell him anymore than I had to. Damn it, he could still read me.

"Yes, I am. Do I have your word this stays just between us?"

"Same as your rules. I won't say or do anything unless I believe that someone's life is in jeopardy. I know you now cross the lines occasionally." He gave a wry smile at that comment.

"Yes, I do. Now I have more leeway than you do, as long as I am not caught. Okay, we have an audio tape of two Chinese men breaking into our clients' home, they spoke Chinese and we have the translation. They mention they'd also bugged our clients' office; we had the office swept and found the same type of bug in both places. We believe they are the men found on the Golden Gate."

"That makes sense, but it's still not cast iron. Which is why you need my help, right?"

"Yes."

"What do you actually need…the minimum?"

"The easy stuff first, a full copy of the ME's report including DNA. We are going to get an independent lab to go over our clients' places. We would also suggest you get someone to sweep Mr. Clegg's place for bugs. I assume it's still a crime scene?"

"Yes, it's officially a crime scene, and no one else has been in it since he took the long drop. Good suggestion. Anything we should look for?"

"Is your team on this one?"

"The Clegg thing? Yes. The bridge no. That's Gomez, in the Pacific division."

"That may have been done deliberately. We got lucky…a stray comment when working with our client. Without that, we wouldn't have made the connection between our client and the separate deaths. That's what brought it all together for us."

"Better to be lucky than good. Best to be both."

"You got that right. If any bugs are found, my money is on old style Russian, or Eastern European equipment."

"What?"

"That's what we found. This stays between us."

"Yeah, yeah. What the fuck is Russian equipment doing in the hands of Chinese burglars in San Francisco?"

I laughed. "Welcome to the global economy."

"Yeah, great. You still haven't asked what you really want."

"Well, I was leaving the best for last." I took a deep breath knowing it was a big ask. "Can you get us a copy of Mr. Clegg's hard drives, laptop, and desktop?"

"Jesus, Mas! You don't want much. Anyway, there was no laptop found in his apartment. Are you sure he had one?"

"That's been confirmed with our client."

"The burglar or killers…whichever, must have been taken it. If, and it's a big if, I will try to get the hard drive from his desktop copied. Not a promise, Mas. That's a big ask."

"Fair enough. Remember, Sophie is better than the best tech you have, and I promise to share anything we find, as long as it doesn't impact our client negatively."

"That covers a lot of ground. How's it working out with Sophie as a partner?"

"Much better than expected. We both have our issues."

That brought a guffaw. "No shit, Mas, we all do. You two have had more than your fair-share. I hope it works out. Don't call me. I'll call you if I can work something out. Thanks for lunch."

"My pleasure."

We shook hands, bowed, and then laughing, hugged. It was good to be back on an even keel relationship with Kenzo. He left first. Staying I finished the tea and cooled pot stickers.

A thought hit me. Idiot! Sometimes you just have to wait for the right moment for a thought to come to you.

Tara said she was introduced to Mr. Clegg by Kasagawa. The probability of Mr. Clegg being a member of the kink community increased the minute I realized he was Kasagawa's friend. Kasagawa had compartmentalized his life in the U.S., mixing with the SF Japanese community for his home language fix, but visiting the kink clubs for his BDSM fix. If Kasagawa's KinkInc profile was still up, maybe Mr. Clegg was on his friend list.

Calling Sophie, I was surprised when Marie answered. "Sophie has asked not to be disturbed. Is it urgent Mas?"

"No, just take a message and give it to her. She can decide what to do with it, if anything, until I get back. 'In KinkInc are Kasagawa and Clegg friends?' Read it back."

She did.

"Perfect, on my way back, now."

Going down the stairs two at a time, I was in hurry. I paid the tab and waved goodbye to Wanatabe.

The drive back was easier, but still awful. Sophie was waiting for me with a smile, "Good thought, Mas. Thanks for the message. I was getting frustrated with the lines of enquiry I was following and not getting anywhere. I've come across some interesting names to work on. I pulled up Kasagawa's KinkInc profile. It's still open. As we knew, he didn't have many friends on that site, but Clegg was one of them. Clegg's profile is there. He did a nice job, very accountant like, no surprises. He was a switch. But selective with his friends. He had a lot following him, but only a couple of dozen or so friends. Kasagawa being one."

"Any other names jump out?"

"Not immediately. You can dig at those. You have a better feel for that site than I do."

"Wow, praise indeed."

"Nope, just the truth. So, get to it."

"Yes, ma'am."

"That was a clever idea, and the break has given me renewed enthusiasm to get back in the trenches. This accountant stuff this is not easy to get your head around."

I sighed. "That's why you're doing it and not me."

"Thanks! I am also following some e-mail trails to other folks who may or may not be connected to Tara's project, if they are connected it has to be peripheral. Bye."

Sophie blew me a kiss and disappeared behind her computer screens. The snacks at Wanatabes' had not filled the hungry hole, so I asked Marie to run out and get me a sandwich or something. KinkInc was the go-to site for Kink events and kinksters in the Bay area, more for connections than for dating, thankfully. The site was international, and not particularly well designed for ease of use, not very intuitive getting around it. Navigating took practice, and in this case, I had more than Sophie.

Mr. Clegg had a detailed profile. Using the KinkInc name of 'Mr. Numbers' was apropos, I guess. The profile page was well put together, and his proclivities probably had nothing to do with his death. We had to follow all and every lead, you never knew when something interesting, or vital would show up. Looking through his list of friends and followers, nothing and no one jumped out to me as suspicious, however I would delve into each one of them.

Thankfully, he didn't have that many friends.

Looking into each one was time consuming, taking the name plugging it in the search function, open the profile and read everything posted. Some people posted way too much, others kept it brief, here was the usual mixture of everything, leaning to the more is better side. The mix of people and ages was interesting, he was obviously liberal in his tastes people wise, and very selective quality wise. Each profile I looked at was very well constructed. Literate in describing the owner and the persons wants and needs, open and up front. Better vocabulary and detail than most

No one stood out until I hit Ms. Doubleentry. In the BDSM community that could be taken in multiple ways. She seemed too young for Mr. Clegg. He was in his mid-forties, and she was in her mid to late twenties, according to her profile.

Her main picture was a partially hidden face, the others on public view were a mixture of photos of her in various BDSM scenes, never showing her full face, images pulled from the internet. One thing that caught my eye was her hobbies, math puzzles and problem solving, as in any, numerology, video gaming, solving the unsolvable equations. I wondered if she had ever worked with Mr. Clegg and if they mixed BDSM pleasure with math pleasure.

She listed as a switch, same as Mr. Clegg, other than age they seemed a good fit for each other. The list of what she was into was very specific—both giving and receiving. She was thorough in listing and delineating what she wanted—a 'yes' with soft, medium, and hard limits—and what she was curious about or willing to try with the right partner, male or female.

Her public calendar of events showed she was not particularly active. Only two events were listed as "going" and a "maybe." Checking the dates and locations, I noted one of the "going" events was an open play party the following night at Sorcerers, I knew the club, though not as well as The Cauldron. This may be worth investigating. The "maybe" event was on Sunday. A bondage workshop? Not easy to have a conversation at a workshop. The other "going" to was not for two weeks, and then nothing else was on her calendar. Not wanting to wait that long, I decided tomorrow night was our best opportunity.

Pulling up the event, I checked "going" and sent an e-mail to Sophie letting her know we had a date at Sorcerers and the reason why. Ping, that was fast.

She responded, "Good idea, we should probably scout it out tonight."

Uh oh. That could mean a lot of things, knowing Sophie. My cock started hardening in its restraint. Being controlled by her got me going every time. In public, it caused me all sorts of anxiety, and turned me on beyond belief—a contradiction I had yet to resolve.

Business first. If Ms. DoubleEntry had worked with Mr. Clegg, hopefully she would give us some insights into his work. It could also make her a target, if any one discovered that she worked with him— assuming she wasn't already targeted. The fact that Clegg's laptop was taken, made me believe whatever they were looking for hadn't been found, and if it had, someone was making sure there were no copies of his work. Tara was targeted after he was dead.

More bloody questions than answers.

Our one problem was we didn't know what Ms. DoubleEntry looked like, because she always hid her face, or most of it. Checking her list of friends on her profile I didn't know or recognize any of them. I'd have to figure out another route. Going back to Mr. Clegg's profile and checking all his friends to see if there were any in common with Ms. DoubleEntry, there was one couple, but again I didn't recognize either participant. It was worth a shot. The whole BDSM community was interconnected. Six degrees of separation, and all that. KinkInc was a good place to find a lot of those links.

Back to Ms. DoubleEntry's profile, I scanned all her posted public images looking for clues to help me recognize her in a real-life situation. Hair style, size and shape of her body, the kind of clothes she wore or didn't, favorite colors…anything I could find. Making a list, I built a profile.

Of course, there was a lot of black, the basic color of choice in the kink-fetish world. Ms. D.—I couldn't handle calling her Ms. DoubleEntry all the time. The name was too long. She was varied in her choices, going with various shades of green. While some photos partially showed her face, there was no hair to be seen. So, she was either bald, unlikely, or my money was on her being a red head. Looking at all her images again, not one showed hair, heads chopped off, hoods, masks, and head coverings. Being a red head was a natural *look at me*—an identifying mark.

Next observation, there were none of her standing, they were all kneeling, seated, or laying down. Looking at the poses and the position she had been placed in, in relation to the equipment like the spanking bench. She had to be tall, a lot taller than average. Six feet for sure.

Damn she would be imposing in heels. You would see her a mile away. Impressive, with a figure to match without being cartoonish or fake, everything about her looked real. At first, I thought at that height she could be Trans, not that it mattered, I was looking to find her, not judge her. I discarded that idea after reviewing the images of her naked.

The profile was not a long one, but I could hang the information I had on it and figured we had enough to identify her in person. It didn't take long to get a response once I sent my profiles of Ms. D. and KinkInc to Sophie for her feedback and comments.

She looked up at me from her computer. "Wow, she's a tall one. Your profile makes sense, but I'm not sure I agree with your assumption about the hair color. Wanna make a bet? If you're right, I get to pick our play date. If you're wrong, you get to pick the play date."

That was a twist, usually in our wagers, the winner got to pick. Beginning to wonder if Sophie actually thought I was right about Ms. D's hair after all.

"Ah, I don't think so. No bet. This is business."

"Let's put that one on hold until tomorrow? This profile is a good start, I can't think of anything to add, I will look at her profile when I get a chance."

"It's definitely on hold."

Sophie laughed and went back to doing her stuff. Going back to Ms. D's profile, I looked to see if something had caught Sophie's attention, if there was, I didn't see it. Sophie was devious in her Dominant role. Mixing business and pleasure could be an explosive mixture. Her computer world was much safer than the messy real world. Now she had joined the real world, she still didn't completely understand all the risks.

The rest of the day passed without incident, all three of us doing what we were supposed to, and tomorrow was another day, another day to resolve the threat. With the additional pressure of finding the reason behind Mr. Clegg's death-it had to be connected.

Toward the end of the day Sophie looked up, "I would like us to explore the space at Sorcerers tonight, I checked there is an open play party." It was a statement not a question, and I had no problem with it, just anxious on the timing.

"Why tonight?"

"You said you haven't been there in quite a while, me either. I want to check it out, get the lay of the land, before we hopefully meet with MsDoubleEntry."

"Any other reason?"

"Oh, you will just have to wait and see."

That convinced me it would be a play night for us. We both could use the distraction to decompress and clear our minds. The following night would be all business.

We ate an early dinner. Sorcerers opened at 8:00 p.m. but wouldn't be busy until 10:00 p.m. at the earliest. That was fine for our purposes. Get in early, check out the place, then make sure it was the same as I remembered it.

Sophie changed into Ms. Circe. The metamorphosis never ceased to amaze me. She was the same person, but different, in a good way. Like me, kink was a part of her, an essential part, not a defining part. She was a complicated person, and that was one of the things I loved about her. Thankful for how lucky I had been to meet her, even under tragic circumstances.

101

The way she was dressed it would be an active evening. The corset she chose was not a restrictively tight one and covered more of her, although when she got swinging a flogger, a boob had been known to escape. Wondering if she would use me as her target for release tonight, or find someone at Sorcerers for pick up play, then just use me as her goffer and clean-up crew. Whatever she wanted was fine by me, I trusted her.

In Circe mode, she instructed me to tighten the laces of her gold brocade corset. Tightened to her satisfaction, she said good enough. Stockings pulled up and attached to the six garters attached on each side of the corset. Circe chose her shoes, she handed them to me, black patent five-inch heeled pumps. Circe standing in front of me, her pussy, level with my face, neatly trimmed blond curls, tantalizing me. Feeling a hand grab my hair, she balanced herself and raised one foot, slipping on shoe on. Foot down, the other foot lifted, and the shoe slipped on.

Remaining in my position Circe pondered the rest of her wardrobe, finally selecting a pair of loose wide legged Japanese style pants, semi-sheer, down to her ankles leaving her shoes exposed. She was ready, I knew she would cover up with a light coat, for the night chill when we left the club.

Dressing for me was easy, as instructed no underwear, or socks. Black shirt, pants, and slip-on shoes. My cover-up was a black leather blazer. We were ready to go, I picked up our play bag and we grabbed a ride share. The evening was drawing in, and the lights of the city glowed, getting ready for the night's excitement. I can't say it enough, I love this city for all its faults, and it has many, but I love it, and wouldn't want to live anywhere else.

Arriving at Sorcerers, the doors were open, and a few people going in. We paid our entrance fee and signed the usual waivers. Switching off our phones, which was a painful exercise for Sophie. Not so much for Circe, it meant she was about to play. We stored them in one of the available lockers along with our coats. As expected, there were only a few people milling around, couple here, couple there, singles moving about.

Going upstairs I noticed a change, the place had been cleaned up, tided up, and painted. One wall had been stripped down to the brick and it looked good. All the equipment looked refurbished. The Saint Andrews crosses, glinted with new varnish on the wood and the leather pads shone. The whole place had a new look of care and attention. The huge play space was overlooked by the lounge. Only soft drinks and mocktails served along with lite bites. All the furniture had been replaced with a mixture of comfortable chairs and sofas.

A new feature at the far end of the play space was an open loft like level, accessed by a spiral staircase. Two beds and two chairs were the only items on that loft. The beds, one was a vacuum-bed the other had tie down rings all around it. The chairs, one a Queening chair, and when in use the submissive was trapped by the head inside the chair. The other a restraining chair, the person sitting was retrained in place by multiple straps, not able to do anything but wait for release.

The excitement for tonight began to increase, whatever Circe wanted to do, let's get it on. Circe sat on one of the sofas, I stood at her side, holding both our drinks, our toy bag by our side. Being in role and submissive to Circe was always a turn on, and I was thinking that she was doing this deliberately. She knew the effect she had on me in this situation. Would we play together, or would she keep me hanging? As I was pondering, a young woman approached us. Stopping in front of Circe, she curtsied introduced herself as "Pearls" and asked if Circe was open to doing a scene.

Circe responded by asking her to sit, offering to chat. The woman was probably in her early thirties, and well put together and would probably be described as well rounded, she already had wrist and ankle cuffs attached. Circe and Pearls sat close and began to chat. Negotiation was required on both sides for them to progress from a potential to an active scene. Not being able to hear much of what was being discussed I began to drift. This was a meditation for me, letting go the stress, being someone else's responsibility for a while, it was freeing. Hearing my name brought me back to reality.

Circe was standing holding Pearls hand, she said, "We need to get you parked, so I can have some fun with Pearls."

"Yes ma'am, as you wish."

"There is a black velvet bag in our toy bag, please get it and hand it to me."

That was new, I didn't recognize that item. Opening the bag there it was on top, lifting it out it had weight, and circular, a collar perhaps for Pearls to use for the scene. Handing it to Circe, she immediately opened the drawstring and pulled out a substantial collar. She instructed me to turn with my back to her.

Feeling the collar encircle and close around my neck, the leather was cool against my skin, the collar felt heavy for leather. Circe explained.

"Your collar is steel, covered in leather. It has a substantial lock. The collar is not coming off until I decide it is."

Circe locked the collar on. As I heard the lock click shut, a jolt went directly to my cock. Instructed to pick up the bag and follow her. Obediently I followed her and Pearls down to the play area.

Circe strode through it to the end and carefully ascended the spiral staircase, saying over her shoulder, "I don't want you getting into any trouble while we girls have fun."

She was going to put me in the chair. Shit, as much as I wanted it, the humiliation of being strapped down in view of everyone, was going to turn me on, and make me want to run away, unresolved contradictions.

Reaching the chair, Circe told me to look directly at her, she said one word, "Strip."

What! She was going to strap me down naked, exposed. and in view of everyone. My face burned hot, my cock filled my cage, and I obeyed her, undressing quickly. Sitting on the bare varnished wood, my back against the pad and legs spread wide open. Pearl saw my chastity device and giggled in appreciation.

Circe told Pearls to strap me down. Pearls began at my neck, threading the strap through the rings set in my collar, pulling my head back against the head pad, firm but comfortable. Next came the chest strap. My back was snug against the back pad. The hip strap pulled my ass deep into the back of the seat. My torso was now fixed—left arm strapped near the elbow, forearm and wrist straps fixed in place. With each strap tightening, I could feel myself letting go. Right arm was a repeat of the left, and only my lower body remained free.

The wide V of the chair split me open, my encased genitals open to view, the light glinting off the shiny metal cage. First the right thigh strap pulled my leg outward and was strapped in place. Moving downward, next was the strap around the top of my calf just below the knee, pulled firmly against the smooth varnished wood…she finished my leg with the ankle strap. Pearls moved to my left leg and quickly had me completely immobilized. Circe complimented Pearls on the neat job she had done and kissed the top of her head, she dropped her head and blushed.

Circe was not finished with me. She went into the toy bag searching for something specific. My anxiety started to rise, needing to be released from this chair, so I could get some relief. Circe knelt in between my wide-open legs, I could feel her playing with my cage, not teasingly. When she let go of my caged cock, the chastity device was heavier and pulled down. Circe smiled and said,

"Enjoy. I'm sure everyone watching will have a good view of you."

A buzzing started and vibrations hit my groin, she had attached a vibrator to the cock cage. The low throbbing sound assaulted my ears and the waves of vibration invaded me. As the vibrations washed up the cage, my dick felt as if it were at the center of my being. The vibrations intensified as my erection pushed into the slots of the cage, filling it to capacity. Futilely, I tried to move away from the tormenting machine. I wanted to come, but not in public. Resisting was not an option. At this level the machine would eventually make me orgasm, as it had in the past, but that had been in the privacy of our home, not in front of an audience. As they moved away from me, I saw a remote in Circe's hand, the vibrations decreased to a level that would maintain a constant erection, but not push me over the edge to orgasm. This was going to be torture.

Circe told Pearls to pick up the toy bag and follow her. Fixed in position, I could see most of the lower play floor. Would Circe hide from me, to tease me by not knowing what was going on, or worse perform in front of me? Allowing me to see her in action, while not being able to join in. My balls felt like they would explode at the slightest touch, I was so horny.

Straining fruitlessly against the straps and trying to get a glance of her. Circe came into view, leading Pearls to the furthest Saint Andrews cross. Pearls was turned facing me, Circe commanded Pearls to undress. Slowly, taking her time. Pearls removed her clothing piece by piece, and carefully folded and placed them to one side. Naked, Pearls, her pale skin almost luminous, backed up to the cross. Circe fixed her wrist cuffs to hanging clips. Her tits lifted with her arms. Her large nipples, even from my distant vantage point, were hard and visible. With her ankle cuffs fixed to the lower clips, she was spread, open and vulnerable.

Circe pulled two soft leather floggers out of her bag, showing them to Pearls, her eyes widened in anticipation of what was to follow. Circe showed her a blindfold and asked a question, Pearls shook her head in the negative.

Standing in front of Pearls, Circe began the ritual of flogging a willing participant. Slowly and deliberately, she swung one of the floggers, and after a while she switched to the one in her other hand. The blows were light, barely touching Pearls. As Circe warmed up, she continued by using both floggers and alternating them. She built up a rhythm. Pearls reacted to the ministrations. Her shoulders and breasts started to change color. The paleness began to change to a rosy glow. The blows began to change direction and land between her legs and inner thighs, making her rise up against her bonds to avoid the leather tongues that lapped at her. She called to Circe, a denial. Frantically Pearls moved, rocking side to side, and again with a desperate call out. Circe gave permission. Pearl slumped into her restraints and shuddered against them in orgasm.

Waiting a few minutes, Circe released her, pointing to the clean-up cart. Pearl wiped down the cross and sanitized it for the next players. While Pearl was cleaning up, Circe prepared the spanking bench. Picking a paddle from the bag, she tapped Pearl's ass and pointed to the bench. Laying her rouged front onto the cool leather. Circe attached Pearl at wrist and ankle.

The first blow made Pearl jerk violently forward, and all the breath went out of her. As she inhaled, Circe struck again. Pearl gave the same jerk forward, this time issuing a scream from her open mouth. Circe played her, never letting her settle into a rhythm, keeping her on edge with the interrupted frequency and intensity of the blows.

Because Pearl was sideways to me, I could not see the change in color of her ass, only her reaction as the blows landed. She was grinding on the bench's smooth leather padded top and finding no relief.

Her shoulders pulled her body up and forward, in a humping motion. Now Circe was using a lighter touch and a more sustained pattern of stokes. Pearl orgasmed against the bench, each wave slightly less than the one before, until she was still. Circe freed her from the bench and covered her with a light blanket. Standing unsteadily, Pearl was supported by Circe, and together, they walked out of my sight for after care.

Without Circe to focus on, my sight wandered over the entire club. Seeing many of those in the lounge looking my way. I quickly averted my eyes and focused on the main play area, trying to enjoy the sights and sounds of the now filling club. Most of the equipment was occupied, and scenes were in various stages of play. Time drifted slowly. The captured erection throbbing between my legs continually reminded me of my predicament, still reinforced by the vibrator attached to the cage.

A couple came up the spiral staircase and went to the vacuum bed. He helped her naked form in between the layers of rubber. Seeing only what my peripheral vision picked up, I concentrated on the sights before me and the sound of the vacuum bed being turned on, hearing the air being sucked from around her supine body.

Due to the sound of the vacuum, I didn't hear Circe, before she was suddenly standing in front of me. Smiling she asked, "Did you enjoy the show?"

"Yes, ma'am."

"Of course, you did. The question is what do we do with you?"

"Whatever you wish."

"A proper answer. You will get a release tonight. I will give you the choice of places. You chose the place, and I get to choose the how. That seems fair."

"As you wish ma'am."

"I know. Isn't that a delightful thing? Choose between here and now, or home later."

Without even thinking about the consequences, I said, "Here and now, please."

"Excellent choice, I was hoping you would choose here. Stay put."

In my rush to agree to her option of choosing a location, I ignored that she held the how of my release. Now I began to worry. What was she going to have me do, in accepting my release?"

Daring a look at the lounge, I noticed there were several people watching me squirm in discomfort. I eagerly waited to see if Circe would allow an orgasm, or if she'd spoil the orgasm. I looked away, squeezing my eyes shut, fighting the consistent waves of sensation going through me. Knowing I couldn't hold out forever, I wanted this to be over. With Circe, there was always a price to pay for pleasure.

Hearing her voice, I opened my eyes. Leaning in toward me one hand either side of my head, she said, "How about some encouragement."

The intensity of the vibrations increased, and changed from constant to a random pattern, with one hand she folded the upper part of her corset inward exposing her nipple, switching hands she repeated the action. Her nipples hard and centered in a pool of crinkled aureole just out of reach of my parted lips.

"Would you like a taste, here let me help you."

With her hand she held her right tit, just at the edge of my lips. Stretching to my limit, I managed to lick the very end of her nipple. She pushed forward, and I took her breast into my mouth. My body pulled against every strap restraining me. The vibrator continued pushing random waves of motion and sensations into me, through the metal cage and my filled flesh.

Retreating, she removed her breast from my mouth, replacing it with her other, alternating, now twisting my nipples with her free hand. The vibrations were back to constant and each time she changed the breast in my mouth, the vibrators intensity was moved up a notch. Finally, this pushed me over the edge, feeling my balls tighten and rise up, quickly I asked with a mouth full of her breast for permission to come. Nothing, again I asked, louder, but still muffled my mouth gagged by the fullness of her breast. At the point of no return, I heard the magic words

"You may come now."

She pulled back from me allowing a clear view to all observing us. My body contracted in a spasm as I expelled my cum out through the end of the cage. It spilled out, slid down over the tormenting vibrator, and dripped down to the floor, pooling between my spread legs. More spasms followed, each decreasing in intensity. The feeling of the ejaculation was one of awesome relief. Vaguely, I heard applause of appreciation coming from lounge. Feeling physically and emotionally drained, all I wanted to do now, was go home and get into bed with Sophie.

Releasing me slowly and methodically. Circe talked me down, and as each strap was released, I felt myself return to earth. Clean up materials were on a small table against the wall. Still naked and on my knees, I cleaned up my cage, and the pool of ejaculate. Wiping and sanitizing the chair, where I had just been restrained, for the next recipient. The process of cleaning up was therapeutic in its own right, a transition from one state to another. Circe hugged me, saying it was time to dress and go home.

On the way home, Circe returned to being Sophie and said, "I wasn't sure if bringing you off in public was going too far, knowing you are circumspect about some public stuff. I'm very happy that you trusted me that far."

"Sophie as you, or as your alter ego Circe, I trust you with my life."

"I know, and that's scary. I have never had that much responsibility before. With you though, it doesn't seem to be a weight I can't carry.'

"Good, back to reality. We have a busy day tomorrow."

She laughed, "And you say I'm the one who compartmentalizes."

"You are. I am just picking up your bad habits."

We crashed into bed, cuddling we were out in minutes.

Chapter Ten

After the previous night's adventure, I felt refreshed and more relaxed, a hot shower, free of my cage, but observed by Sophie. With the cage replaced, I was ready for the day. My first call of the day was to Tara, for once she sounded pleased to hear from me.

"Mr. Hammet any progress?"

"Please call me Mas. I think we are beyond the formality of Mr. Hammet."

"Well Mas, any progress?"

"Some, we are sure it's somehow connected to the 3DMedia project. The death of Mr. Clegg is part of it, and we think he found something significant in his research, which put him in jeopardy and by extension you."

"There was nothing in the flash drives?"

"Sophie is still tearing them apart. We will probably have to get a forensic accountant to help with that stuff. That is way out of our wheelhouse, and we may have a lead on one of those."

"Kristen told me about the extra drive's Robert sent. Why would he send them to me, the project was closed?"

"Whatever he found started with that project. He used you as a safe haven. He knew your process, about archiving projects so that was a safety measure, what he didn't count on was the efficiency of Kristen. You didn't know anything about the extra work he was doing. If you had, would you have contacted him?"

"Absolutely. I would have wanted to know what and why. I still do. Especially now, after what has happened."

"Anything odd or suspicious occurred since we started looking into this matter?"

"No. I use my old computer for everything that was already compromised, so it's in use all the time. Hopefully, that should keep whoever hacked me busy. My new computer is only for new business."

"Good."

"Sophie mentioned it. She is very good. She set up my new computer quickly, and I feel safer, at least digitally."

"Good to hear. Still staying with McCarrigan?"

"Yes, and I think you can also use his first name, Kevin. This is the first real relationship I have had since my divorce." She paused. "You don't need to hear about that."

"No, I don't, but trust me I am happy for both of you. How is Oso making out? Any problems?"

She laughed. "He is a sweetie. I like him. He doesn't talk a lot, but once you get past his accent, what he says is usually thoughtful and down to earth. He really appreciates what people do for him, especially you."

"Me?"

"He told me a little bit about you, and what you had done for him. Seems he had a pretty tough childhood and some bad breaks."

"Yeah, he also made some dumb choices, but he is basically a good guy."

"Why does he only go by Oso?"

"I'm not sure. He picked up the nickname in prison. Oso means bear in Spanish. Guess he wanted to leave the life before prison behind. The name fits."

"It might sound crazy but when this is sorted out, I might keep him on as a driver, if not full time, some good hours."

"Really?"

"Yes. He is a good driver, so I get work done while he drives. It impresses my clients that I have a driver, and it doesn't hurt that he is the size of a small building. I can't lose."

Laughing, I ended our call, thinking that was the Tara we knew, playing the angles and using them to advance her business. I couldn't argue with her reasoning.

Next, I wanted to call Kenzo about the full autopsy, even though we could get a copy via Sophie's back door into the Police department. Getting the report from Kenzo would be best. If we got a full copy and he found out, he would be suspicious and start nosing around where he wasn't wanted. Our back door was our secret, and we wanted it kept that way.

We also needed to know if he could come through with a copy of Robert Clegg's hard drive, our real ask. Calling his office, I was told he was out and asked if I would like to leave a message? Nope, no message. His cell went to voice mail, I left a message. Pondering why he wasn't answering, it had to be a significant meeting for him not to answer. Getting up for a coffee refill, I was thinking there would be a logical answer when Kenzo got back to me.

The office door opened, and in walked Kenzo, he

quickly shut the door behind him saying, "I haven't been here, and you haven't seen me, got it?"

Marie and I echoed. "Got it."

"Good, is Sophie here?" A loud yes from the other room, she came out to the front reception room.

Kenzo dropped two envelopes on Marie's desk and continued. "Full final autopsy report on Robert Clegg. I also threw in the reports on the two Chinese guys as well, seeing that you think they're connected. The hard drive in Clegg's computer had been removed, but we found an external hard drive hidden. It was a big sucker. I had the hard drive copied in house for 'preservation' reasons. I copied the copy." He looked at Sophie "Is that good enough?"

"Should be fine. If the first copy of the original was done correctly, then we should be good."

Kenzo bridled at that comment, "Our tech team did the first copy. I copied that, I'm not a complete idiot when it comes to tech stuff."

Sophie smiled. "Congrats on the promo. How do you like being in charge?"

Kenzo snorted. "Huh, not even close to being in charge, just more political bullshit to dig through. Have some good people to work with though, and I can pick my team. Look this is so far off the books, I've put my career on the line-again with this, but I owed you, both of you. Now we are even."

I interjected, "You owe me, us nothing. Did you check Clegg's place for bugs?"

"Yes, and yes, we found some, actually a lot, every room. The Tech team was surprised when they realized they were such an old-style, even though they were new, if you see what I mean."

"Yeah, we get it, Sophie said, "To be honest, I'd have been surprised if you hadn't found anything."

I was curious why Kenzo hadn't answered his phone when I called, "How come you didn't answer your phone. You always answer the damn thing."

"Switched it off and took a personal ride share. Had her drop me off a block away. I bought a book in that corner bookstore with a credit card, so I have two receipts. Now I can deny I ever came here, and no one can trace the visit, if it ever comes out that you have police property."

We were impressed for a lot of reasons, and Sophie said, "Good thinking with the phone." She added, "You really don't owe us anything."

I followed up on that. "You gave us leads when you didn't have to, and that helped a lot. We appreciate this as well…anything we get, you'll get, as long as it doesn't compromise our client."

"Don't suppose you will tell me who your client is?" He smiled as he said it.

"Not a fucking chance."

"I had to ask." With that exchange he said goodbye, we said thanks, and he was gone.

The whole exchange took literally a few minutes, yet the payoff could be huge for all of us, depending on what Sophie pulled out of the hard drive, and I could get out of the autopsy reports.

Kenzo had been thoughtful to include the two Chinese vics' reports even though we had already seen them. Sometimes a hard copy is better, and to be honest, I preferred the hard copy. It was the way I was used to working in the police department, and that habit had stuck with me. With a hard copy, I'd make notes on it. I guess I was old fashioned.

The rest of the day we spent going over the goodies that Kenzo had dropped off. The autopsy reports on the two Chinese found on the Golden Gate bridge were as we had seen with a few extra notes by the medical examiner. She was slower than anyone liked, but she was thorough, and her work stood up to any scrutiny, much to the dismay of many a defense attorney.

The additional notes and comments were confirmation that the off-shore Chinese man had a heart attack, which was the cause of his death. The ABC victim had been tortured. Maybe they were mutilated to disguise that. No that didn't make sense. Dumping them in such a public place with faces, teeth, and DNA readily available? The ME's report proved the mutilations had all been done postmortem

The ABC victim had been easily identified from military records. I figured the mutilations were done for deflection and publicity value, and they had gotten that in spades, you can't keep something like that quiet in this town. Too many people around with phones...meaning cameras...a lot of official folks too, who can't keep their mouths shut. The bane of police work. Not much here that we didn't already know. Still confirmation is a good thing.

Next the autopsy report on Robert Clegg. Taking it slowly and reading carefully, the actual cause of death was no surprise—massive trauma associated with a fall from a great height, like nine floors. The drugs found in his system probably led to hallucinations. Again, thankfully for the pernickety ME, she did a thorough tox screen, and some of the drugs in the tox screen were never used for recreational use, only in chemical interrogations—more evidence to change suicide to homicide.

Even a mangled body like Clegg's gave up its secrets to the right person. Signs of wrist and ankle restraints on Clegg became visible, under the intense examination of a formal autopsy. Whatever had been used was wider than the usual zip ties, but still narrow enough to leave telltale signs of use, showing bruising and some slight abrasions on his wrists.

Interesting, so why throw him off the balcony?

Maybe they didn't. The two Chinese were hired muscle at best. They may have been present, but they didn't have the smarts to run a chemical interrogation. Thinking all this through, there had to be at least four people present, the two Chinese, someone to administer the drugs and monitor Clegg, and lastly the person asking the questions.

So, what went wrong? The autopsy confirmed the fall killed him. The person in charge hadn't got what they wanted, and that lead them to go after Tara. This always came back to the question, what had Clegg found that got him killed?

Looking at the timeline in the police report, it looked like they had been at Clegg for several hours at best. Chemical interrogations can take a long time. Moving Clegg to a more secure and undisclosed location would make sense, so why not do that first? Maybe the decision to move Clegg had come later, and he had escaped them during the transfer. If he had escaped why jump? Maybe the drug cocktail had more effect than expected? And why the hell were the hired help so sloppy, letting Clegg get the better of them? We'd probably never discover the real reason on that one.

More questions than answers. The only thing for sure, whoever was in charge was pissed, they'd lost their target and had taken it out on the two Chinese. Which meant this was definitely a bigger operation than we thought.

Tara had to be the next target, even if she didn't realize it. This would be a capture, not kill mission, which led me to wonder why she hadn't been snatched already. Probably, it was the increase in her digital security, and the changes in her routine, like staying with McCarrigan and Oso driving her. Oso was protecting her, but he wasn't bullet proof. I had to warn him to be extra vigilant.

This was not how I wanted it to play out. Interrupting Sophie, I said we needed to talk, and now. The tone of my voice grabbed her attention.

"No problem, what is it."

"We need to get hold of Tara and get her more protection. I think she is going to be snatched by whoever went after Clegg, and they'll try to get what they need from her. This will be a clean-up job now. They still want anything and everything connected to that project. Which also makes us targets when they find out who we are…if they haven't already."

"Well, I may be able to assist in that. As we know, the e-mails came from Russia. I can now prove they came from Saint Petersburg. Could be an individual, or even a government sponsored team. More interesting is the list of names associated with the Media Company that Tara represented for the merger-acquisition. I need to talk to her about them and see what information she has on them. It looks like the offer was higher, and way out of spec for the value of the company. My antenna went up. This has to be money laundering, and it may be connected to the Russian mob."

"That's good and bad. The info good, the Russian thing is bad. Why use Chinese locals? Russia and China are not exactly friends now."

"Layer of insulation," Sophie said. "The front for the buyout was Chinese. Only the front. Besides, money has no enemies."

"True, money has no friends, either. Do you get the feeling we're missing something?"

"Yes, and it has to be what Clegg was researching. We will definitely need accounting assistance to translate his stuff into something we can understand."

"Let's wait on that until we have contacted MsDoubleEntry. She could have an insight into his world. That's tonight"

"Trust me Mas, I hadn't forgotten not for one minute."

"That worries me, on several levels."

"You know me by now. You trust me with your life remember?"

"Yes, I trust you, but you are still new to my work world. Together we will make it work."

"Yes, we will, for the first time in my life I feel complete. I'll call Tara and set up a meet."

"Tell her to be careful."

"I will."

Marie brought in lunch. Each of us working on our own tasks gave the office a monastic quiet. That sense of something not quite right and not being able to identify it was bugging me. Returning to the autopsy reports and reviewing them and my notes, made me feel like I had gleaned as much from them as I could for now.

Telling Sophie I would see her at home and Marie that I would see her tomorrow, I left. Leaving I wandered the long way home thinking about all the issues and the mess of information we had. It didn't add up. If it was money laundering, it wasn't only about that, there was something else deeper behind it.

Enough! To get ready for tonight's work at Sorcerers, I would make an early dinner. We would arrive early at the club and wait for MsDoubleEntry to show up.

Chapter Eleven

For our foray to hopefully meet Ms. D, I quickly changed. For me it was easy, black shirt and pants, black shoes, topped off with a black leather blazer, same as last night except this time I was wearing underwear and socks. I was ready. Sophie on the other hand took time to turn herself into her alter ego Ms. Circe, and that was always a spectacular sight for me.

Her hair piled up high and held in place with enameled metal spikes. Make up stark, contrasting, and effectively a mask. Her corset, one I hadn't seen in a while, red brocade, pushed up her tits, exposing lots of cleavage and stopped just above the nipple line.

Seeing her go through the process was getting me aroused. She asked me to assist in getting her corset tightened to her satisfaction. Pulling on those long laces, and her exhaling as I tightened the beautiful, figured fabric tighter against her body, her waist narrowed into an hourglass shape. With a corset this low cut and snug, I knew she would not be doing anything active tonight. Tonight was all business.

Sophie completed her outfit by tying a loose long sheer wrap skirt around her narrow waist, tying the big bow on her left hip, no top. Her cover up, just a light coat, and she was ready.

I asked, "Ready for battle?"

"Of course."

Leaving the house, we were anxious for more and varied reasons. First, MsDoubleEntry actually showed. We needed to meet her and get information from her.

We arrived at Sorcerers before the club opened, which was a good thing. We would see everyone who came in. The person staffing the front desk was someone I recognized, but not to speak to. She welcomed me, saying she recognized me from The Cauldron.

We introduced ourselves, and I asked, "I don't suppose you know MsDoubleEntry?"

"Sorry, I know the name, not the person. One of the Dungeon monitors probably will. I'll ask when they get here. Only Big Boots is in right now. He has first shift."

"Thanks, appreciate it. We know him."

That was a piece of luck. Knowing Big Boots would give us credibility with the others. We entered the club, and I left my jacket and Circe's coat with the coat check. Picking up our non-alcoholic drinks from the upstairs lounge we spotted Big Boots already on the play floor chatting with a couple. Downing our drinks, we went to say hello to him.

Catching Big Boots attention, then because we were in this setting, I introduced Sophie to him as Circe.

"Nice to see you Mas." As he took Circe's hand, kissing it. "A pleasure to meet you Circe."

"I am sure it is." That brought a smile to my lips and a chuckle from him.

"Mas, are the rumors true? You played a big hand, along with Kenzo, in solving the bodies in the bay killings?"

"I can neither confirm nor deny that rumor."

"Very politic of you, and thanks for the confirmation."

"We do have a favor to ask regarding another case we're working on. Hoping to meet a community person who goes by the KinkInc name of MsDoubleEntry. Do you know her?"

"Know her by sight, and enough to say hello. That's about it. One of the other dungeon monitors on tonight knows her well. Do you know Whiphand?"

I shook my head. Until meeting Sophie, I hadn't been involved in the Kink community for quite a while. In fact, not since my departure from the police department. The kink community in San Francisco is huge, and there were always new people, people who moved in different circles, both private and public.

"Not an issue," Big Boots said, "I'll introduce you to her. She's been around a while and has been doing a few workshops at Specter. You know that place, right?"

"We know of it but haven't been yet."

"Nice space. Really well set up for bondage of all sorts, anyway, she is usually early and if she doesn't know her, she'll know someone who does. I gotta get back to monitoring, safety first."

He said it seriously and meant it seriously. Non kink folks just don't understand how seriously the community takes the mantras of *'safe, sane, and consensual'* known as SSC, and RACK, *'risk aware consensual kink'*. Playing in the kink world could be amazingly fulfilling, and with that, there were risks, risks that everyone should be aware of. That included predators, and they didn't usually last long. The community grapevine was wide, long, and deep. Bad news traveled fast.

We thanked him and wandered around the space as various people were starting to occupy the dungeon equipment. You could feel the energy increasing as more people entered the space. Having seen enough we retreated to a spot with good visibility of the entrance and a view the stairs up to the lounge. If she showed up and we recognized her, it would be better if we could get an introduction, rather than approach her cold. If we didn't recognize her, we would need Whiphand for an assist.

There she was. It had to be her. I nudged Circe and nodded in the direction of the coat check. MsDoubleEntry was as strikingly tall as I predicted, especially as she was wearing high heels. She was making an entrance. Red head. I was right about the hair color, with long lustrous curls hanging halfway down her back. It had to be natural. She was proud of that hair. The way she moved and shook the long curls, it moved so fluidly. Definitely a glorious and intimidating sight.

MsDoubleEntry looked completely at ease in this environment, knowing many of the people already in the club, greeting them with kisses and hugs. We needed an intro to Whiphand, who hopefully would intro us to our target. Keeping an eye on her, I asked Circe to find Big Boots for the intro to Whiphand if she had arrived. Sophie left on her mission, and I kept sight of MsDoubleEntry as she went upstairs, discreetly waiting until she had reached the top of the stairs before I followed.

Sophie returned with Big Boots and a woman dressed in old fashioned fox hunting gear, top to bottom, and carrying several horse-racing whips. She looked confident and curious. Big Boots did the introductions and left. We all found a fairly quiet corner and sat.

"The only reason I am talking to you is because of BB. I know and trust him. He has vouched for you, that gets you my attention and time. We'll see how it goes from there."

Answering her, "Fair enough, I will explain what and why, and you take it from there."

She nodded in agreement.

"We represent a client who is in some jeopardy and probably the people closely associated with them. There has been one attack on someone who is an associate of the person known as MsDoubleEntry. We would like an introduction, just to talk, and apprise her of the situation, nothing more right now." No way was I going to give away more than I had to.

"Is she in any danger?"

"Possibly, can't say for sure."

"Okay, but if you are bullshitting me, you will regret it."

Sophie said, "Listen, we are part of this community, and we understand it as well as you do. We do not gaslight, catfish, bullshit, or any of those other things to scam people. This is more serious than spanking a willing ass. Sorry if I offend, but we need to talk to her tonight, are you willing to help your friend?"

"Okay, okay, yes! I am protecting her that's all. We in this community have to stick together. Hold on. I'll ask if she wants to talk to you. If she does, I want to sit in."

Sophie looked at me.

I shrugged my shoulders, "As long as she doesn't mind, and you follow the standard community rules by keeping everything confidential, saying nothing to anyone. Can you give us your word on that?"

"Done, word given."

"Not good enough. I want to hear you say it out loud."

"Fuck, alright. I give you my word, nothing I hear or see will be divulged to anyone for any reason, unless I have permission from you. Everything will remain confidential. There satisfied?"

"I will be if nothing leaks."

"Stay here, I'll talk to her."

We watched her walk over to where MsDoubleEntry was talking to another couple. She looked over to us as Whiphand spoke to her, Sophie waved. She smiled at Whiphand and put her arm around Whiphand's waist as they walked over to us. As they approached both Sophie and I stood, offering our hands and names in introduction.

Once seated, I started by saying, "Thank you for taking the time out of your evening, we appreciate it."

"This is intriguing."

"Well, let me start by saying we do not think you are in any danger at this point. Our agency represents a client who we feel is in imminent danger. The fallout from a project they undertook."

"How is this anything to do with me."

"Well, it's not actually you we are interested in, it's one of your associates. The accounting consultant our client used. He continued researching after the project was archived. We think he discovered something significant, and it was this that led to his death."

She fidgeted uncomfortably and said, "Again, I still don't see what this has to do with me?"

"Do you know a Mr. Robert Clegg, known on KinkInc as MrNumbers?"

"Yes, why?"

"He was killed. It was initially thought to be a suicide. It will soon be announced as a homicide."

Stopping, I wanted to see her reaction, and I got it. She didn't know Clegg was dead, she went pale and started to shake. A tear rolled down her cheek. Sniffing, she asked when it happened.

I told her the timeline, and the initial thought that he'd committed suicide, and she sobbed out loud, "Bullshit, he would never do that. Hits too close to home. His brother did that when he was a teenager."

"You hadn't heard about it?"

"No, I've been on vacation, and out of touch with everyone. Besides, Robert, when he is-was working, is so focused he often ignored calls, texts, and e-mails for days, if not weeks. I thought he was busy. Oh shit."

She broke down sobbing, two people came over, looking suspiciously at Sophie and me. Asking Whiphand and MsDoubleEntry if everything was alright. Whiphand said, "Yes," and they left, hovering close by.

Sophie moved next to her and said, "Believe me, I know how you feel. I lost my sister earlier this year. We want to find who did this and protect our client. To do that, we need your help. We are very good at what we do, but we are out of our depth with the sophisticated nature of these accounting financials. Can you think of anyone who would be able to do the forensic accounting for us?"

Her eyes were red, and her face tear stained. She answered in a quiet strong voice, "Yes, me."

I asked, "You can do this?"

"Yes. I met Robert a few years ago, he was my mentor in this community, he guided me and protected me until I gained experience. We hit it off because we both love, loved numbers. He was the practical one. He is, was a CPA specializing in accounting forensics. I chose the more academic path. I am a dissertation away from getting my PhD. That was why I took a break. I was working on it. Seems a little pointless now. What do you need from me?"

Sophie said, "We need someone to review Robert's research and break it down into understandable bites for us. We think the answer to all this is in his work, but if we can't understand it, it's not much use."

"When do you want me to start?"

Thanking her, I asked, "When can you start?"

With a wry smile she asked, "Would now be a good time?"

"No, you need to process what's happened." I had a follow up. "Is there anyone you want to call, or someone you can stay with?"

"Yes, my apartment share. I think I want to go home now." Whiphand said she would take her.

I countered, "We'll make sure you get home safely. We don't even know your given name." I let that question hang.

"Erin, my real-life name is Erin. I live just off Haight. How do I know what you have told me is true?"

"Do you know Big Boots?"

"Of course."

Turning to Circe, I asked her to find out if Big

Boots would mind coming over when he was done with his shift. She immediately left to find him.

Sitting silently in our corner, Whiphand was comforting Erin by holding her. The volume of the club had picked up, and the sound of people enjoying themselves was incongruous with the situation.

Big Boots put his hand on my shoulder and sat next to Erin saying, "You know I'm a cop, right?"

She nodded. "Well Mas here, was a really good Inspector, and now a really good private investigator. His partner is good people. She's had her own losses. You know about the bodies in the bay thing?"

Again, she nodded.

"They helped break that case. You can trust them…good enough?"

Looking closely at Big Boots, she said in a subdued voice, "Yeah, good enough. Thank you."

He took her hand. "You need anything, just ask, got it? Whiphand can always get hold of me."

Erin smiled. "Got it." Looking at Sophie and me, she said, "Let's go, I want to go home."

Picking up our coats, I gave Erin our business cards, and she gave Sophie her number and e-mail address. I logged on for a ride share, and it was there in minutes. After helping Erin and Sophie into the back, I sat up front with the driver. He was good and got us through the evening traffic efficiently.

Erin's home was an apartment on the second floor of a Victorian. With shaking hands, she got her keys out and opened the door. We walked her up to the apartment door making sure she went in, and we heard her greeted with, "What wrong?"

Erin started crying, and we left hearing the other

voice say, "OMG," as the door shut.

Meeting Erin had been the point of the evening, and that had been a success. The depth of her reaction made me want to re-evaluate her relationship with Robert Clegg. This was more than high jinks with kink. It went deeper. Telling someone that a person they cared about was deceased sucked. It sucked when I was a cop, and it still sucked. I, for one, was not up for anything other than a drink and sleep.

Erin's reaction to hearing about Robert Clegg affected Sophie as well. It picked the scab off the memory of her sister's death, and we agreed we needed a drink and a talk about the next steps. Then sleep.

We stopped at a local watering hole, ordered our drinks, and discussed how we should integrate Erin into the case. Sophie offered to take it on, since she was the one with the tech skills to run through the flash drive material. It made sense.

As we walked back to our house, Sophie commented, "We will have to protect Erin as well as Tara. Working with us could put her in danger."

"Agreed."

Helping Sophie out of her Circe clothes did not have the usual arousing effect on me. We both knew what loss was like. Sleep took us both quickly as we spooned naked against each other.

Chapter Twelve

My sleep was broken by my phone going off like a fire alarm. My head hurt, and it wasn't from alcohol. Groggily I looked at my phone. Not a number I recognized. I answered, "Mas Hammett how may I help you."

"Mr. Hammett, Erin. When can we meet, I am pissed-off! In fact, I am fucking angry. I want the son of a bitch who killed Robert. Can you get them?"

Sitting straight up in bed, fully awake, I said, "Meet us at the office as soon as you can get there. We'll be there in twenty minutes max. Then we can talk about it."

"Screw talking about it. I want to be involved."

"You will be if you can help decipher Robert's research. See you soon."

Sophie came into the bedroom with a quizzical look on her face. "Who was that this early?"

"Erin, she is meeting us at the office. I said I'd be there in twenty minutes. You can take your time. I'll need to explain everything to her, and what we want from her. That includes the potential danger. We also need to find out more about her, what she does, other than academics. She has to earn a living somehow, that apartment isn't cheap, even splitting the costs."

"Dream on Mas. I'll be there as well. it only makes sense. Remember, I'll be the one working closely with

133

her."

"Fine, let's go."

Dressing quickly, I ordered and paid for breakfast as we walked to the office. Sophie texted Marie, asking her to call in and pick it up—all paid for.

Marie texted back. —What's going on, too early!—

That brought a smile to both of us. Sophie responded. —Case moving forward.—

Opening the office, Sophie warmed up her computer, and I put on the coffee. Hearing the main door open I expected it to be Erin. Nope Marie. She must have broken all sorts of speed records to get here so quickly and pick up breakfast as well.

Breathlessly, Marie said, "You didn't think I was going to miss anything did you."

God, I hate waiting, even if there is good reason. This waiting for Erin to show-up was killing me. It shouldn't be taking this long for her to get here from her place, even with the rush hour traffic. What if something had happened to her, an accident. I began to think of all sorts of bad scenarios. Coffee up and a hearty breakfast, later helped take my mind off Erin.

Finally, in she walked. She looked a mess, hair disheveled and red-eyed. I doubted she had slept much.

"Sorry I am late. There was an accident on the way over."

Marie, who we had updated, offered her coffee and food. She accepted coffee, declining the food.

Sophie took the lead. "You have our condolences. You were obviously very fond of him."

"Fond does not really cover it. I loved him. He was the older kinky brother I never had. We were there for each other. We hit it off from day one. Of course, we had our spats and arguments, but they never lasted. He was always there when I needed him, especially after a relationship crashed and burned. He was brilliant and quiet. Odd, but he was a genuinely kind person. He was old fashioned in some ways, opening doors for you, and straight as an arrow." She saw Sophie and I look at each other. "No, I mean in the moral and ethical sense. He would never do anything even slightly illegal. I think that's why he liked forensic accounting, catching out what he called the 'foolish-felons'. You will be able to get the person who killed him...right?"

Answering for us, I said, "That is our aim. Protecting our client and finding out who killed Robert are all part of the same problem. We must warn you, the people who actually killed Robert, or allowed it to happen, may already be dead. Not the principal behind it all, that is who we are after."

"Good. Where do I fit in?"

Sophie spoke up, "Erin, like we said last night, we have Roberts's research, but can't decipher a lot of it. That is where we need a forensic accountant. How good are you?"

"Very. Top of my class undergrad, post grad, and soon to be a PhD. If you want references there is the head of department where I teach undergrads, my PhD professor, and lastly the owner of the accounting firm I work for in tax season. Robert was mentoring me, on forensic accounting."

"Fair enough, do you feel up to starting today, you look tired."

"Didn't sleep much last night, I'd feel better doing something. I want to start, even if I am not much use.

Today, I thought I would do an overview and get a feel for what Robert was looking into, is that alright?"

Sophie agreed, "Working is better than doing nothing," and asked, "What do you need?"

"The source material. I have my own computer."

Leaving the two of them to do their respective things, I called Tara to up-date her and generally check in. She answered on the first ring and said she appreciated the update and that there was nothing negative to report on her end.

I told her to be careful. It was too early to discount further action against her. To keep myself busy, I took the analysis of the drug cocktail to a private lab who had done work for me in the past, thinking the drug cocktail had to be custom, and maybe get a lead off that. Cathy the lab manager seemed pleased to see me, for a change. Asking her if she had a few minutes to spare for coffee. She did, but not for coffee.

Following her, we left the building and went to a small local café, of which San Francisco is thankfully blessed with many. Getting my coffee and her tea, I handed her the tox report on Clegg. She scanned it quickly, then sat down to read it thoroughly. Her forehead creased in concentration. After reading it and going back and forth a few times, she looked up. "Where did you get this report? It's an official police report out of the ME's office."

"You don't want to know. Even if you did, I am not telling you."

"I had to ask. It's very thorough and a bit puzzling. Most of this cocktail I recognize. There are a couple of components that I don't recognize, at least for use in chemical interrogation. Could be a personal preference.

A lot of experimentation goes on in this field. Not all of it kosher, very off the books. This is dangerous stuff to play around with. Can I keep this?"

"No, but you can make a copy if you want."

"Good enough. I'd like to run this cocktail mixture by a few colleagues. Something is tickling my memory, but I can't pin it down."

"Hey, go for it, as long as no one knows where you got the data from. I mean no one. It could be fatal."

"What the hell have you gotten yourself into now, Mas?"

"To be honest, I'm not sure. We are covering all the angles and following every lead we can."

"Mas, you are a pain in the ass, but an interesting one. I'll be in touch if anything pops with this. Be careful."

Laughing, "Why thank you, I love you, too."

We walked back to the lab. Cathy copied the report and I left, not expecting much if anything from that lead, but ya never knew.

On my way back to the office, I thought about Erin. I needed to know more about her. How close was she to Clegg? Why did he only send his research information to Tara? To protect Erin? Maybe, or maybe he had sent them to her, too, and she was keeping secrets. Two people could play that game.

Getting back to the office, I walked in to a *shush* from Marie. Erin had crashed out on the sofa.

Good, that would give me a chance to talk to Sophie about my suspicions, or paranoia, whichever. I asked Sophie to go for walk, and she looked at me quizzically and said *yes*.

Walking around the block, I asked, "Can you hack

Erin?"

"I can, but why would I?"

"Because I asked nicely"

"Not good enough. You have a good reason?"

"Just thinking, if Erin and Clegg were as close professionally and personally as she claims, why would Clegg only send his research to Tara? I'm thinking she was working with Clegg, and he was sending stuff to Tara as his back up."

"Sadly, your cynicism actually makes sense. She is very good, but I had the feeling she was too familiar with the material for a first scan. We do make a good team. When she leaves, I'll look into her."

We returned to the office to find Erin awake, weary but awake. We suggested she call it a day. She agreed, saying she had to check in with her professor tomorrow. Once that was done, she would come back and work on Robert's research. We let her know it was no problem.

"Take care," Sophie said as she left.

Erin turned as if to say something, shook her head, and left, closing the door quietly behind her.

Before Sophie could start digging into Erin, Marie said, "I have some info for you. While Erin was sleeping, I went through her purse, and found a list of three e-mail addresses, and an IP address."

One of the addresses we already had from Erin. Putting all that info together would be a good start. The fact that we knew Erin's KinkInc name, the odds were that she used the same computer for everything. Sophie would tie it all together.

Being the smart investigator I was, I left Sophie alone to do her thing. I admonished Marie for being underhanded and sneaky, and then thanked her for being underhanded and sneaky. My reward was her middle finger. So much respect for the boss. Ha.

There was nothing much for me to do. On the way back to my desk, I thought about Clegg. I wandered through his KinkInc account again, but nothing stood out. He wasn't a big joiner, only in a couple of groups and visited only one munch. Next was to check out if he had been Yelp'd for his business. Only a couple of Yelps and both were glowing in their praise of Clegg's work. He seemed exactly what Tara and Erin had described. LinkedIn next. This was more fruitful...a lot more information, academic history, work history, and business.

Clegg had done business with, worked with and for some of the big names in the San Francisco business world. Impressive. He was *the real deal*. This confirmed that whatever his suspicions were, they had to be significant, and they'd gotten him killed.

Sophie called out to get my attention, "Mas, got her. Erin was lying, at least by omission if not outright."

"How so?"

"She is sneaky clever. I'm in her computer. Lots of accounting stuff, her PhD project, contacts, lots of folders and files. Well-organized and logical, nothing there that shouldn't be. However, when you get into her private stuff, KinkInc for instance, she is interesting, similar to Clegg, a little more outgoing, wider pool of contacts under the private tag. I'll get you access so you can review them for anything interesting."

"Get to the point."

"Patience, my dear partner. Remember in her profile, she liked puzzles. Guess what I found tucked away in that maze of math crap?"

"Robert Clegg's research."

"Fuck, how d'you know."

"You gave me too many clues, leading me along, and it was my paranoia that led us to dig into her. Only made sense."

"Well, Mr. Smarty Pants, you are correct. From what I can understand from her notes, it looks like Clegg is convinced it's money laundering and also campaign finance irregularities—donations and the like. But it doesn't say how it's being done, only big dollars."

"Back to the Russians again?"

"Maybe, there's a note attached to the file, and it's a list of names. Some I recognize from the files we got from Tara, principals and investors in the Media Co. They're all California based. You'll have a better chance of recognizing them. To me they're just a bunch of names. The ones we don't recognize, we'll Google to start, then go from there."

"Sounds good. Shoot me the list."

"Open your e-mail. Already there."

"Okay, thanks."

Opening the list, the names were listed in alphabetical order along with their position in relation to the company. For a smallish company, there did seem to be a lot of people involved at a fairly high level, and two names did stand out. Hunter Pollard, a congressman representing a coastal seat in Southern California, and James Rivers, a congressman representing an inland area in the Central Valley, both politicians on the right of their party in a sea of California blue. What were they doing being involved with a liberal San Francisco Media company? Assuming it was a liberal company. Even San Francisco has its share of racist and political nut-jobs.

This couldn't be what I immediately suspected. Putting all the pieces we had together, and joining them, the picture they made was not pretty and perhaps not even accurate. Doing a recap in my mind, I listed all the items I could remember. E-mails sent from a Russian location. Soviet made bugs. Chinese burglars now deceased. A dead forensic accountant involved in a failed sale of a U.S. company for a price over the going prices. Probable money laundering and campaign finance irregularities with big dollars. Now we had two California U.S. Congressmen tied to the company in question. Yeah. Maybe this was enough to kill for.

If any of this was true, it still didn't answer the question about what someone was looking for. Dubious or illegal financial links to the two politicians or something else? They wouldn't want illegal links to come out. And unless the money was already flowing, or had, through the company, the buyout was to cover up the past actions in order to make it easier for future transactions.

This was a mess, and we were in up to our necks. We needed to find out what Clegg had discovered, and quickly. Erin was going to get a "come to Jesus" conversation tomorrow. I needed a conversation with Tara to confirm these names and their connection with all this.

I put in the call. Kristen answered and told me Tara was out for the afternoon, but she'd relay a message to her to call me back.

Thanking her, I clicked off and called Sophie over.

"We need to talk, get Marie in here as well."

"What's going on?"

"Putting all the pieces together and making an ugly picture."

Marie joined Sophie at my desk pulling up a chair. I started by taking in a deep breath then laid it all out the way I'd put it together. They were both quiet until I finished.

Marie started, "Mas, there's a lot of supposition and assumption in that theory."

Sophie agreed, "A hell of a lot. Unfortunately, it actually makes sense. Our system is corrupt. We just happen to be better at hiding it than other countries. Don't forget, I have worked contracts for some of the faceless ones."

"I really stretched some ideas here, and I'm hoping I'm wrong. Look at any crime—it's always a matter of motive, opportunity, and suspects. Always ask, who gains from the crime and remember that good old chestnut, 'follow the money'. The point is, if I'm right, this could get fatally dangerous. We could be talking about foreign state agencies, or even our own."

Sophie said, "Erin will be able to analyze the information, and if anyone finds out about her, she will be a prime target, like Clegg."

Marie added, "And it didn't end well for him."

"We will be having a come to Jesus' talk as soon as Erin gets here tomorrow," I said. "Sophie, can you see what you can find out about these two congressmen, particularly financials and donations who, where, and how much. I know they have to disclose a lot, which doesn't mean they are completely open."

"Sure, but I am going to hand off to a third party as

well."

Before she could tell me who, I asked, "Shouldn't we keep this in house?"

"If you had let me finish, I am giving it to Fiend. You know he's good, has great resources, and I trust him. We need all the help we can get on this. These guys didn't get where they are by being stupid and staying there by getting sloppy."

"Ok fair enough, but make sure you let him know this could be dangerous."

"I will and that will only make him more interested. He already thinks there is a deep state, but at least it's our deep state. If he thinks another country is playing in our government, he will be very pissed off. However wacked out he is, he's very patriotic about our country."

Looking at Marie, I said, "Marie, this could get dangerous, you didn't sign up for this. If you took a leave of absence, it might be smart."

"Fuck you, Mas. You guys are going to offer me a partnership. Yes, I know about that. I take full part in the business and the risks, or you can screw your partnership, your job, and yourself."

Sophie and I sat there stunned and speechless for a minute.

Marie continued, "I want to be involved. I really love you guys, and I want to be a part of anything you get into, not just a paper pusher sat behind a desk wondering what's going on. Worrying if you are going to get hurt and stuff."

Sophie and I looked at each other and burst out laughing, so much for keeping a secret.

We both asked, "How did you find out about the

partnership?"

"Well, you guys are not as good as you think you are at keeping secrets, and I have sources too. Am I in? Or do I need to start looking for a new job?"

Quickly I said, "Hell no, you aren't going anywhere. We need you."

Sophie added, "While we are at it, Mas, shall we tell her the rest of the good news?"

"Why not, she probably knows anyway."

Marie looked at us with a frown and asked. "Know what?"

Sophie looked at me smiling. "Go on, you're the boss." Another time I might have questioned that comment, I let it slide.

"Marie, we, that is Sophie and I decided, that you should have an equal share in the finders' fees we received for monies we recovered from the Bodies case. You were involved, and you went over and above. We couldn't have done it without you. Due to the nature of the dollar amount, we need to get the money to you through the business. Minimizing the taxes, we all will have to pay. Making you a partner is what you deserve" She looked stunned.

"What?" she squeaked out, and another, "What?"

Sophie chimed in, "We figure before taxes, your share will be a shade over two million-dollars."

"Whaaat? Fuck, are you shitting me? You're just messing with me, aren't you?"

Together we said, "Nope." I added, "Fact jack. You just made millionaire."

She shot up out of her chair, dissolving into tears. Not the reaction I had expected from hard shell, Marie. Sophie stood and went and hugged her. I joined in.

Sophie had tears running down her cheeks as well. My eyes teared up, thinking of Simon my deceased partner, sure Sophie was thinking of her sister Suzanne, one of the victims.

We settled down, and Marie asked through sniffles. "Why are you doing this?"

I answered, "Because we can, and it's the right thing to do. You are as much a part of this office, even with your disrespect of the boss...that's me by the way."

That comment broke the tension with both Marie and Sophie. Laughing, Marie quietly said, "You guys are the best. You don't know this. We were putting off having kids cos we couldn't afford to get a place of our own. Now we can."

Sophie said, "There are still a lot of details to work out, bits and pieces, but the money will be coming available, probably within six months, and not all at once."

"Whatever, whenever. Can I call Chung?"

"Sure, go ahead," I said. "What the hell, we need to celebrate something. This is as good an excuse as any. Dinner is on Mas Hammett and associates, oh and that name will be changing to something more corporate, inclusive, and anonymous. Go call Chung and make sure he's okay for dinner."

Marie went back to her desk, and we could hear her call, then she put the phone on speaker, a stream of Chinese erupted from the speaker with more voices in the background. We didn't need a translator they were obviously happy sounds. Sophie and I looked at each other, our own thoughts lost in Marie's joy.

Back to reality, Sophie said she would send the

names and request for assistance to her friend Fiend, back in Philadelphia. Meanwhile I would put out feelers here in San Francisco for anything on any the names on the list. Careful to avoid any direct mention of the congressmen, I asked my sources with the main city newspaper, round-about questions regarding which state and federal electors had well-funded campaigns, and their income sources. Of course, they wanted to know if I had anything to offer in return, and I said nothing, this was peripheral to a case I was working.

The reporter-police relationship was always a difficult one to traverse, they wanted more than was often smart to give them, and they had to protect their sources when they gave the police information. Now, me being out of that loop and having more freedom to play their game to my advantage, I owed nothing to either side.

None of us at the office felt like really cranking the work for the rest of the day, so we didn't. Marie disappeared for a while without saying a word. On her return she said it was break time. She had bought small Black Forrest cake to "celebrate". We sat and demolished half of it and chatted as we enjoyed every mouthful—chocolate, more chocolate, and sour cherries. Nothing wrong there.

The conversation of course turned to the case. It seemed to be getting bigger every day, and Tara's part grew smaller—smaller but a significant part. My feeling was, she was still in danger until we could understand her connection to the failed project files.

Erin was going to have to come clean about her part in the research. Talking it out was a good brain cleanse. Marie asked good questions, many of which we couldn't answer because we didn't have the answers.

With plenty more to think about, we called it a day, and headed to Chinatown to meet Chung. We showed up early so we waited in the Li-Po lounge, where, without doubt, they served the strongest Chinese Mai Tai's in town. Trick was, they don't taste as strong as they are—dangerously so. The place was not luxurious. Not even close. It was always lively and a great start or finish to the night. Marie texted Chung to tell him where we were, and he joined us by the time we were into our second drinks. Thankfully, the cake helped absorb some of the alcohol.

Chung said he had chosen the restaurant. I had my favorites, but why not let someone who really knew Chinatown's best restaurants pick? As we walked back into Chinatown proper, Chung asked, "You have cash, Mas? This restaurant only takes cash."

"I do."

So, he turned us up a side street and into an alley— a sketchy alley. He knocked on a sturdy red door. It was opened by a little old lady, who bowed to Chung.

Entering a different world, the décor was luxurious, carved wood, silk hangings and paintings, and alcoves with jade carvings. We were ushered into a small room containing only five tables, two of which were occupied. We were the only non-Chinese and looked up and down by everyone in the room, like we didn't belong. Chung said something in Chinese, and it was all smiles with the other clients going back to their dinners.

I had to ask, "What did you say."

"You don't want to know, trust me."

Trusting him, I said no more. The waiter came over

bringing the owner, who spoke in heavily accented English, with him. Welcoming us for honoring his humble establishment, he bowed.

Returning his bow, I said, "We are the ones who are honored, and we thank you for your hospitality."

My comment surprised Chung and the owner, who then spoke in rapid Chinese. We sat while they went at it. It sounded like an argument to me, but it was all smiles.

When he was finished, Chung said, "That was nicely done, even if it was in English. Why did you say that?"

"One thing I learned as a police officer. It never hurts to be polite and follow other people's customs."

"Well, it sure didn't hurt. I took a chance on bringing you here. This place caters only to Chinese clients. The only reason we got in is because he has known my parents forever, so he said he would do me a favor and allow you in. If you aren't the only non-Chinese ever in here, I'd bet the number is less than a dozen total. This place has been in business since 1913. He is the fourth generation of his family to run the restaurant."

Sophie said, "It's so small, how do they make it pay."

Chung laughed saying, "Wait till Mas gets the bill. The big commercial restaurant is out front. They share a kitchen, but with different menus. This place is sold out period. Normally, you probably have to wait six to eight months to get a spot. This is a favor repaid."

The door opened and more guests filled the two remaining tables giving us odd looks. Quickly the waiter spoke to them, and we were ignored. Drinks arrived at our table and the volume of conversation rose as the other tables were served with plates of food. We had no idea what it was, but everything had an aroma that got the juices flowing.

Sophie asked, "Are we were getting menus."

Chung smiled. "No menus, this is a celebration. We are going to having a ten-course feast, and no you will not have had anything like this before. Get ready for an experience."

As he finished speaking, the first course arrived, and the conversation dwindled to just the sound of chop sticks clicking. The dishes flowed one after the other, nothing rushed and the portions big enough to really savor without filling us. Every dish was different, integrated into the entirety of the menu, and working with the one before and the one to come. Aromas, textures, and flavors invaded all our senses and were incredible. The wine was a California chardonnay, which was not so much a drink as a palette cleanser.

Sophie was the quietest she'd ever been during a meal. We usually chatted throughout. There was conversation, but it revolved around the food. Time seemed to stand still, only the now and the people around this table mattered. This was not so much a meal, as Chung had voiced, it was an experience.

Eventually, when it came to an end, looking around the table, we all had this look of satisfied amazement on our faces. No one wanted to break the magic.

Finally, Chung spoke, "I hope this shows a little, of how much Marie and I appreciate what you have done for us. Thank you isn't enough."

I said, "Chung, it was and is deserved."

The check was delivered to my right side in a red

envelope. Opening it I expected to see a large bill. It was a zero. I looked up at Chung in surprise. He had a big shit-eating grin on his face.

"What's going on? This is our treat."

Marie answered, "No Mas, this is our way of saying thank you. Hope you enjoyed it."

"Are you kidding? You just spoiled Chinese food for me for the rest of my life. I will never eat like this again."

Everyone laughed at that, causing the other guests to turn and look at us. I was sure that commenting with *gwei loh* was a sometimes-insulting comment if you took it that way. I never did. I was thick skinned and have been called a lot worse.

We left the restaurant and parted ways, with hugs and kisses all round. Sophie and I made our way, meandering through the streets, in no particular rush to get home. We talked about how cute Marie and Chung were. That brought the conversation around to us. The reforming of the partnership to include the three of us was a big step for me, her, and Marie. This was the most anchored Sophie had been…ever. I wanted to know how she felt about it.

"Scared. I've never had to think, or worry about another person before, at least not for longer than the time a kink scene takes. This is different with you. It's not a comfortable feeling for me, but it does feel right, so I am going with my gut. Being in control is the way I'm built. You seem to understand that, both in the real world and in the kink world, and it doesn't bother you. It takes a strong person to give up control or be willing to."

"You are all I ever wanted in a person, top to

bottom. Can't believe you are really here. I was worried once we found Suzanne's killer you would hot foot it back to Philly."

"That was the plan. Then I realized there was really no one and nothing there I needed. Besides, you made me an offer I couldn't refuse. No regrets, I love you Mas."

"Let's go to bed."

"Another offer I can't refuse."

Chapter Thirteen

The previous night had been fun and a distraction. Today we had to get back on track to get some answers. Erin would be in to "assist" us, and we needed to have our come to Jesus' chat to make sure she understood what we knew and what we needed to know.

Everyone in the office early, and the atmosphere had a lightness, and it wasn't just the beautiful sunny day. Something had changed between all of us, and it felt good.

E-mail popped, it was from Erin, she would be in later, probably after lunch. Not a problem as along as she showed. Sophie was still deep in a thorough review of the research. Fiend said he'd work the list and dig into all the names, so little was expected from that side for a while. The highlight of the day was an email from Cathy at the lab, the drug mix was one developed by the DoD for use in black site interrogations of terrorists, not good news for us.

The office door opened and slammed shut, Erin stormed in and shouted, "Who the fuck do you think you are, trying to hack me? I trusted you bastards, and this is how you pay me back. Fuck you."

Sophie beat me to it. "Trying to hack you? I did hack you, and you lied to us. So shut the fuck up and sit-down, bitch. We are going to have a come to Jesus' conversation now!"

Couldn't have said it, better myself. Sophie had taken the wind out of Erin's sails. She sat, still bristling and angry.

Sophie brushed her hands off. "Now, we have that out of the way, we can have a nice calm conversation. Starting with why you lied to us?"

"I wasn't sure I could trust you. You said Robert was killed, and it's still listed as a suicide. I checked. How could you know that?"

I answered. "Easy. Because we have a relationship of sorts with the police, plus several other sources of information, not readily available to the public."

She looked at Sophie. "Did you really get into my computer?"

"Of course, I said so, didn't I?"

"You must be pretty good. I have good protection. How did you do it?"

"I am very good, and it's a trade secret. If we get to be friends, I might show you some better protections."

That seemed to break the tension, and Erin said, "Sorry, I am a bit of a mess. My professor agreed to delay my dissertation until I get sorted out about Robert."

"We are sorry about what happened to Robert," I said, "We really do need your help to sort his research. We are convinced he discovered something that is valuable or seriously damaging to one or more people, and we need to understand what it is. We know you were helping him. Do you actually know what the 'It' is?"

"No. I just assisted, ran numbers, crunched data. I never saw the whole thing, and I got bits and pieces. I figured out he was looking at several avenues at the same time, and it had to be complicated. He concentrated on several lines: money laundering, dodgy campaign donations, foreign interreference, and associated financial irregularities. I think he linked it all together at some point, but I don't know where."

"That is where we were leaning," I said. "We also believe it's complicated. Are you ready to work on this, hundred percent transparent? This could be dangerous for you. If whoever is behind Robert's death finds out you have access to this information, you'll be a prime target."

She visibly paled. "What do you mean?

Pausing before continuing, "Whatever Robert found is potentially lethal. Sophie and I don't think they meant to kill Robert. They were doing a chemical interrogation, and something went wrong."

"What are you talking about, chemical interrogation. That's spy novel stuff?"

"Right, until it happens to you. We think this goes all the way to Washington, as in D. C."

"If you're trying to scare me, you are doing a good job."

"Good, that is why we need to get ahead of this, so we have protection and leverage."

"You need me to review all of Robert's research, right?"

Sophie said, "Right."

"What if it's not there?"

"Too much has happened for it not to be. He stepped on some toes, someone found out he was snooping, and that started all this."

"Okay, I want to get the ones responsible for Robert's death." She choked and started crying again,

Sophie put her arm around her.

"Let's get to work, it will help I promise. It helped me." They went into the inner office and set up on Sophie's desk.

There was not much for me to do, so I started running down the names listed on the 3DMedia paperwork that Tara had provided for her project. All the ones in the day-to-day operations and running of the company seemed open and up-front. The silent partners were a different matter, the two congressmen, James Rivers and Hunter Pollard were involved with this company. I began to wonder what other pies they had fingers in.

Looking into that was not as difficult as I thought. They had to declare business interests, and there were not many for either of them, and only one in common other than 3DMedia. A real estate company, Golden Realty Union, dealing in California real estate, specifically in business and industrial properties around California. That was an interesting enough company to dig into. A thought struck me, nah it couldn't be that simple or that stupid. Golden Realty Union, the initials were the same as the old Russian military intelligence service GRU. That had to be a coincidence. The Russians were never, *ever* that dumb. The company had to have been created in the U.S. by Americans. This was insane, and I was clutching at straws, but I had to follow that straw further.

Golden Realty Union was a shadowy company, with very little information available on-line. The two congressmen were listed as board members. There was a good front and lots of nice pictures, and not much else other than marketing flim-flam. This was definitely something I would need help with.

"Sophie, you need to see this, and I need help."

"What have you found?

"I am not sure if it's anything, but it smells and needs a good look at," I said, explaining what I was looking at, and how I got there.

Sophie picked it up as I was talking. "Damn right it needs a look. Erin is wading through Robert's files and data, looks like it's going to take a while, a lot of it's new to her. I can do this while she does that. Anything specific you want me to look for?"

"Anything that doesn't look kosher. It's too much of a coincidence these two congressmen are linked to 3DMedia and the Realty company. There has to be something there big enough to kill for—like foreign money."

"What about the Chinese connection?

"Smoke and mirrors, deflection, distraction. I think Russia's involved, or at least Russian money."

"Okay, Mas, I'll take a look."

"Thanks, what are friends for?"

Now I was starting to get really worried, no way we could take on an adversary like the Russian government or the Russian mob, and I wasn't sure there was much difference. I wasn't sure the U.S. authorities wouldn't be set against us if the congressmen got wind of us and our suspicions. Shit, give me an uncomplicated homicide case. That bad feeling was creeping up on me again, and I didn't like it.

The day dragged by with nothing much for me to do except keep the coffee pot filled and fresh while all the women around me worked away at their tasks. Feeling like a spare dick at an orgy I left. Target practice would do me good, relieve some tension, on the way to the range I put in a call to Kenzo, needing a clarification on what would constitute grounds for a RICO case, I knew money laundering was one aspect of it, but not all the ins and outs of it, that was usually brought by the DA's office, it never hurt to have information. Kenzo was out and I left a message, saying it wasn't urgent.

The range was busy, so I couldn't practice rapid fire. If I couldn't do that, I would do the opposite and take my time with each shot for placement and accuracy. Shooting differently had its advantages, using both right and left hands, I banged my way through two hundred rounds, the targets were shredded, and I was covered in GSR. Back to regular habits, home, clean my weapon thoroughly, stashing it away, where I could access it quickly and safely. Usually, I had it in its case with a safety lock on it. Today, I decided to keep it loaded and handy, hoping I wouldn't need it.

After showering, I reviewed all the information we had. Noting a lot of gaps which needed filling, but I was sure they'd fill in as we pushed forward. Convinced the congressmen were up to their lobbied balls in it—bias on my part. Politicians in general pissed me off, and proven corrupt ones were even worse. My personal feelings didn't mean I'd underestimate how dangerous they could be, though.

I cleaned up and readied to go back to the office, hoping the girls had found something for me to go on and sink my teeth into.

Walking into the office, it looked like my wish was realized. Immediately I was verbally assaulted by Sophie, who was quickly followed by Erin.

Sophie asked, "Where the hell have you been? We got stuff. Erin found some things of interest. The Chinese corporation that was bidding on 3DMedia was a front, a shell company, all the financing for the deal was coming from the holding company and financed through a Maltese bank." She let that hang like it should mean something to me.

"And?"

"Jesus, Mas. Malta's banks have a rep for fronting Russian money, government money, and 'not so government' money. You can even get a Maltese passport if you have the cash. This is another link to Russian involvement."

"That's great, can you link the money to Russia or just the Maltese bank, because up front it's a Chinese corporation."

"Right now, only the bank. Erin is still working on that trail, looking for any names that raise red flags. Robert found the new bidder on 3DMedia. It's a different division of the same holding company, and that deal looks to complete in the next couple of weeks or so, once the SEC has finished their look see. Oh, I have looked into those names you wanted. Seems like 3D is a real company, and on a quick scan looks above board. I need to do more work on that end, some of the company officers bios seem as little thin. Marie had a clever idea. She's looking into Golden Realty's purchases and sales. They will all be in the public records. She is going to go over the local deals first and then work her way to San Jose and down to L.A."

I commented, "That was a really good idea. Does she need anyone to do leg work?"

"Don't know. Ask her. We have some good leads

to follow up, but they will take time. I'm going to set up an appointment with Tara for tomorrow to go over all the names we have. She can short cut us to the ones that we should look into first."

"Nice job, this is excellent progress. Call me if anything else comes up."

"Yup, sure will." Sophie seemed excited at the progress, being a little, less jaded. I knew we would have to get a big break, or this was going to be a long slog. Even with the research Robert had done, his suspicions, and data, we needed hard proof.

Marie said there was nothing for me to do yet, but probably tomorrow both she and I would need to go to the city records department and put in requests for the information we needed. She was making a list of all the properties she could find on-line first. There were not as many as I expected, but they all seemed to be in the higher value range…millions with an 's,' that was not a surprise knowing the property values in San Francisco and the surrounding counties, I knew it was also true for San Jose, and pretty sure it was the same down in L.A.

Helping Marie compile the list of properties, consisted of me reading off the property names and addresses that were of interest, while she keyboarded. She was a lot faster than I was. That done, she left for the day, and I went home to get dinner ready. Sophie called and asked me to make enough for a third. Erin was coming for diner. The more the merrier. I never had been able to cook small, even when it was just me. We always had leftovers.

Okay, what did we have that would work? Rice always a good standby, chili, hmmm beef, pork, or chicken. Decisions, decisions. Half pork half chicken, I would hold off on the heat, in case Erin was not up to the heat level we liked. We would add hot sauce to ours if need be. Cooking is meditation, cutting and chopping, adding ingredients, the sum of the whole greater than the individual parts. Like our office. The three of us were better together than separately.

Pot on and simmering, I grabbed a beer and put on the news. Nothing much, a big tech convention messing up traffic around the Moscone Convention Center. A stalled car on the Bay Bridge—good luck with that one. An accident on 880. A normal day in the Bay area.

Hearing keys in the door, I stood up to greet Sophie and our guest saying, "Hi honey, how was your day?"

Sophie laughed, "Very funny, Mas." Turning to Erin she said. "See the crap I have to put up with from my sub." That brought me up short. Sophie continued. "Erin wondered why we were so comfortable at Sorcerers and knew Big Boots. I explained the situation."

"Oh." Was about all I could say to that. While I felt comfortable with my sexuality and kink, I wasn't going to advertise it, either. Even though I had looked Erin up on KinkInc, a web site is very different to reality. Fuck it, done, next.

Erin used our spare bedroom and bathroom to freshen up. While she was out of ear shot, Sophie said she had started to really like her. "Erin is smart and driven."

My comment was, "And if we get in the way of what she wants."

"Not going to happen. She wants closure for Robert. Anyway, she's cute don't you think?"

"You're nuts, if you think I am stupid enough to answer that question." We both laughed at that. Erin walked back into the kitchen, as we were laughing. It looked as if she had been crying.

She covered it well, and I said, "My partner here was trying to get me in trouble."

"How so? If that is not too personal a question?"

Sophie spoke, "Not at all. I asked him if he thought you were cute. Smartly, he declined to answer."

Erin looked at us in surprise, "What? I don't feel so cute right now. Actually, I am not sure what I feel. I'm kind of numb."

"That's called normal," I said. "If you felt differently, I would be worried."

She added, "Big Boots said you were an Inspector in the SFPD before you became a private investigator."

"I was. It's a long story." I needed a distraction. "Let's eat." Sophie laid the table while I dished the chili into one serving bowl, the rice into another, and the tortillas on a warm plate.

We sat and dished the food, poured beers into glasses, and we dug in. Even if I say so myself, I make a good chili. After a stilted start, the conversation became easier, and the food disappeared. After the conversation covered everything from San Francisco to our work and hers, we eventually ended up at kink. By acknowledging we belonged in the community, it gave Erin a higher level of trust in us, simply because the Kink community runs on trust.

Sophie surprisingly, was more open than I expected, knowing her penchant for privacy, and her history of being off the grid, any grid as much as possible. San Francisco was having its effect on her.

The conversation included Robert. It turned out Erin had met Kasagawa, only briefly, while working with Robert.

With the meal ended, Erin left to go home. Sophie and I agreed she was *cute*.

We didn't have much of anything new to discuss with the case, so watched some TV, a comedy. We had enough reality every day to last us and laughing was good medicine.

Chapter Fourteen

The next day, we had plenty to do and places to be, so we left in short order. Me to the office, and Sophie to meet with Tara. Marie had beaten me in and put the coffee on. Erin walked in just behind me. She looked better than the previous day, but still tired. I would bet she hadn't had a good night's sleep, yet.

She asked me where Sophie was.

"Chasing down other leads and hopefully looking for a short cut to useful information. Are you okay to carry on with your tasks? Do you need anything from me?"

She smiled. "With coffee, I am good to go."

Leaving her to it, I called the realtor who I'd dealt with when I first bought my place. I hoped he'd help us with our real estate questions and save us some leg work.

Andrew answered on the first ring. I explained what we needed, but not exactly why. He explained that he'd look into it and agreed to assist us, saying he would get back to me ASAP. He did warn me if something came up, he'd drop it. The San Francisco Real Estate market was cutthroat.

"I understand and thank you for the assist."

Marie was off to the hall of records. She wanted to look into the whole real estate thing herself, anyway. Now that she and Chung would be able to actually buy a place, she wanted to understand the entire process. I felt sorry for any realtor who tried to put anything over on her and Chung.

Erin was tucked away at Sophie's desk and tapping away on the keyboard, reading, and making notes. Feeling good about where we were headed, I saw McCarrigan's number come up on my phone.

Before I could say anything, McCarrigan said, "Someone's taken Tara. What happened to her bodyguard? Shit, I got a message, you need to see, get over to my office and make it quick."

He hung up before I could say anything. I was off, telling Erin, "Lock the office down as soon as I leave. Don't answer the door for anyone other than Marie, Sophie, or me. No one. Got it?"

"Got it, Mas. What's happened?"

"Emergency. Sophie was supposed to meet Tara this morning, and I haven't heard from either. Going to McCarrigan's office. Call me if you hear form Sophie."

"Sure. I will.

"Lock us down."

That was taken care of…now to sort out our client. The trip to McCarrigan's office took longer than I wanted. If I had been transported instantly it would have been too long. Wondering what had triggered the snatch, we had been careful in our approaches and what we were looking into. The opposition had to have tracked her back through the merger deal itself, as Tara was the primary. She was not high profile, or wealthy enough for a straight kidnapping. Her ex-husband was now on reasonable terms with her, so no motive there. This had to be connected to 3DMedia, and damn what happened to Oso and Sophie? Neither answered their cell phone, and that worried me.

A worried assistant showed me directly into McCarrigan's office. He was pacing and turned as soon as he heard the door, saying, "Look at this."

He brought up a text from that morning, with an image The image was a of a disheveled Tara bound to a chair and gagged, a note pinned to her shirt. "Deliver all files on 3DMedia or she dies." In the background to one side, I saw a piece of clothing that looked like what Sophie was wearing that morning.

Where the hell was Oso, this had to be bad, if they got both Tara and Sophie, and no Oso to be found. McCarrigan was speaking, but I wasn't listening, I was already thinking next steps and moves. McCarrigan didn't know it yet, but Sophie being taken as well was a blessing.

Calling the office, Marie had returned and answered in the usual way, no secure word for trouble. Giving Marie rapid instructions on what I wanted. She took it all down and said it would be done by the time I got back.

Next calling Tara's office, a distraught Kristen answered in tears. She had received the same email as McCarrigan, followed up by a telephone call telling her to get all the material associated with the 3DMedia deal.

"Have you gone yet?"

"No, I'm scared, how do they know I can get them?"

"Probably because they bugged the office and have had access to Tara's computer for a while. It doesn't matter. All you need to do is get what they asked for and bring it back to the office. Put it in the safe for now.

Don't say anything to anyone-got it?"

"Yes, what if they harm Tara?"

"If you follow exactly what they tell you to do, we should get her back without any problems."

"Really?"

"They want those drives, not her," I said, wishing I really felt that way, but scaring Kristen didn't serve any purpose, other than potentially screwing up the entire deal. I was about to turn to McCarrigan when my phone went off again—Oso.

"Oso, are you okay? What happened?"

"Sorry, Mas, I blew it. I let you down."

"We can play the blame game, later. What happened and are you okay?"

"Yeah, I'm fine. I couldn't do nothing, man. They lit me up with their Tasers and banged me head. I couldn't stop them. They took Ms. Tara and Sophie. I really fucked up."

"Oso, get it together. I need your help. Can you do that? I'm going to need you. Got that?"

"Si man. Whatever you need."

"Okay. Get to my office and stay there. I'll call ahead and let them know it's okay to let you in."

I called Marie to let her know Oso was on the way and to be nice to him. "He feels it's his fault, and it isn't."

That done, I could turn my attention to McCarrigan and concentrate on getting Tara and Sophie back as unharmed as possible.

"Alright, what about the phone-call that followed the text?"

"What?"

"Don't play silly buggers, they called with a follow

up to the text, giving you instructions for a drop, right?"

"Yes, how did you know?"

"Because I'm not stupid. You're now playing on my turf. They have Sophie as well as Tara, and if you fuck with me, I'll take you out. Our job is to get them both back, safe and sound. If you try this on your own, you'll fail. They called on your cell, yes?"

"Yes, on my cell. Alright, I didn't know about Sophie, how did you?"

"The photo, I saw the clothing she wore this morning. What were the instructions given?"

"Wait in my office. Tara's assistant would contract me. I'm to wait for further instructions. Do not call the police etc. I didn't, I called you instead."

"Good, how is your driving?"

"What?"

"Pull yourself together. How good is your driving? Can you drive like you mean it?"

"Yes, of course. It's good, I think…why?"

"You may need to drive like a local asshole if it all works out. What do you drive?"

"Porsche SUV."

"Mind if it gets a few dents?"

"Not if you get Tara and Sophie back."

"Good answer. I'm going back to the office. Let me know when they call or text you."

Getting back to the office, I expected a text would be coming soon. I entered my building and called Marie as a heads up. Cautiously, I unlocked the door and entered, calling out so she knew it was me. After shutting and locking the door behind me, Oso came out from the inner office. He hung his head. I couldn't stand that look. To take him down, it must have taken multiple Taser hits, and he had a nasty lump on the back of his head, which says a lot about him. No blame there. I should have been more aware and gotten more protection. It was my fault if anyone's. Now I had to fix it.

"It's okay Oso, not your fault. Now I need your help getting them both back, safe and sound. You in?"

"Anything Mas, anything you need."

My phone dinged with a new text. Same image. My phone went off, showing Sophie's number. Answering it with, "Yes." An electronically distorted voice came out loud and clear.

"We want the copies of the flash drives. Give us those and no one gets hurt, don't and they die."

"No problem, when and where?"

"Not that easy Hammett. We need you to wait and think about the consequences of non-compliance."

"I already said you can have them all."

"Patience, while we have a chat with the ladies. You'll get further instructions when we're ready. Be ready to deliver."

My body froze—my mind shifted to all the physical images of other hostages I'd seen. I had to hold back the violence welling up within me and gather my control. The kidnappers wanted to make sure what they got was the total package, which meant they'd question Tara and Sophie. I didn't feel good about that scenario. Sophie could be pigheaded and obstinate. They'd put a lot of hurt on her to get the information they wanted. I hoped she realized this wasn't a game. None of that improved my disposition toward them, so I'd be ready when the instructions came.

Oso, Marie, and Erin looked at me, waiting. First, I

asked Marie. "Did you copy the flash drives?"

"Erin did it." She handed me two baggies' with exactly the same type of flash drives.

Good that done, I needed to eat. "Oso, tell me what happened."

He started relating the events. "We were driving to the office, and Ms. Tara says we have to detour to pick up somebody, Ms. Sophie. We picks her up n' they chat away in the back. I's keeping an eye out for tails like you said, and I thinks I sees a tail, but I'm not sure. I do the usual. *Nada.* We continues to the first appointment. Stopping, I gets out to open Ms. Tara's door, and I sees someone but too late. I felt like I wuz lit up, man. Turning to the dude, I wuz hit again from the front, and back as well. Then I don't remember too much after that. When I woke up, they wuz all gone. Doors open, and all gone."

"No one saw anything?"

"The garage was underground and looked empty."

"You were set up, man. Someone made a bogus appointment. It was a trap. You didn't have a chance."

Kristen would know about the appointment. She answered my call immediately. "Any news? I have the flash drives. They're in the safe. I haven't heard anything since I spoke to you."

"Don't worry. I'll let you know if anything breaks. Hang in there and wait for further instructions. They are going to make us sweat for a while. Who made the appointment for this morning?"

"Tara made it herself. Then she had me add it to her schedule. She said it was an initial consultation about a property with a Real Estate company."

"Owned by Golden Realty Union."

"How did you know?"

"Lucky guess. I want you to come to my office, bring your laptop, and the flash drives. It'll be safer for you here. Pick a cab up off the street, like now, okay?"

"Yes, I'm on my way. Thank you, Mr. Hammett."

With that done, next was McCarrigan. I had a plan forming, and I needed all the pieces in place before I could weigh the odds to make sure they were in our favor. He answered, agreeing to come to the office. I told him where he could park his vehicle, close and available as needed.

With everyone in one place, it would be easier to coordinate and easier to execute. When the instruction calls came in, it would give me critical information. If all the calls were made at the same time, it would mean there were more kidnappers than I expected. One after the other, was what I believed would happen. Now I was about to take a big risk. Oso still looked like a dog that had been beaten once too often.

Getting his attention, I asked, "Hey Oso, you want to help, right?"

"Sure, Mas, anything *si*."

"Do you happen to know a few people who would cause a disturbance on request? Nothing too extreme. Just noisy and aggravating?

"*Si*, no problem. Where and when?"

"Not sure, yet. It'll be short notice. Would that be a problem?"

"Na, it's cool."

McCarrigan arrived slightly out of breath and looking disheveled. We settled him at my desk, and he was back on his phone. Kristen arrived with a worried expression and sat with Marie who took the flash drives from her. This was coming together nicely.

All that was left was to engage Erin into helping me find Sophie. An easier job than I expected, thanks to Sophie. Now I was grateful for what I originally thought was an extreme measure. When she agreed to become partners, she had us both chipped with GPS trackers, just in case she lost me, so she would be able to find me. I thought it was extreme, but I complied. She had agreed to move to San Francisco and move in with me. If she had asked me to walk on water, I'd have tried.

Speaking quietly to Erin, I asked her if she would help me open and use the GPS tracking system on Sophie's computer.

She nodded. "I can do that, if you know how it works."

"Sophie showed me a couple of times. I'm not that good with tech, but you're fairly good. Between us, we should be able to get what I need."

We sat at Sophie's computer. I knew her passwords…Yes plural. Next thing I knew, we were in. In theory, I had an idea of what to do and where to go. With Erin looking over my shoulder to check on me, we slowly made our way through the maze of stuff on her computer. Sophie had set it up, so it was simple to use. Erin only had to correct me once, and we got to the GPS activation screen, hit enter, and there she was. Wherever that was. Loading in the GPS coordinates, I hit locate on the map icon. Blip…up popped a street map of San Francisco with a pulsing light in the center of the screen.

Shafter Avenue in Silver Terrace. Not an area I knew, but I had a location, and that was what I wanted.

The area looked industrial. Warehouses and the like. Couldn't be too complicated. I wanted as much information as I could get—a floor plan would be perfect.

"Marie, can you do a search for floor plans if I give you an address?"

Before she could answer, Kristen said, "I can do that. I am always doing stuff like that for Tara."

Shrugging, I said, "Go for it." I didn't care who did it, or got it, as long as I had it, and quickly.

Marie piped up, "If we both search, two people will double the chance of success.

Oso said, "Nineteen people be enough for what you want."

"Shit, Oso, I said a distraction not a riot." He thought that was funny, at least he now had a smile on his face.

Once I got everyone together, I said, "I have to run a few errands. It's necessary I go, but please stay together. I'll be back as soon as I can.

McCarrigan responded with a snide smile, "Not running out on us are you, Mas?" His nerves were showing and that surprised me. He must care more for Tara than I gave him credit for. Still, it was an un-called for comment.

"Just be ready to do your part when it needs to be done, and don't fuck it up. Lives depend on it." That wiped the smile off his face. "No one gets in here while I'm gone."

Saying it for everyone's benefit, but I aimed the order at Oso. He nodded.

Once I heard the door locks click behind me, I went home, grabbed a change of clothes—everything in black, shirt, jeans, leather jacket, and black Dr. Marten boots. My weapon was the next task. Collecting it, I cleared the chamber and dropped the magazine, removing all the full metal jacket rounds, and put them back in the bullet tray. I took out a box of hollow point and reloaded the magazine with ten rounds, adding an extra one in the chamber, and filled my two spare magazines with the same. A thought crossed my mind. Knowing where Sophie stored her pistol, I opened the box and took that one too, as back up. If my thirty-one rounds, plus Sophie's ten rounds weren't enough, nothing I had would be.

What I was about to do next, was completely legal but my intention was completely illegal. Taking my Mossberg 590 shotgun from its hard case under the bed in the guest bedroom, I loaded it, and put it in its carry case. So far, no problem. Only, I was going to give it to Oso, and as a felon, it was illegal for him to own or carry a firearm of any description. To make it clear, I would still ask him if he'd be willing to take the risk, knowing what his answer would be. Still, I had to ask.

I took that receiving no calls from the office as a good sign. This would now give me time to reconnoiter the location where GPS tracker put Sophie and, more than likely, also Tara before we attempted a rescue. Before going into the office, I decide to leave the shotgun and spare rounds covered in my SUV.

The silence in the office was deafening. Each person morose and trying to look busy. When McCarrigan closed his computer and glanced at me, he looked tired. A different type of stress, one he wasn't used to, showed in his eyes and the lines on his face. Kristen and Marie worked at their laptops. Erin looked up with a small smile. She had something. The look on her face was positive, but that could wait.

Marie asked, "You need anything?"

"Only everyone's attention. Oso and I are going to take a look at the GPS location. All of you stay put. Same rules apply. No one leaves. If the kidnappers call with instructions let me know ASAP. I should get a call as well. We'll get back before dark depending on traffic. Everybody okay?"

McCarrigan said, "Not really. I want to do more— be involved." He was serious.

"You'll get your chance, and we'll need you to be ready. Trust me, you'll get all the action you can handle."

Erin asked, "Mas, can I have a word?"

"Sure, here is good. We're all in the same boat."

"Okay. If you're sure."

"I'm sure." Anything she said would be heard by people with skin in the game, and it would distract them from what was going on outside.

"The funds for the purchase of 3DMedia are coming through the Maltese Bank and probably dirty. I'm still not sure exactly of the source. Why is another matter. They already have a system for funneling money into our electoral system, at least to specific candidates. Two congressmen are tied to the 3DMedia deal, and so is the Real Estate investment company. The investments they're involved with really got Robert going. Basically, it's a front for money laundering and delivering funds to a PAC. I am still working on the details. That trail is convoluted."

"You mean like the Russians allegedly putting millions into the NRA as a conduit to the presidential campaign?"

"Kinda. It's more subtle. More long-term planning than the other."

"All good stuff. Keep digging. We'll be going, or we'll get trapped in traffic both ways."

Oso and I left, on the way to my SUV. I asked him the question. "Oso, there's a shotgun under the cover in the back, it's yours if you want to use it. You can't legally have it on your person. If you don't want to, that's fine. Your choice."

"No problem, Mas. I take you up on that, when we needs it. Thanks for asking, an' meaning it. This is my problem, too. We fix it together. I got debts to pay back."

"Not to me, Oso. I made that clear."

He smiled a very nasty smile. "Not you, Mas. I wants payback on the *pendejos* who tagged me."

"Then try not to kill anyone unless you have to.

"Na, a beating down will make me feel much better. Shooting ees too easy."

Wouldn't want to be on the wrong end of Oso, ever. With that comment we lapsed into silence. By taking the back roads, it was longer by distance but quicker than being stuck in highway traffic. Turning at Shafter Street, I thought the map was wrong and it was a dead end, then noticing a narrow lane at the top of the street, which went around the back of the industrial buildings. Comparing the reality with the map on the internet, it all matched.

Slowing my vehicle, we both looked over the building identified by GPS. Industrial and run-down looking place, with a substantial lock on the roll up door, and on the sturdy looking main entrance door.

Not so run down, after all. Windows only on the front of the building.

As I drove up the lane and concentrated on driving, Oso used his phone to take video of the side and back of the building. It was a clever idea I should have had, still now we had information we could use. There were two vehicles parked on the side of the building. Time to get out of here. We didn't want to be observed and arouse suspicions. The information we gathered should be enough for me to put together a plan of action.

Oso texted Marie the exact address of the building where the GPS said Sophie was located, and we were banking on either Marie or Kristen getting a floor plan of the building. Even a floor plan could be deceptive if alterations had been made without pulling a permit. It could throw off my plan. Then again, no plan was perfect, and too much planning was as bad as no planning.

On the way back to North Beach, I had Oso call in an order of Chinese food. On the way we picked up the order, and Oso carried the two bags of food inside, while I carried the shotgun. The plan for tonight included using McCarrigan and his SUV, and it had to be tonight, regardless of the instruction we'd get from the kidnappers.

Back inside the office, the bag I carried got curious looks, but no one said anything. The food was welcome. Marie went to get paper plates and disposable cutlery, and Kristen offered to assist. We sat wherever we could. The office wasn't large. Six adults, seven if you included Oso as two people, meant the setting was quite cozy. This was probably the most people who'd ever been in the place at one time on business, yet alone here sitting to eat.

Kristen's cell went off. Everyone froze in place—food halfway to mouths, jaws ceased chewing, and all eyes went to her.

"Recognize the number?" I asked.

She nodded. "Yes, it's Tara's phone."

She answered it on speaker. "Hello."

The metallic voice asked, "Do you have all of the project files?"

With a trembling voice, she said, "Yes, all of them."

The voice asked, "Digital and hard copy?"

"Only digital. All hard copies were shredded after being digitized."

"Excellent answer. Wait for instructions." Click. The last comment convinced me they had encouraged Tara to tell them everything, and it would have been a physical interrogation. Not enough time for a chemical one.

Whose phone would go off next? McCarrigan's or mine? My bet...mine. Even though I was expecting it, the sound of my ringer surprised me.

I also answered it on speaker. "Are they unharmed?" I demanded.

The metallic voice said, "Do you have all the digital archive you copied ready?"

"Yes, everything. Are they unharmed?"

"How many?"

"Five original flash drives. We condensed them down to three."

An eerie metallic voice said, "Excellent answer, wait for further instructions."

The line went dead.

Everyone was looking at me. That was good, two calls in sequence, together. That told me this was a small operation, one maybe two with brains, and then some additional muscle.

"McCarrigan, you'll be next. They are going to use you as a courier." He looked at me with a questioning look. "They'll assume Kristen will be too scared. You have Tara to lose, so you'll play nice, and you don't have any experience in this type of situation. They don't want me, a P.I. and former police officer, doing a drop when they have you."

Sitting in silence, most half-heartedly went back to eating. Oso and I continued eating as before. We both would need our energy later. Seeing us tuck in encouraged the others to continue. Soon the conversation started up, and Marie asked the question that was on everyone's mind.

"Mas, do you think they're okay?"

"They should be. Like I said, I think Robert's death was an accident, not meant to happen. They are more interested in getting what they want, than hurting Tara and Sophie."

"What about after they get what they want?"

Shit why did she have to be so smart.

"Depends on what they saw, and who is running the show. Killing them would cause a lot of unwanted attention. Once they have what they think is all the data, no one here is a danger to them or their principals."

She looked at me. "Okay, put that way. It makes sense. But you are going to get them back before anything happens, right?"

Smiling a confident smile I didn't entirely feel, I said, "Yup, that's the plan."

178

McCarrigan asked, "You have a plan?"

"Yes, I do."

"May I ask what it is?"

"Well, it's not fixed yet. Depends on what the next set of instructions are."

"That's pretty sloppy, isn't it?"

"Call it flexible and adaptable."

Looking as if he was going to say something, his phone interrupted. He answered it on speaker, "This is McCarrigan."

The same metallic, emotionless voice gave the orders, "You will be our courier. Any mistakes or errors, and you will not see your girlfriend again, alive. Write this down."

I handed him a note pad and pen. The voice continued, giving Kristen's cell number then mine, saying, "Call these numbers and arrange to pick up the assets. You have one hour to collect everything. We'll call back in one hour with more instructions."

Making a sign to him for more time, McCarrigan played along asking, "I'll need more than an hour. Traffic is bad, and I don't know where they are. What if they don't answer?"

There was a pause.

"Two hours, no more." Gone, the line went dead.

McCarrigan actually looked shaken.

"Nicely done, and an extra hour. Any change is in our favor. This also means they aren't locals. Anyone who lives here knows how bad the traffic is at this time of day...every day."

Everyone laughed at that, and the tension eased, if only a little.

McCarrigan asked, "Does this help your plan?"

"Don't really know. This changes their timetable, and that could make the difference."

Marie said, "We had better put everything together and be ready for the next instructions."

"Do it. And thank you," I said. "Make sure you use two different types of bags or containers. If they are both the same, it may arouse suspicions. They don't realize we are all together, so we are probably not under surveillance. That was a mistake on their part, or they are running a very slim operation and don't have the manpower. Either way, it's an advantage to us."

That made me feel better, and this time I did feel more confident. Whoever took Tara and the woman I loved was going to regret it. That was a promise.

Two hours on the dot, McCarrigan's phone went off. He answered on speaker, and the disembodied voice asked, "Did you collect everything?"

"Yes, only just, I told you I needed more time."

"Enough. Listen carefully. You will put everything in one bag and take it to the following address." The address was the one on Shafter Street. "Put the bag through the mail slot and drive off."

"When will Tara be released?"

"When we have confirmed the contents of the drives are what they're supposed to be. You will be notified when and where. If anyone follows you, or you involve the authorities, they are both dead."

"No nothing, I promise no police."

Hearing the truth in his voice, I was sure of his feeling for Tara. I already knew what mine were for Sophie. If they hurt her, I was going to seriously fuck them up.

Calm down Mas, don't get emotional now, save it

for later. Cold, calm, and collected will get them back.

The metallic voice gave one last instruction. "Make the drop at precisely 2:15 a.m. Not before and do not be late, that will mean serious consequences for the ladies."

Silence. McCarrigan stared at his phone.

Bringing all my players attention back to the present situation, I said, "Now, we have a timeline. Let's get this thing rolling. Oso, can you get your associates to roll up on that street at ten minutes to one AM?"

"Si, no problem. What you want them to do?"

"Be loud, do donuts on the road, create a party."

Oso smiled. "They specialize in loud 'n' obnoxious."

"Not too obnoxious. I don't want anyone to get hurt or have the police involved."

"No *problem,* Mas."

McCarrigan stepped forward. "And my part?"

"You will be doing all the driving. Bring the bag of flash drives with you in case we have to call this part of the plan off. You will then do the drop as per instructions."

"What's the plan?" he asked.

That was something I really didn't want to divulge. It was an iffy plan at best. I had to trust him to do his part, and for him, knowing up front would be better than any surprises. So, I told him. "We get there early, going in the back way, down a narrow lane behind the building, completely hidden—no windows on the back side, only a rear door. Oso and I will enter through there when the distraction is at its max. All their focus will be on the front. I figure they'll have a max of seven or eight people inside."

He asked, "How did you figure that number?"

I counted off on my fingers. "A principal, one interrogator, plus five or six for muscle. The snatch was well-planned. They set a trap. So that means they have *some* training. Three took out Oso, one each on Tara and Sophie, probably at gun point. If it wasn't, Sophie would have created all sorts of hell. And a driver, another vehicle to transfer them. Cuffed and bagged, it probably took seconds. You don't want any more people involved in something like this than absolutely necessary."

McCarrigan asked, "Two of you to take on eight-armed people? That is not good odds. Shit, Mas, I know my way around a gun. I'm coming in with you—no arguments. This is Tara." He added, "and Sophie."

Not sure if he was serious, I was about to ask him about his experience with guns when Marie spoke up. "I can drive. Mas, you know I can drive."

"That's settled then." McCarrigan tossed his keys to Marie saying, "Don't worry about dents or scratches. It's a car. I can always get a new one. Got it?"

Marie nodded with a smile.

That actually made sense. I could rely on Marie's driving because she was a natural and could easily maneuver her way around San Francisco. The driving taken care of, I handed McCarrigan Sophie's CZ pistol. It looked small in his hand. He handled it, showing he knew what he was doing. He was proficient but not well practiced.

Hoping this plan didn't end in anything fatal. The last thing I asked about was if there'd been any luck with the floor plan.

"Sorry, I was distracted," Kristen answered, then pointed to her computer screen. "Yes, here. It's an old one from the late eighties. Nothing more up to date, which means it is the same, unless changes were done without permits. Will that do?"

"Perfect, this will give us an idea of what we will be walking into. Print up some copies. Everyone needs to memorize it." Oso and McCarrigan nodded. I would do the same. Paper plans are never the same as seeing it in real life, but better than nothing.

We had hours to while away. Erin and Kristen were to stay in the office. As a backup, I gave them Kenzo's cell number. In case we didn't call in by a certain time, they were to call him and have him send out the riot squad. I hoped the women wouldn't need to make that call, but if they did, it would mean something went very terribly wrong.

Resting as much as I could, I suggested everyone else do the same. Oso was too big to be comfortable anywhere, he rolled-up his jacket as a pillow and crashed on the floor. Marie took the sofa, and Erin covered her with her coat.

Chapter Fifteen

Time ticked away slowly, as I reviewed this very sketchy plan, wondering if there was a better way to execute it. *Blank.* This was it, with the resources and time we had. The kidnappers were on a tight timeline to get what they wanted. They knew the information was readily available to us and therefore to them. The chances of the two women still being alive, on this timeline, were really good, and why we needed to act tonight. The kidnappers had chosen the time for the drop deliberately, a shitty time of night when your body was at its lowest ebb. We had the element of surprise on our side. I'd configured our procedure, so I had the lead followed by Oso, and McCarrigan brought up the rear. Each of us had specific tasks and responsibilities.

I pulled out my bullet proof vest from the supply cupboard and put it on under my jacket. The only other vest we had was Sophie's, and that was way too small for either of the other two men. Besides, I would be the main target. My key gun would handle any lock we encountered.

Searching around for the office cutters, like pliers but with cutting edges, I couldn't find them. Marie sleepily asked what I was looking for.

"Cutters."

She pointed. "My desk, bottom drawer, right side, and please put them back when you are done."

Right where she said they would be. Even tired, Marie was on the ball and busting mine.

"Why cutters?" McCarrigan asked when I handed them to him. "Why not a knife?"

"Robert Clegg had marks on his wrists and ankles that looked like wide zip ties. Cutters are better to get them off, more efficient. A blade can slip and cut the person you're trying to free."

He continued, "How do you know they'll use zip ties?"

Patiently, I said, "I don't. Ask yourself, would they change a habit that works and are comfortable with? Zip ties are easy to use, efficient, quick to put on, pretty secure, and can't be picked like handcuffs. Less risky than rope. Knots can be undone."

"I guess you know what you're doing."

"Sometimes. Let's get going, I would rather be early and get bored, than rush and screw up."

Waking Oso was like getting a bear out of hibernation, slow and easy does it. He came round quickly when I said it was time to go. They all got up— some more bleary eyed than others. Marie put on yet another pot of coffee for those staying behind. Erin said they wouldn't need it. "The adrenaline is already pumping."

Marie was ready jingling McCarrigan's keys. I handed the cased shotgun to Oso. We trooped out and walked the short distance to where McCarrigan parked. Marie opened the door locks as we approached, and we all quickly got in. Oso laid the gun case across his legs pointing at the door. McCarrigan sat behind me, giving Oso more room behind Marie, who was adjusting everything to her liking, seat, mirrors, and steering wheel.

Marie pulled the SUV easily out into the minimal night traffic. She tested the brakes and acceleration, steering in and out of the traffic to get a feel for the SUV. From the look on her face, she liked the vehicle. No conversation, only the GPS voice giving directions to the location she'd plugged into the car's system.

Heading south toward the Peninsula, the trip was about what I expected at this time of night. The area around Shafter Street was quiet. All the businesses were closed and dark. The only illuminations were the few sour yellow streetlights, and one or two over the entrances to shuttered properties. Driving past the street we made the next right, the one that ended in the narrow lane running past the back of the buildings. Marie managed to turn the SUV around facing the way we had come in—parking lights off and engine running.

Saying I was going to have a look at our target, I eased out of the vehicle—my weapon out and ready, just in case. The night was cloudy, damp, and noticeably quiet. Traffic on the 101 was a distant, constant buzz. Nothing stirred.

Hearing a noise, I froze, carefully looking in the direction the noise came from. *Goddamn raccoon in a trash can.*

The only other thing I noticed were two vehicles parked on the side of our target building: an SUV and a commercial van with no windows. They would have to be taken care of and disabled on our way into the target. No point letting them chase us if we could prevent it. Slashed tire walls would do.

Nothing looked any different from earlier in the day. Returning to the others, I took out my tactical knife and handed it to McCarrigan saying, "As soon as we get to the vehicles, slash the side wall of at least one tire on each vehicle.

He looked like he was about to say something.

"Yes, I know it's redundant to go over it again, but we are going to go over everything again and again. I will take care of the door locks and open the door. Oso goes in first with the shotgun. I go in right after, then take the lead. We don't know which room or rooms Tara and Sophie are being kept in. Chances are they will keep them together…easier to guard, and they hear what's being done to the other. It works on their heads. When we find them, use the cutters on the zip ties. If it's rope, you have the blade. Got it? Any questions?"

McCarrigan asked, "What will you be doing while I do all this?

"Making sure you don't get shot and watching your back as you get the women out the way we came in. The floor plans are only a guide. We don't know if any alterations have been done. Probably haven't, but that's not a guarantee. Stick close behind until we get the women. That answer your question?"

"Yes. Sorry I'm more used to a desk."

"You asked to be here."

"I did. I will not let you down. Trust me, I want them back as much as you do."

"Good enough. Let's keep it tight. We should hear evidence of the party starting in about fifteen minutes."

They had to be some of the longest fifteen minutes of my life. With five to go, I said it was time to get in position. We exited the SUV. Oso slid the shotgun out of its case and used the sling to carry it, steadying it with one hand, leaving the other free. McCarrigan checked the cutters in his pocket, carrying the pistol out and ready in one hand and the knife in the other. Quietly closing the vehicle doors, I led the way down to the edge of the lane waiting for the distraction to begin.

Soon as the first pick-up truck rounded the corner onto Shafter Street, we heard it—loud Mexican music blaring, followed by another loaded pick-up truck, then a series of low riders, bouncing and honking up the street, and ending with a last pickup truck loaded with a sound system. If this had been a cemetery, the dead would have been up and dancing.

Giving them a few minutes to circle the trucks and give notice they were not passing would attract the attention of the occupants of the targeted building. It should bring all of them out front, or at least focus their attention on the front. Wondering if anyone would be stupid enough to challenge them was not my problem.

Moving quickly around the edge of the lane and into the shadows cast by the building, I pointed to the two vehicles. McCarrigan moved to the side of the first one, and Oso stayed back while I moved to the door.

Two substantial locks. Not complicated. Within seconds I had the first one open, and then the second one clicked open. Signaling I was ready, a hand on my shoulder told me Oso was ready to breach. I opened the door slowly until it was full open and clear. Oso had the shotgun up and in front of him, leaving me enough room to duck down and step in front of him.

Entering the dim, safe lit hallway, I confirmed it looked like the floor plan. That meant there were two rooms off to each side—the two rear doors in the hallway faced each other, and the front two doors faced into the main building. My guess was that Tara and

Sophie were being held in one of those two.

Which? Right or left?

Easing our way along the passage, we could hear the music, covering any sound we made. Reaching the corner first, I took a quick look right and left. No one in sight. Some work had been done in the main area, and it obscured my view of a majority of the front of the building. That was good and bad.

Taking a chance, I went right. The room had a big window and nothing in it. I backed up left…no window. Pistol ready, turning the door handle silently, I opened it sharply. Telling the woman standing over Tara to be quiet and move away. She saw my weapon un-waveringly pointed at her. She moved away, hands raised in compliance. Giving McCarrigan credit, he did not move in front of me. He went around me and knelt by the side of the two women who were zip tied to heavy, back-to-back metal chairs.

I motioned to Oso to cover the woman. When he did, pointing the shotgun at her torso, I closed the door. I wanted as much privacy as possible for as long as possible. Both women looked worse for wear— disheveled hair, split lips, and their clothes had been ripped open down the front, exposing them. I could see bruises starting to form on breasts and abdomens. Feeling the bile begin to rise up my throat, I had to move before I did something we would all regret.

McCarrigan was as good as his word, using the cutters efficiently. He had both women freed of the zip ties, but they still sat in the chairs. Tara groaned, coming around. She must have been drugged, as well as physically abused. Trying to stand, Sophie seemed in better shape than Tara. McCarrigan helped her to her feet. Sophie was unsteady, not even trying to cover herself. When she looked up at me, I saw the damage. A swollen eye and dried blood on her lips and cheeks, and clamp marks on her breasts didn't stop her from trying to smile and talk though puffy lips. She mouthed the words, "Thank you," to me silently.

I turned away from Sophie and toward the woman standing with her back to the wall. I assumed she was the interrogator. Taking a step closer to her, she opened her mouth to scream out a warning. Before she could make any sound, Oso punched her square on the jaw. Her head bounced into the dry wall, and she dropped to the floor like a bad habit. Out cold. She looked like a broken doll, arms and legs splayed out at all angles. I didn't feel sorry for her in the slightest. I only hoped Oso hadn't broken her jaw because I'd need her to talk, later.

Now all we had to do was get out of there alive. We could still hear the loud music and the cars squealing tires. Opening the door cautiously, looking both ways, I saw no one in sight. Signaling the others to move, I sent McCarrigan first carrying the unconscious woman. He'd zip-tied her with ties he found. Her hands behind her and her ankles together, she was just a dead weight. Sophie helped the insensible Tara. I stood guard on one corner and Oso on the other. We had our retreat covered. This time, with Tara dragging her feet, there was more noise.

I heard a shout and a gun shot went off. The round whizzed passed me, barely missing my head. I dropped and returned fire, shouting for the others to get the hell out—now. The boom of the shot gun was like a cannon going off in the enclosed space, then I heard a scream.

At least one went down, if not out. More shots came our way. The shot gun was keeping the attackers at bay, for the moment. Standing to assess the situation, instinct made me turn. Not fast enough. A thud in my left ribcage, knocked the wind out of me and slammed me into the wall.

Fuck, I'd been hit. Taking fast shallow breathes, I realized it hadn't penetrated the vest—cracked a rib at worse, maybe. I returned fire in that direction and emptied my magazine, dropped it out, and replaced it smoothly, ready to go again.

Quiet. A lull in the action. They were trying to figure out how many of us there were and how to get to us. Using the lull to pick up my empty magazine, I motioned to Oso to get back to the rear door. I would cover him, and when he was safe, he would cover me. For a big man, he was light on his feet, making it down the hallway swiftly.

As I was about to move, I noticed movement to my right. I fired a couple of shots and as I did, instinct made me turn to my left. A man rose with a weapon. I fired and watched him go down. Hit center mass. I turned into a crouching run and made it down the hallway. As soon as I was safe, Oso fired down the hall behind me to discourage anyone from following us. I closed the door and jammed it shut with a piece of wood that was probably used to prop it open on hot days. The others were already out of sight.

Shaking with adrenaline and breathing heavily, I asked, "Oso, you okay?

"Si, better'n fine. We got da ladies back." He stopped and looked at me. "We go back and finish them? No? They's put a hurt on Ms. Tara an' your

Sophie."

"Not tonight, Oso. We got what we needed. The ladies are back, and we got the person who put the hurt on them."

"This bitch did that? Can I have her?"

"Let's just get the hell out of here."

Retracing our route back to McCarrigan's SUV, I was surprised to see my SUV also there, parked behind the Porsche. Marie must have called for reinforcements. It was Erin driving and Kristen standing at the rear lift gate. She was covering the woman with the rollout cover. Good thinking.

McCarrigan had helped Sophie put Tara in the back of his car. Sophie sat next to her holding her, both under a blanket. I waved them to take off.

After they did, Kristen closed the hatch on my SUV and returned to the front seat. Oso and I got in behind them and Erin took off, no spinning tires, smooth and easy.

Coming down from the adrenaline, I began to feel my ribs start to throb with pain. Feeling around the left side, I felt the ragged edge where the fabric was pierced and dug around for the flattened round. It felt like a cannon ball, but was probably only a nine mm. Damn it, I was sore, and I was thankful it was a body shot.

We got lucky, real lucky. No one was hurt, and at least two bad guys went down, one permanently, for sure. Killing anyone is never a good feeling, even if it was them or me. This case was getting way out of hand for me and Sophie to handle on our own. We would have to inform the authorities, and the only one I trusted was Kenzo.

I glanced at Oso. "You want to check in with your

friends, thank them, and make sure they're all okay?"

"Si. I guarantee, they are okay. At the sound of the first shot, they rabbited out of there." He laughed a big booming laugh, releasing the tension. "Man, you were cool in there—like a rock. Me? I was shaking."

"Practice, Oso. Shaking is all part of it."

Then I asked the reinforcements how they came to be there.

Erin and Kristen answered together, with Erin winning. "Marie called us. She figured you'd need more space on the way back. How were you all going to fit everyone in the car? She asked if we were up to helping out." Looking at Kristen she carried on. "We both agreed we had to do something, so we said sure. Marie told us where all the keys were. We picked up your car and came here. Good job, huh?"

Responding, I said, "No argument from me."

Oso commented in admiration, "Mas, you knows ladies with cojones, that's for sure."

Where to now? I needed to see Sophie and get her checked out, along with Tara. I also had a prisoner, and this had to be all on me. What to do with her? She would have some information, Probably, not enough. She was obviously a subcontractor used for the interrogations. Still any information would be useful.

We still had Simon's apartment, my old partner's place. Sophie had stayed there until she moved in with me.

I told Erin to drop me and Oso off at the that address and gave her the directions. I began to think out a plan. The series of events would have to fall into place according to priorities. Calling Kenzo at this hour was not an issue, he would answer seeing my number and guess it would be important. Why else would I call him in the middle of the night?

He picked up just before voice mail. "What the fuck, Mas? You in trouble again?

"Kinda. Can you meet me at Simon's old place?"

"Now?"

"No. Get a crew over to Shafter Street—top end left. Then, can you come over to Simon's place in a couple of hours?" Giving him the exact address, I continued. "There should be at least one body, possibly two, plus lots of bullet holes. When I see you, you'll get the full story."

"Fair enough. See you in a couple."

After hanging up, I said, "I'll keep everyone out of this as much as I can, certainly out of anything that's illegal. Oso, make sure you wash all your clothes and take a shower to get rid of the GSR. Okay?

"Got it, Mas."

"Erin. after Oso and I take our guest into the house, would you take Oso home?"

"Got it. Do you want me to come to the office same as usual?"

"We keep everything as normal as possible."

My phone went off. Marie's number. "Yes."

Sophie's hoarse voice asked, "Where are you? Do need me?"

"Going to Simon's place. All I need to know is you're alright. You need to get checked out by a doctor." I heard McCarrigan in the background say he knew a doctor who would be discreet, and it's where he was taking Tara and Sophie.

"Go with them and no arguments."

She said she would, and that closed the call.

Chapter Sixteen

Exhausted, I wanted to sleep but couldn't, not until I'd had a chat with my guest and met with Kenzo. At Simon's place it was quiet. Erin turned off the lights, put the SUV into neutral, and coasted to a stop almost directly outside Simon's place. Erin gave me my set of keys, and I ran up and unlocked the door. Oso picked up the woman, wrapped her in the old blanket I kept in the car, and tossed her over his shoulder. We were in the house within seconds. He unceremoniously dumped her on the sofa, and she groaned.

Oso gave me a hug and left, saying, "I'll check on Ms. Tara and Ms. Sophie, tomorrow. Be good, Mas."

I tossed my keys back to Erin as she was leaving, and Kristen ran in with my shotgun, silently handing it to me. Nodding my thanks, she left. The house was quiet. The woman was conscious and pretending not to be.

Sitting her up, I spoke directly to her, "Make any sound I don't like, and I will hurt you."

She sat awkwardly, hands fixed behind her back, and her ankles crossed and bound. She looked at me, not afraid but not at ease, either. Placing the barrel of the shotgun under her bruised chin, I lifted her head. She was small, not quite petite, and attractive in a hard, used way.

She dressed in a mannish business style, a collared

white shirt, dark jacket and pants, and low-heeled, lace-up black patent shoes. Her dark hair was styled to be practical. No doubt, she was a professional. I wondered who had trained her. My money was on one of our own "initials only" government departments. I was furious about what she'd done to our client, and to my partner.

My phone went off distracting me from my observations. McCarrigan spoke, "I forgot to tell you, as we left that place. I picked up a brief case and a small medical bag. Thought you would probably want to look into them. Sorry, I wasn't functioning properly."

"No apologies necessary. You held up your end, and yes, I'd like them very much. When can you get them to me?"

"Soon, we are at the doc's now. I'm going back to my place to get new clothes for Tara and Sophie. I'll drop it off then."

"Great. I'll text you the address. It won't be too far out of your way."

That was interesting news. Looking at the woman, I smiled my best "I got you, bitch" smile, and asked her name.

"Won't do you any good."

"Humor me."

"Sandy Wright, and no, I won't tell you who I work for."

"I figured that. Doesn't matter, I already know." That comment while not strictly true, got her attention. "What I want to know is why kill Robert Clegg?"

She smiled before answering, "We didn't. It was as suicide."

"Bullshit. You pumped him full of drugs, and he

flipped out. You're as responsible as if you had pushed him yourself."

"Never be able to prove that. You don't know how high this goes, and to be honest, neither do I."

"Good try. We are going to have a conversation similar to the one you had with my client and my partner." A look of concern came over her face. Good, I wanted her to sweat a little. She would have an idea of was what was coming, or she thought she did.

Using an old pillowcase, I put it over her head as a hood. She was thinking water boarding, wrong. I'd done it to hide what I was doing, puttering about the place, getting my implements ready for our conversation. Laying out a selection of knives and other household items, improvising as I went, hoping I wouldn't have to use any of them.

Good as his word, McCarrigan showed up, calling me as he parked. I opened the front door, and he handed me the two bags, saying, "Not stopping. Going back to the doc's. He's not happy with the situation but will be very discreet. Sophie insisted the doc draw blood, in order to preserve any evidence if drugs were used on Tara. She'll be with Tara. We will catch up, later. Bye and thank you, Mas."

I shook his hand. "Good presence of mind…to pick these up. Thanks. Call you, later."

I shut the door, making sure it was unlocked. Kenzo would be here too, soon, and I wanted the first conversation to be private. Returning to the dining room with the bags, I put on latex gloves and opened the briefcase. Not much. A spare magazine with nine mm rounds, some papers I would examine later, and two photographs of Tara. Two business cards tucked into a clip, and some receipts. This was the organizer's case.

The medical bag was like a good-sized purse. I opened it then carefully took out the contents. A case contained a row of small, capped vials, each labelled. I pocketed one of the vials for comparison with the drugs found in Robert Clegg. In another small case, I noted three small metal and glass syringes, along with several packets of needles. A box of small clamps. These would match the clamp marks on Tara and Sophie. A small hand generator with leads ending in clamps. Turning the handle would generate an electrical current, portable, and effective, depending on where the clips were placed.

Now it was my turn. Taking the sharpest knife and without saying a word to Sandy Wight, I took to slicing off her jacket. She flinched at my first touch, relaxing as she understood what I was doing. With the jacket in shreds on the floor, I pulled her up to a standing position. She had difficulty maintaining her balance with her ankles crossed and bound. Not my problem.

The knife parted the fabric of her pants easily, as if it had never even been there, and so far, I hadn't drawn a drop of blood. With her pants removed, her breathing changed, turning shallow and more rapid. Panty hose. As I pulled them down, she almost lost her balance. Pants as rags and topped off with a mess of shredded panty hose, her feet disappeared. Slice, slice, and her panties were gone. Her bush was dark and trimmed. Deliberately exposing her lower half, after taking the jacket first, I wanted to let her know I was in charge, and no she couldn't predict what I was going to do.

After carefully cutting off her lower clothes, I just

took her shirt and violently ripped it open. She let out a cry and did lose her balance. Saving her from falling, I stabilized her and peeled her shirt back down over her arms exposing her bra covered breasts. The bra came off next, two cuts and the straps were parted. Sliding the knife blade up between her tits, I pulled gently, and the fabric parted exposing her tits. Her nipples hardening with the temperature change, the aureole crinkled up, dark against the paleness of the rest of her, no tan lines. Pulling the bra out from behind her, she was basically naked, standing with a hood over her head, not knowing what was going to happen next. Unable to cover herself in anyway and vulnerable to anything I wished to do to her.

Pushing her backwards she collapsed back onto the sofa with a squeal. This was not about sex. This was only about getting the information I needed. The table with all my improvised implements was now in front of her.

Taking off the hood in one swift motion I asked her, "Do you like my tool set."

Blinking at the light, she said, "You can't do this. I'm working for the government."

"No. You are not. You may be working for someone in the government, but certainly not for 'The' government. You're as dispensable to them, as the two unfortunate gentlemen who ended up on the Golden Gate Bridge could attest to—if they were alive.

"I was only doing what I was trained to do."

"Ever been on the other side of the street, or is it the flip side, I forget. Now we need to get serious, or I will be forced to start using my tool set. From the look of things, what you did to the two ladies in your care—I use the term 'care' loosely of course—your *care* caused a lot of pain but not too much damage. That was good. However, I'm not as sophisticated as you, so I will probably cause you as much damage as pain. Apologies for that up front."

She was agitated and unsure of what was going to happen. That was exactly what I wanted. Her bravado was slipping.

"You know people will come looking for me," she said. "They will take it out on you."

"Oh, don't be silly. They are never going to find you. No one knows exactly who took you. One of my associates has a private plane. We can take your body parts to Mexico, and you are a mystery never to be solved."

Her head dropped. I was getting to her, and I hadn't even touched her other than removing her clothes. She didn't know I could never do to her what she had done to Tara and Sophie, not even after seeing the results myself. When running a bluff, one had to be convincing, and that I could be.

"Now I'm going to start with your extremities. Do you prefer to walk or write? Or one of each? You can choose. Think about it while I turn on the stove. Some of my tools will take time to heat up."

Leaving her to ponder her anticipated fate, I went into the kitchen making noise and turning on the gas stove. On my return I saw a tear in the corner of her eyes.

"Have you decided where I should start?"

"Nowhere."

"Sorry, that's not an option. I need information you have."

"I'll tell you what I know. It isn't much."

"Well, that's a sensible decision. As long as you tell the truth, you'll be fine."

"I was contracted for one interrogation. That one went terribly wrong. Those two idiots let the subject get the better of them and escape. He took off running, went out the balcony side, and flew off the railing. He didn't know where he was, or what he was doing. It was an accident."

"Why release him?"

"He was more resistant to the medications than expected. We were going to move him to the building where you found us. How did you find us?"

"Trade secret. Keep talking. Who was asking the questions?"

"The person who hired me asked the questions, I only knew him as Steven, most of the others called him 'sir'. I was to medicate the subject while Steven asked the questions."

"You heard all the questions. What was he after?"

"I was concentrating on making sure the subject was doing okay and responding as he should."

"He was Mr. Robert Clegg. He was a person, not a fucking subject. What do you remember about the questions?" She flinched at my raised voice.

"Most were about finances, where the money came from and went. He spent a lot of time on those details. He asked specifically about a deal with some company. I think called 3D. He also wanted to know about a Real Estate company. I don't remember which one or even if the name was mentioned. That's all I know."

"Not quite. What did he want from Tara?"

"A lot of the questions seemed the same."

"But this was not a chemical interrogation, was it?"

She paused, "No, she was drugged, but Steven wanted answers quickly. He said we had to short cut because there is a timeline coming due.

"You rigged up Tara with clips and used the hand generator on her, correct?"

In a quiet voice she responded, "Yes."

"Who was responsible for the physical side of the questioning? Steven?'

"Yes."

"Did Steven get the answers he was looking for?"

"I'm not sure. I know he really wanted to get hold of the flash drives. Tara and the other woman held out for a while. Once Tara had given up the information about her set of drives and said they'd been copied, the other woman said she was the one who had the copied set. He seemed satisfied that once he had them, it would protect whoever he was working for. I overheard him on a call. He apologized for the time of the call, saying they would be covered by that night, and the deal could go through."

That meant the call was to the east coast. "Who else did he have working for him?"

"Local muscle, thugs basically, and not very smart. He already had the two Chinese men when I met him. One had a thick accent and seemed foreign. The other one…I got the impression he was local. All of them seemed to have some sort of military training, but not rank…or not the quality I have previously work with."

"How many of these have you done, and how did you end up with Steven."

"A lot in the middle east. There, we had time and could be careful. This was my first free-lance, off the books. It was suggested I help out as it would help my career. It came down through people who do not wear uniforms."

"Sorry to hear that. You are still in a lot of trouble, and anyone you name will deny any involvement and let you swing. A friend of mine will be here shortly, a San Francisco lieutenant, and you can trust him. Tell him everything. Only way you survive this is to come clean and give up everything you know. Is there anyone in your agency who will have your back?

"Maybe, I'm not sure."

"Your information is useful. It fills in some gaps. I'll get you some clothes when he gets here."

"Can I ask you a question?"

"Sure."

"Would you have used those tools on me?"

"Nope."

"You were bluffing?"

"Yup."

"Bastard."

"Right again."

She lapsed into sullen silence. That suited me. I was thinking about what she had told me. Somehow, we had to sabotage the 3DMedia deal, which should buy us time to link everything together and to the congressmen and get what Clegg discovered out into the open. The sound of the doorbell broke my concentration. I hollered that the door was open.

I met him at the top of the stairs. Kenzo walked in looking tired and pissed off. He went directly into his rant. "We visited the address you gave me, nothing and no one there. Good call on the bullet holes and no bodies. Someone had cleaned up, not well enough to get rid of all the blood in one area. Are you sure you hit one?"

"I'm sure. Center mass. He went down. He must have been wearing a vest. Sure, as hell glad I was. You can have the round."

Kenzo stopped short, and I walked into him.

"Who the hell is this, and why is she naked."

"Kenzo, meet Ms. Sandy Wight. She was the one who administered the chemicals to Robert Clegg and tortured our client and Sophie today. She came clean to me and will spill it all to you. You may have to get her into protective custody."

"Fuck, Mas. What the hell? Is Sophie okay?"

"Sophie's doing okay. I'm waiting on the doctor's report. When I've gotten some clothes for Sandy here, I'll explain everything to you."

Raking through some of Simon's old clothes...I realized I had to clear out this place, sell it, and move on. I grabbed a couple of t-shirts, a SFPD sweatshirt and sweatpants that were clean and serviceable. That was about it. Nothing else would fit. Cutting Sandy free of the zip ties, she rubbed her wrists where the ties had been and dressed quickly, facing away from me, modestly. This time I did take the time to look her over. There was no softness to her.

Kenzo made coffee, no milk, but plenty of sugar. If she thought she was free, she was wrong. Hooking her up with a set of Simon's handcuffs, arms in front of her, I sat her on the sofa. Finally, I placed a set of headphones on her and tuned to a local rock radio station. No way was she overhearing the conversation I was about to have with Kenzo. I positioned her so I could see her, but she couldn't see me or Kenzo.

He handed me a cup of coffee. "Mas, you really got a talent for getting into deep shit. I'm listening."

Starting at the beginning, and laying it all out for him, I only omitted the bits about bugging Tara's home, and Oso using the shotgun. Laying it out logically for Kenzo was not a bad exercise for me, it helped me visualize the whole picture, or at least what we had of it up to the present. He was a good listener, making notes rather than interrupting the flow of my narration. When I finished, we sat in silence for a while as he reviewed his notes.

Flipping back and forth, he looked up and said, "You did all right, except for the snatch. You couldn't have prevented that with the resources you had. One question...how the hell did you find Sophie and Tara so quickly?"

Wait until he heard my answer. "Sophie—when she moved here—she insisted we both get GPS chipped. No, I don't know where she got them. We had them implanted by someone who does body modifications, no questions asked."

"Wow, Mas, you picked a winner with her. About time your luck changed."

"No question. What do we do now? We're still working on the flash drives. We have to stop the merger, buyout or whatever it is, and throw a wrench into their plans."

"You've got no proof the two congressmen are involved in anything illegal, yet. Everything is circumstantial, assumed, a lot of maybe's and hope-so's."

"Don't do this Kenzo. You know this stinks, and we are on a short timeline."

"I agree it stinks, but still no proof. Look, the best that could happen is you create an anonymous threat or accusation about the 3DMedia deal with the SEC, Treasury, Justice, and anyone else you can come up with. But without a crime, I can't get involved."

"Yeah, I get it. We are on our own with this one. You still have a homicide to solve, and Sandy will clear that up for you. The two on the bridge are out of your district, but you will get it as well because it's linked to the homicide-suicide, and that one came first."

He nodded in agreement. "If you...or we can prove that everything is linked, then it becomes a bigger issue. I would need to work with White collar, RICO or even DHS."

"Not sure I'd trust anyone else. Too much money involved. Looks like Washington, D. C. is in it up to their nuts. If these two are dirty, how many more are? We got lucky because someone screwed up. Twice. We can't rely on that to keep happening."

"No, *we* can't." Kenzo was unofficially on board. I liked the sound of "we." I was more relieved than I expected. He continued, "We need to have each other's backs on this if it goes as high as you think."

"Agreed. So, what do I do with my guest? I don't want her. I got what I needed from her, which wasn't much. Confirmations more than anything. Can you use her to clear up the Clegg case?

"Not sure, a lot of unanswered questions on that one if I take her in. What happens if you just cut her loose?"

"Ends up dead or disappears back under the stone she came from. Probably the latter."

"My thought exactly. I can't let that happen. Shit,

Mas, you dropped me in it again."

"What are you going to do?"

"Have a chat, a private chat. You can't be in on this one. Go for a walk. If I'm or we're not here when you get back, I'll call you. Promise."

"Okay. Thanks for being there... When we have anything more, you will be the first to know."

"What did you shoot the perps with?"

"Shotgun and my nine with hollow points."

"So, minimal forensics on the guns, good. I won't ask who had the shotgun."

"Thanks. See ya."

Walking back into the room with my guest, I wanted to hurt her, knowing I couldn't. She was in big trouble, and she knew it. Kenzo, he had her on kidnapping and torture charges. As leverage, Sophie would be a witness. She was in big trouble with whoever hired her, and she knew what happened to the muscle. That could happen to her. Rock and a hard place.

Not my problem.

As I walked down the steps to the street, I shivered in the damp air. The night was cold, and I was tired. Walking aimlessly, I replayed the events. Damn, we'd gotten lucky. My ribs hurt. Proof I was still alive. Tara and Sophie—I hoped they were resting, but I couldn't. Steven, probably the one I shot, was still on the loose. We'd both survived. It was an even playing field till the next time. I may not be able to interrogate Sandy's way, but I would have no qualms about doing Steven.

By my watch, I had been gone twenty minutes plus, time enough for Kenzo to get things sorted. Not sure what to expect when I got back, I warily went up the front steps. The front door was slightly open.

Shit. That's not Kenzo. Pulling out my weapon I pushed the door fully open and entered. The lights were out. Flipping the switch, I found Kenzo face down on the floor. Quickly checking for a pulse, a strong one, I used his phone to call nine-one-one.

"Officer down."

Giving the address twice, I hung up and wiped his phone down. Looking around there was nothing to show Sandy Wight had ever been there, her purse and the brief case were gone. That had to be how they found Sandy—a tracking device in the case, smart move. The question now, was Sandy alive or would her body show up. Waiting until I heard the siren, I picked up the shotgun and left, I would follow up in the morning, I figured Kenzo would say as little as possible until we had spoken.

I called McCarrigan. He answered on the first ring. "Everything okay?"

"Mostly. More developments. How are Tara and Sophie?

"Beat-up, tired, and they're both very angry, but sleeping now. What will you do?"

"Stay at the office tonight. Tell Sophie I need to speak to her as soon as she feels up to it. Thanks for the assist tonight. We couldn't have done it without you."

"No problem. If I can do anything else, don't hesitate to ask. I'm really pissed off. Nobody fucks with me and mine and gets away unscathed."

"Got it. Think about political contacts who would listen to you."

Hanging up I decided to walk to the office. Simon's place wasn't that much further from the office than mine—besides, the walk would do me good. Hiding the shotgun by wrapping it in my jacket, I walked briskly and made good time.

When I arrived at the office, the lights were still on. That worried me, and I cautiously entered the building. I slowly tried the office door. Locked. Calling out, I identified myself.

Marie responded, "Are you okay?"

A "yes" would have set her off. The correct response would be "not in this lifetime."

The door unlocked, and the relief on her face was easy to see.

"Thank God you're okay. Is everything kosher."

"No, Kenzo came to take custody of the woman, and sent me out for a walk. When I got back, he was face down and the woman was gone. He'd been attacked, but he'll be okay. Probably concussed, and he will be definitely pissed."

Hearing someone moving in the inner office I looked at Marie.

She said, "No one felt like going home or being alone tonight, so we camped out here, that's okay, right?

"Yeah, no problem. I haven't had a chance to thank you for tonight. Good job."

"All in the family, Mas, all in the family."

Suddenly I was tired. Feeling drained, I needed sleep. The floor was looking really good. I locked the door, stuck a chair under the handle, grabbed a blanket and lay down. The dead would wake before me.

Chapter Seventeen

The fragrance of coffee slowly permeated my consciousness. While I attempted to get up, my ribs complained, and the soreness had spread. I figured nothing was broken or cracked, I was just badly bruised. I could deal with that, but I still felt like shit. Marie helped me up. As I started to remove the bullet proof vest I'd slept in, she noticed the hole in it.

"Mas, you were hit! Are you okay?"

"Yes, just bruised, and we have the round to give Kenzo when he is up and about."

I finally managed to sit up, and Marie handed me cup of steaming *wake up*. The caffeine hit me in a rush. Alive and pissed off, I realized again how lucky we'd been last night, and so had Kenzo. Killing a cop was never a good idea, even for *our* adversaries.

"Would you call and find out where he is, which hospital?"

She nodded. "Are you sure that you're okay?"

"Yes. Where are our other guests?"

"Kristen went over to McCarrigan's place to assist Tara. Erin went home to get a change of clothes. She's going to be staying with me and Chung."

"Chung doesn't mind?"

"Not after he heard what happened. It was his idea."

That was all good news to me. It left me free to

concentrate on Sophie and get some answers before anyone else got hurt…or killed.

First, I needed food, or I wouldn't be good for anyone. "What would you like for breakfast?"

"Already in hand, Mas. It'll be here any minute. I figured you'd need it, and then would want to see Sophie ASAP."

"You're a gem. Tell your boss to give you a raise."

We laughed, and that hurt my ribs. I hoped the man I shot was in as much discomfort as I was. No…worse. Breakfast arrived, we demolished it in no time, and once I felt better, I called McCarrigan. "I'm on my way over."

****

Parking wasn't a problem this early. The security guy at the desk recognized me and buzzed me in. McCarrigan was waiting for me, door open, with a finger to his lips.

"Tara is still out. The doctor gave her something for the pain so she could get some rest. Kristen is with her. Sophie refused the meds. She's tough. We were going over the recent events and the situation in general. Sorry I got you involved in this."

"No time for sorry. How about we go on the offensive?"

"What?"

"Where is Sophie?"

"In here, Mas," she called out. I followed the sound to the living room. As soon as she saw me, she walked slowly toward me, and we hugged. My ribs complained. I didn't. It was good to see her and hold her. We kissed and held each other in silence.

It was Sophie who broke the silence. "I knew you

would come for us. Those chips aren't so dumb, now, are they?"

"Not dumb at all, and we have a lot to go over."

"Do you have coffee on?" I asked McCarrigan.

"Yes," he said, "fresh cups all round, and then let's talk."

Sophie noticed how I was favoring my one side, so I told her what happened. "I got shot and the vest worked fine, only left bruises nothing else."

She looked like shit, but I was relieved to see her. I wanted payback for this. Calmly, we sat around the dining table. Starting at the beginning, I laid it all out to Sophie and McCarrigan. He wasn't an investigator, but he was smart, and both were silent while I talked. Taking a quick breather at the end of the summation, I started to give my analysis and conclusions.

"The bottom line is that whatever Mr. Clegg found caused all of the recent events." My thoughts were on money laundering, using real estate deals to funnel illegal, possibly-probably Russian, money into at least two congressional campaigns and for the purchase of 3DMedia. Everything connected to those two, even if it was a tenuous connection, indicated the congressmen were also laundering money."

McCarrigan started first, saying, "Well presented, but a lot of your conclusions are supposition. There's no actual proof of any wrongdoing."

Bridling at that, I said, "The proof is that your girlfriend was kidnapped and tortured. Good enough proof for you?"

"Mas, you have to look at this dispassionately. You, we have nothing. Yes, I'm pissed, but you have to look at this coldly." He turned at Sophie for support.

She nodded. "He's right Mas, we don't have enough to go on, yet. We can't just go around accusing those congressmen of crimes without evidence. Is Kenzo going to be all right?

"Thanks for asking. Marie will call as soon as she finds out anything."

McCarrigan asked, "Anything useful in the brief case from the warehouse?"

"It was taken when Kenzo was attacked, along with Sandy."

"Well, you screwed that up, didn't you?"

"Probably why I took photographs of everything in the case. You do your job, we'll do ours. The case would have gone with Kenzo anyway, so I took the pics for our use. You really are a prick."

Sophie interjected, "Calm down. There was probably nothing incriminating in the case anyway. This wasn't the organizers first rodeo. Still, there might be something useful."

"There was." I said, "The car rental company where the transport was rented. We have the license plates from the two vehicles and the rental person's business card info. The renter will have used a fake ID, but what was still worthwhile is that we should be able to get a photo from the security camera. That's a Kenzo job." Just as I finished, my cell rang. Marie.

"Yes."

"Kenzo is going to be fine. Mad as hell. He wants to see you now at the hospital. Concussion and bruised pride. I'll text you the hospital and room number."

"Got it, we're on our way."

"Is Sophie, okay?"

Sophie heard the question and answered loud

enough for Marie to hear. "Worse for wear but getting better."

Realizing Sophie was dressed in big sloppy clothes, we'd have to get her a change of clothing before going to the hospital. Feeling the blood rise again. We said our goodbyes to McCarrigan with promises of follow up meetings.

I reminded him to get Oso back as protection, and he agreed saying, "I'll call him as soon as you leave."

In the elevator, I studied Sophie. She was tough, stoic, but she had been through an ordeal. "Are you really, okay?

"I am now. I was scared, and I don't mind admitting it. Fucking scared. I knew you would find me. But everything happened so fast I couldn't react. It was just like the self-defense trainer said, 'You have to practice until its second nature.' I guess I need more practice."

"Bullshit. Unless you are actually expecting it, no one reacts in time to do anything. All I can say is thank you for thinking of the trackers. I thought I was going to lose you, Sophie." I choked up as I tried to complete my thought, "I couldn't bear the thought of that." I squeezed her hand in mine. "First, a change of clothes, and then Kenzo."

Sophie changed in record time, and we were soon getting our guest passes at the hospital. Kenzo had left instructions that I was to be allowed in as soon as I got there. When we got to his room, he was sitting up in bed with a laptop.

He looked up as we entered. "This is turning into a shit show, and I have a lot of questions for you two. I played dumb when I was questioned by my captain because I needed to talk to you first."

"You first, then us. What happened?" I paused,

Kenzo said, "I was getting Sandy ready to move, when I heard a noise. A male, white, average height, dark hair, and trained. He didn't realize that I was. Sandy hollered that I was a cop, he smiled and attacked me. I was handling him and probably could have taken him. Then the lights went out. Bitch hit me from behind. I woke up in the ambulance. Thanks for that. PD sealed up the house. I have a concussion, dented pride, and a lot of questions."

"Sorry about the head. We are still putting all this together ourselves. We have a set of information put together by Clegg, the suicide/homicide victim. It's complicated. We have an asset who is doing a break down for us. As I said last night, it involves the congressmen. We think the proof is in Clegg's info, or at least clues to getting proof. The man who attacked you was sent to clean up, by retrieving all the copies of Clegg's work. That takes clout. We have some leads you'll need to follow up. Hopefully, you'll ID your attacker and maybe discover who he works for.

"So now you are using SFPD as support for your investigation."

"No, I'm trying to find your attacker."

He sighed saying there were no leads, no Sandy. "I'm running her name now. Apparently, there was nothing left in Simons' place. No clothes, no briefcase. I asked. That was my best bet for a lead."

"You can use the photographs I took of all the contents. I figured you would want the actual briefcase, so I took photos of everything. Happy to share. And the round from my vest to check out." I tossed him the baggy containing the bullet from my vest.

"Shit, Mas, the PD should never have dumped you. It was unfair and a waste then, and now. Thanks, looks like a nine mil."

"My thought exactly. The vehicle rental place should have video of him. Sandy's DNA will be on the sofa, she was naked on it for a while, and maybe if you are lucky fingerprints."

Kenzo looked at Sophie. "Are you, okay? You look like you had a rough time."

"Getting better by the minute. More of a mind fuck than the physical signs. Bodies heal faster than minds."

"Too true. Don't be a stranger. And Mas, don't let anything happen to her."

"I'd never. Over my dead body."

"And I need all the info you get."

"Anything we get, you get...my word." We said our goodbyes and left for the office. Both quiet in our own thoughts on the drive.

"Did you mean what you said to Kenzo?" Sophie asked.

"Sure, what we get, he gets."

"No, I mean about over your dead body."

"Yup."

She started to sob, quietly into her hands.

"What's wrong, I meant it."

Between sobs she said, "I know you did. I've never had anyone love me like you do, and it's scary."

"That's what love does, I guess."

We held hands all the way back to the office.

The door was locked. Opening it, I faced Marie facing me holding the shotgun. Relaxing when she saw us, she told us Erin had returned and was working on the thumb drives. Erin heard us and came out to greet us, and Sophie hugged her and thanked her for her part in the rescue.

With old home week over, I suggested Sophie and Erin needed to get back at it. One, it would take Sophie's mind off what had happened, and two, between them, hopefully we'd discover what Clegg had found. I cleaned the shotgun and reloaded the magazine to capacity. I went over its use with Marie.

First job for me, I sent the photos to Kenzo. Easy and done. The next was not so easy. Waiting for results from any of Kenzo's inquiries, and finally for Sophie and Erin to do their thing.

I asked Marie if she had any luck with the GRU real estate end of things.

"No," she said. "I've started to look into that and found some information, but not enough. A real estate insider is what we need."

Andrew, my realtor hadn't gotten back to me. I called again, but it went directly to voice mail, so I left a message. Hopefully, he would respond to the urgency in my voice.

Back to waiting, Kenzo texted a thank you for the photos. Lunch time hit with not much accomplished on my end. I went out and picked-up lunch for everyone. Surprise, Andrew was waiting for me when I returned with the food. He apologized for the delay in getting back to me, using the excuse that he had listings to look after.

"I was intrigued by the GRU Company," he admitted. "I looked into them."

That got my attention. It was perhaps why he was here in person and not calling or e-mailing. With

Sophie and Erin busy in the inner office, and Marie spread out in the outer one, I suggested we go to his office where we could chat in peace. He agreed, and we moved the conversation to his office.

Once we settled in, he told his office manager not to disturb us, and we got down to it. Waiting for him to start, I took out a note pad.

"Mas, there's something not right about that company you asked me to look into." He stopped collecting his thoughts and continued, "It looks like a money laundering scheme, simple and effective."

"How does it would work?

"Okay, crash course. Dirty money definition. Any non-legal money placed in the financial system through purchases, deposits etc., that's purposely layered to conceal or disguise the origin. Then it's moved and used, over and over so it becomes integrated in the system. That creates an apparent legal origin for the money. People collect the proceeds from purchases, sales, capital gains, anything used to disguise the true origin and ownership of the assets. Once that is done, the proceeds can be used for personal benefit, investments, liquidity, and of course payoffs, and its clean—hence laundered. That's the quick and dirty overview. It's more complicated than that, but money laundering happens all the time, especially with drug money."

"And you think Golden Realty is involved in this type of scheme?"

"Won't be quoted on it, but yes, I do."

"How would I find out about their business purchases and sales?"

"Easy, real estate sales are logged with official

departments, the city, county, and or state, one or all depending on the state you're in. You would need starting info like companies' tax ID numbers, lists of properties bought or sold, the dates and amounts. All that helps with searches."

"What caught your attention?"

"There was not much to find, but what I discovered was interesting. Golden would buy a property, sell in short order at or just over market, and that is not as noticeable in the LA or SF markets, but it cleans the money. I only found a few transactions, but they all looked questionable to me. A year or so later, they would buy some of the properties back at a discount, then resell later at above market, gaining a nice profit. Clean, washed money. I'll give you the list I pulled to start you off. Is this helpful?"

"More than you know. I may be picking your brains again on this one. Thanks, we really appreciate your help."

With a laugh he said, "No problem, here's the list. Now I am going to sell some more prime SF real estate."

A subtle way of saying *we are done goodbye*. Andrew had given me a lot of food for thought. This had to be why Clegg was killed. He'd found something suspicious, probably illegal, and was looking for proof. Now it was down to Erin and Sophie to retrieve the proof.

My ride back to the office was slow and reflective. We were all going into deep waters here. As an Inspector, I saw all sorts of crimes, but nothing on this scale or with such ramifications. We had to make sure everything we did was copied and deposited in safe places. Once information gets out, it's not possible to contain the spread. The old saying, *"If you want to keep a secret, don't tell anyone."* We needed to make it pointless for the information to be retrieved. Anxious to see what Erin and Sophie had discovered, I wanted to be back quicker than the traffic allowed.

Using my key, I entered the office. It was quiet. Marie looked up as I closed the door behind me, gave me a thumbs up. She had something. Nodding for her to follow me, I continued into the inner office, where all I could hear was the hum of Sophie's computer and the click of her and Erin's fingers on keyboards.

Interrupting, I said, "We need to do an update. I'll start. Andrew, the realtor looked into Golden Realty, found it suspicious, and thinks they are laundering money. The transactions are questionable. He gave me a list of the ones he found and said there are sure to be more. Marie was already looking into that and now she has more to go on. Sophie, you go next."

She took a deep breath. "I heard back from Fiend. He's pulled a lot of data on the congressmen he thinks are dirty. But they're smart. Nothing yet to tie them directly to actual illegal activities. Offshore accounts, investments here and overseas. They look like successful politicians. Still digging, back tracking the money trails, and he will keep at it. GRU seems very profitable, and I'm looking into the sources of the initial financing and where the purchasers financing comes from. It will just take time."

As Sophie finished, Erin chimed in, "The money is coming from the holding company. I suspect Russian money via Malta, but I need to confirm that if I can. The funds are being funneled through several large banks, Deutschland International, Canton, and Macao Banking Corp, NY City Bank, and the Asia Pacific Bank of SF. It's going to take me some time to unravel and check Robert's work. He is—" She choked and continued. "—was, very thorough. Just the volume of work to wade through is daunting."

"Sophie, as soon as Marie or Erin give you something concrete, can you access the congressmen's and GRU accounts?"

"Yes, of course, but I need to be careful going forward. This is where it gets dangerous. In my past life, I worked for these folks, and they do not like being on the other end of investigations. The money trail won't be a problem, but the congressmen and, by association, GRU could be, how shall I say, delicate."

I added, "You mean dangerous?"

Quietly she said, "Yes."

That reinforced my earlier thought of distributing everything we had to safe places. We needed protection and leverage. "We need to copy everything we have. Tara's original files, Mr. Clegg's, everything we have found and documented. Three copies, can you do that now, and make it as condensed as you can? They'll be distributed to safe places, and if anything happens, all the information will be in the right hands." They all stared at me for more. "You don't want to know where they'll be. It's safer that way. How fast can you copy the info?"

They all started to talk at once. Sophie shushed them and said, "Half an hour, max."

"Good, make it twenty minutes. Then, I have some visits to make."

Chapter Eighteen

Left to their tasks, I walked the neighborhood. My calls were made without interruption. First to Kenzo. He picked up on the first ring. I told him what I needed, with the promise that what we would give him would be clean, and useful in an investigation. He agreed to be a holder.

Next was to Colleen, American born Chinese investigative journalist with a reputation for being tenacious and a secure confidante. Our paths had crossed before, and I believed she was trustworthy. She picked up on the last ring.

"Well, this is a surprise, Inspector."

"Inspector no longer, but I'm sure you knew that already."

"I did, and sorry to hear it. What do you need?"

"Straight to the point as usual. I need a favor."

I explained what I needed. She asked smart questions—not that she expected me to divulge the exact nature of the situation. If everything worked out, I promised she would have an exclusive story laid out. If it didn't work out, she would have the start of a great story to finish on her own. She read between the lines and understood what that meant. After a pause, she agreed to be a holder.

The third call was going to be difficult. I didn't want to do this but felt safe doing it. Calling Diana

Garcia-Alvarez, tenured professor of political science at Berkeley, and my prior BDSM relationship brought back too many memories. She had supported and helped me clear myself of the false sexual assault and attempted rape charges that one of my subordinates in the SFPD brought against me. Thinking of those times still made me angry.

No surprise, the call went to voice mail. I left a cryptic message, hoping she'd be curious enough to return the call. By depositing the information with law enforcement, the media, and hopefully a political expert, I figured I'd covered all the bases. That, at least, should protect us. If we didn't survive further encounters with the opposition, the following shitstorm would have to be good enough. Getting the info anonymously to Kenzo, Colleen, and Diana would be simple by using the drop offs and cut outs.

Feeling better about the precautions taken, I relaxed just a little. I figured the packages should be waiting for me when I got back, and they were. Three padded envelopes were waiting on my desk as requested. I left without saying where I was going, because what the others didn't know could protect them.

First, I called in an order to Wanatabe's for take-out. Wanatabe welcomed me with a bow and a smile as we met at the pick-up counter. Slipping him the envelope with Kenzo's name on it, along with my payment for the food order, he bowed his understanding. One down, two to go. My stomach growled at the smell of food all around me. When I got back in the car, I inhaled it as I made the call to Kenzo saying the order was "ready to go" with emphasis on the word "go" so he would know it was at Wanatabe's.

Getting the package to Colleen would be slightly more complicated. Calling first, I asked her to meet me at the Westfield Mall on Market Street and instructed her to carry an open purse. She agreed to be there in twenty minutes. That would give me time to get there before her.

The street and mall were busy, but not packed. I waited by the watch store, with an eye on the mall doors.

When Colleen walked in, I made sure she saw me, but gave no sign of recognition as we made our way to the elevators. Entering the elevator, we moved next to each other at the back, the elevator filled, and everyone faced forward, waiting for their floor. I slipped the small envelope into Colleen's open bag and got off on the next floor. She stayed.

Wandering around the store for a few minutes, I bought a little gift for Sophie, left, and returned to the office. She loved taking a long, scented bath. This bath set would be just the thing to help her relax.

One envelope left to deliver, if my conversation with Diana went as well as I hoped it would, and if she returned my call. Big ifs. So far, I was satisfied, but that was as far as it went. I hoped we'd get some definitive answers about Clegg's work, soon. Assaulted by all three of the women as soon as I entered the office, Marie got to me first. She'd found more transactions for GRU and was compiling the details, dates, buyers, sellers, and dollar amounts.

Before Marie was finished, both Sophie and Erin began talking. Sophie traced some of the money trails back to Malta. She had the thin end of a wedge in the system. Now she would use it to get more source information. Erin had reviewed all Clegg's work and found he had confirmation that the banks in the U.S. were being used to funnel the clean money. They were sending it back out to the holding company and offshore bank accounts before bringing it back into the holding company's U.S. accounts, and then on to donations for a rightwing PAC.

Sophie said she would start hacking the PAC that afternoon.

Clegg was right. He had been one step away from proof, and we were following his trail to the proof. We still needed concrete proof before going after anyone. Sophie and Fiend would be key in getting that, probably by nefarious means. As my years in the SFPD, I always rejected anything illegal when it came to evidence. Since leaving my former position, I'd changed. Now, I accepted getting the proof we needed by almost any means.

After the initial onslaught, we all sat around my desk and talked through what we actually had, what we needed, and the path forward. Marie was set with the GRU leads and trail. Erin would mine Clegg's work and follow up on all the accounting trails, and then create a map of the financial ins and outs. Sophie would start hacking the Realty Company, and the PAC. Fiend would also keep looking into the congressmen's accounts and affairs. So far, he had found nothing out of the ordinary, which only increased his paranoia and suspicions.

All of that made me superfluous in the office. What I could do was try and protect everyone. One thing for sure, the danger wasn't over. Our rescue of Tara and

Sophie surprised them, and set them back, it didn't terminate the threat. They, whoever "they" were, would be planning their next move, and it would be against us for sure.

As I was thinking about what I could do, my cell went off. Diana Garcia-Alvarez.

"Hello, professor."

"Hello, Mas. It has been a long time. This is a nice surprise."

"Yes, too long. I am sorry about that."

"Nothing to be sorry about, Mas. Circumstances somethings are just beyond our control. It's a two-way street, and I knew how to contact you. I regret I didn't. Are you well?"

"I am, and kind of content."

"Aah, you've found a partner." She paused. "One who is worthy of you, I hope."

"Yes, professor. I need to talk to you about a situation. I'd like to meet in person and very soon, if possible?"

"Personal or professional?"

"Political."

"Now you've tickled my curiosity. I'm free after three today, then not for a couple of days."

"Today would be perfect—preferably on campus. If you don't mind, I'll make my way to your office."

"Acceptable. Very cloak and dagger."

"Please do not tell anyone about this meeting. I will explain when we meet."

"Mas, I will hold you to that. See you soon."

Memories welled up. I couldn't stop them, but this meeting was necessary to protect all of us, not about me. With nothing much to do, I cleaned the shot gun and my pistol again. Glancing up at the clock, I realized it was still too early to leave for Berkeley. I re-read all the hard copy of what we had discovered and my notes.

Everyone was right. We had lots of information but nothing concrete tying the congressmen or anyone else directly to anything. We needed a smoking gun, or at least some smoking money. I put our best chances at finding that on Sophie and Fiend. We still had "Steven" on the loose. Fear twisted my gut. He wasn't about to quit his mission without another go at us.

Time to get on the road.

With a mixture of anticipation and dread, I drove over the Bay Bridge and arrived early, parked, then wandered around the campus until it was time to meet with Diana. It would be strange seeing her again. This time, thankfully, it would be all business.

The door to her office was closed. I tentatively knocked. Big, tough, PI extraordinaire—I felt like a schoolboy about to be scolded. Fuck this. I knocked hard, opened the door, and entered.

Diana looked up and smiled. "Welcome, Mas, it's been a long time."

"Yes, it has."

She came around her desk, and we hugged. "I have missed your service. No one since has quite managed to fill your shoes. It seems you still wear a chastity device."

Shit. I thought I'd held myself far enough away from her to keep her from feeling my cage.

Changing the subject, I asked, "Did you get any flack for your support of me? "I asked.

"Nothing to speak of. The police department and the college kept everything quiet. It was in their own best interests. Why the mystery? Not that I am complaining."

"I seem to have gotten myself into something that could be dangerous." Letting that hang, Diana took the bait.

"...and you want my help?"

"...need would be more precise," I explained. "I'm leaving resources in three locations, a trusted law enforcement source, a media person, and hopefully a political insider.

She laughed at the last one. "Why me?"

"Because I trust you. I need information, and you are smart enough to follow up if anything happens to me."

That comment wiped the smile off her face, she said, "You better tell me what's going on."

Laying it all out for her, she made notes and refrained from asking any questions until I finished. We sat in silence while she mulled over the story I told.

With a sigh, she looked at me sadly. "This is the state of politics in our country today. None of this surprises me—only that it hasn't been made public on more occasions. The presidential election was one thing. It's all much more insidious than the public knows. What you've discovered is more of the same. What do you really need from me?"

"A secure place to leave the information we have discovered, and a run down on the political process. What are the rules for donations to political figures, etc.?"

"Mas, the first ask is not a problem. The second...how much time do you have?"

As I slid the envelope across her desk, "Probably

not as much as I need. Please do not look at the information unless I disappear or am dead."

"I promise. Okay, let's get to details."

We spent the next three hours going over the rules of donations and the no-no's. They seemed pretty clear, but as with everything written by lawyers, there were grey areas and loopholes. By the end, I had a good basic idea of how things should be, and how people got around them.

I stood to go. "Then to put all of this simply—if we can tie the congressmen directly to any illegal activities, then we have them. If not, they will be free and clear." I summed up something I already suspected.

Diana held out her hand. "I think you knew that all along." She gave me a knowing smile.

"Just confirming for the record." I turned and left.

The drive back across the Bay bridge was horrible. This time I didn't care. It gave me time to think and mull over the information Diana had given me. Erin's expertise was critical in untangling the financial labyrinth. Sophie and I could hang the other evidence on that—if we could get it.

I got back to the office, surprised that everyone was there so late. They were working but looked fried. Considering the law of diminishing returns, they better stop, refresh, and get back to it the next day.

I clapped, getting their attention. "How about we call it a day? Save everything and close up. Tonight, dinner is on Hammett and Chandler. No arguments. We all need to be sharp at all times. Being exhausted is not an option. Not the way to get this job done. We can debrief at dinner. Ready? Let's go.

Dinner was just what we needed. The food and

wine were good therapy, and the conversation ebbed and flowed. Erin fit in better than we could have been expected, and I basked in the company of three smart women.

Once the meal was over, we each debriefed the others about our day, detailing our accomplishments, what we still needed, and our plans for the next step. Erin was mapping the financial flows from Robert's data, and Sophie was delving into the offshore items. I didn't ask. Marie tracked and collected data on Golden Realty deals, now she had to do some analysis and offered to help Erin.

Finally, I added my opinion, for what it was worth, of the political ins and outs Diana provided, and then told them how I'd created a backup level of protection for us. "By depositing evidence of our work in three different locations, if anything happens to us, the information will be our insurance policy. Our safety will be guaranteed as long as you don't know where it is or with whom I shared the information."

They gave me a little flack about that for a few beats until it sunk in. Sophie eventually agreed. "It's as good a plan as any. If we go down at least we'll take those bastards with us."

With dinner over, Erin went with Marie to her place. Sophie and I went home, both of us too tired for any play. I did give her the gift I picked up at the mall as cover for being there.

"I thought one day soon we'd have time to enjoy this. Then we could enjoy each other, too." I gave her a devilish grin and wiggled my eyebrows at her.

She laughed without much enthusiasm.

"Probably not tonight," I added. "I'm sure you're

as exhausted from all this pressure."

The stress of this case was beginning to tell on both of us, and I knew we would both soon need a release. Once in bed, I held her for comfort, glad she was safely in my arms. We tried to have a conversation, but it faded quickly, and I fell into a deep sleep.

Chapter Nineteen

Jolted awake with a thought or a dream that we were being attacked in our office, I got up and stumbled into the bathroom. I splashed water on my face to rid the image in my mind that had scared me fully awake. I got ready for the day by starting the coffee while thinking through what I could do to attenuate the safety problem. Steven would have to escalate his actions against us before we went on the offensive. Before, their purpose was eliminating the threat, now it would be containment, and clean-up. Us. We were meant to be cleaned-up.

Sophie was still asleep when I put a mug of coffee beside her, and gently shook her into consciousness. "We have a problem."

"Just one?" she smiled at me to let me know she was okay with whatever I said. "More serious than having a target on our backs?"

"No. It's just that. Being a target. I think we need to move our office to another location ASAP." That got Sophie's attention.

"Why, now?"

"We are exposed where we are. One door in and out, with a lot of other businesses on the same floor. We don't know who's coming or going. We need better security, and we can't control that environment."

"You're right." Sophie asked, "Where do you

suggest? Simon's place?

"No, I thought of that, the place is known to the opposition. We need a place with security access. I wonder if McCarrigan would let us use his place. He said he would help if we needed it."

"You've got to be kidding. I don't think he's going to go for that."

"The answer is no unless you ask. Get up, we got places to go and things to do. Meet you at the office."

With that I grabbed my jacket, bag, and left. The office building was quiet this early, and our floor was deserted. No one and nothing stirred. I was careful opening the door, but nothing looked suspicious or seemed out of place. After closing the door, I locked it behind me. An envelope on the floor immediately caught my attention. Thin and flimsy. I tore it open, a single sheet-computer printed message. "Order to 'GO' lunch."

Had to be Kenzo's idea of, "Message received—Wanatabe's for lunch." He had something he didn't want to convey over any phone. After cranking up the coffee machine, I put in a call to McCarrigan, never expecting him to pick up. He did.

"Hello, Mas. This early has to mean a problem."

"Were you serious about assisting?"

"Yes."

"Serious enough to let us move our office into your apartment. It's more secure than our building. We're too exposed where we are. Would that be a problem?"

"You are joking right?"

"I wouldn't joke about this. We are making progress and the opposition hasn't responded…yet, to the other night's activities."

"How long?" he asked.

"Don't know. Probably not too long. I have a feeling this will end sooner than later."

"How many of you and when?"

"Four of us. Sophie, Marie, Erin, and me, plus hardware. Probably today."

"Great, tech squatters wrecking my home."

"We will pay for any damage."

"Not an issue. I will let the security staff know you're coming in. Please make sure everyone has their driver's license, or official ID, for security."

"Thank you. How is Tara?"

"Sore, recovering, and angry. That will probably go to another level when she hears I've sublet the apartment to you. She is still staying with me." He ended that with a deep laugh, and I smiled to myself imagining their conversation.

Most of the hardware was easy to move. Sophie's computer was another matter. That was going to be another interesting conversation. Next call was to Mack, a handy man who had done work for me in the past.

"Hey, Mack, it's Mas. I need a quick job. How fast could you put a sheet of heavy plywood over the front door of our office?"

"Is there a problem?"

"Not a handyman problem."

"That's a quick an easy one. After lunch, mid-afternoon would be the soonest. I'll have to pick up a sheet of wood. Is that good enough?"

"Perfect, and thanks. Any issues, call this number."

Right, now to get all the bodies in order. Coffee poured I called Marie, asking her to bring in some breakfast, and be prepared to move the office, saying I would explain everything when she and Erin got here. Starting, I put together what I needed.

Sophie arrived. Kissing her, I said, "We're moving today. I got a place with better security."

"What the fuck? McCarrigan's agreed? You're kidding me, right?"

"No, no kidding. We're moving to his apartment for the duration. Think about it. The building is more secure, and we can improve on that. Now, about moving your computer?"

"No need. I can access it remotely if I need to. All our data is securely stored elsewhere."

"I hoped you would say that. Pack what you need. I have someone coming this afternoon to screw a heavy sheet of wood over our door. We'll put a notice up referring all contacts to phone, and mail to be redirected to Simon's place."

"Okay. I'll leave my computer on and running. Why the note for Simon's place, we won't be there?"

"Correct. Delay and distract. Steven already knows about that location, but not us camping at McCarrigan's. By the time they find out, hopefully, we'll have enough evidence to start an offensive."

"That actually makes sense."

Sarcastically I responded, "Well thank you, ma'am."

"Be careful, I may be stressed, but I still have a key close to my heart."

That made me smile, and of course, set my cock hardening in its cage. Back to reality, Sophie started packing up what she needed to take with her. Marie and Erin arrived with breakfast. As we ate, I explained what we were doing, and why. They wholeheartedly agreed without question.

It took longer than I expected or wanted, making me late for my meeting with Kenzo. I'd wanted to arrive after him, so there'd be less chance of a connection if I was being monitored. I looked for anything suspicious. Not seeing anything, I entered Wanatabe's and went directly upstairs. Kenzo was already munching on pot stickers and waved me to a seat opposite him.

"Mas, you were right about Sandy's DNA on the sofa. We got a match. She is or was DoD, Army, and probably attached to special forces. All very vague, and we were flagged as soon as the match came back. It more or less told us to keep our hands off, which is not an issue…is it?"

"No, she's not a key player. Steven is certainly higher up the chain, but still not key. His role is action not planning. Someone else is pulling all the strings."

"That's another hands-off situation. We started a search for 'Steven' through the data bases, as soon as we plugged him in, a voice from on high said 'hands-off.' Whatever you got involved with, it goes way over my pay grade."

"What parameters did you use for the search?"

"A physical description and the photograph we got from the vehicle rental place. He avoided all the cameras, except one, and we got a good likeness. I'll send you a copy."

"That's good news, and thanks. Send it to Sophie not me."

"Oh, and the slug you dug out of your vest. No match in any data base so far. If we extend the search, we might step on a few toes that don't want to be stepped on. I suggest leaving that alone for now, before it gets flagged."

"Agreed, don't worry about the slug for now. Be careful. I assume you are concentrating on the bodies on the bridge and Clegg?"

"The Chinese investigation hit a dead-end. It's being called a gang retaliation killing. Clegg will be shut down as a suicide. Mas, we will not be able to solve the bodies on the bridge with what we have, especially not being allowed to link it to Clegg's murder. I will only be going through the motions. I hate being told to lay off police work for politics."

"Even with Clegg's drug cocktail screen being positive? Oh, by the way, I borrowed a vial of the drug from Ms. Wright. If you need it for the Clegg case, just let me know."

"Thanks, for the offer, I meant what I said about assisting you with anything I can...off the record," Kenzo said. "Whoever is behind all this has a long reach and a heavy hand."

"You be careful. We are going to sort this from our end and fuck them over."

"Now it's my turn, Mas. *You* be careful. We still don't know who all the players are for sure."

"Appreciate that. FYI we are closing up the office and camping out at McCarrigan's apartment."

"You're shitting me!"

"Nope, he's very pissed about what happened to Tara. They're an item."

"And he's fine with this?"

"Not really, but he offered to help in any way, and this is what we need."

"Be careful of him."

"We will be. I only trust him so far, and that's not very far. He has held up his end to date. I'll leave first and settle the check. Stay safe."

With that, I left Kenzo, then had a short chat with Wanatabe as I settled the check. Kenzo's information was worth the visit, and especially his offer of help. My priority was to get back to the office and complete the move.

Sophie held off Mack who was waiting for me. She'd packed up my laptop and my hard copy notes were ready to go. Doing a quick once over, I agreed all was clear. I set the alarm system, and we were gone, leaving Mack to screw the plywood over the door.

After we split up to take different routes to McCarrigan's. Marie went on her own by MUNI public transport. Erin went with Sophie by cab. I picked up my SUV, drove myself and some of the bulkier items to McCarrigan's. By the time I arrived, Sophie and Erin were waiting for me, Marie had arrived and held the door. We brought in the equipment and checked in with building security. We showed our official ID's to the security staff who, having been previously warned of our arrival by McCarrigan, were expecting us. They even offered to help us carry our equipment to the apartment. We thanked them for the offer but politely declined.

McCarrigan was apprehensively waiting for us. How could I tell? He was pacing when I got there.

I hoped I could reassure him. "We appreciate your assistance with this. I know it can't have been easy decision to make. How did Tara take it?"

"Volcanic would be a good description." He laughed a genuine laugh. "She threw a fit. until I reminded her that it started around her business, and we all had a hand in her rescue. She is better now. Grateful. Make yourself at home. I'll be at my office if you need me, and Tara is at her office with Kristen, and Oso is babysitting both of them."

"Excellent. See you later. We need to get working. We even brought our own coffee."

Again, he laughed at that. "Plenty of coffee here...milk, sugar and mugs are available, too. Use what you need. I also left out a few surge-protected socket strips. The cameras for the hall and garage are accessible with this code." He handed me a note. "The door has a video phone, so you can see who is asking for this apartment at reception. Anything else?"

"Nope. That about covers it. Thanks again. See you tonight."

McCarrigan left us to our business. The first order was to unpack. I already began carrying my pistol, and so had Sophie. We'd also brought the shotgun, just in case. Unpacking was tedious but went smoothly. Sophie went to the elevators and installed our own remote cameras, increasing the visual coverage. She also put remote cameras in the stair wells and freight elevator. We would not be getting any surprise visitors.

With the computers set up on the dining room table, we got back to work. As we spun up, I explained what Kenzo had told me. I was not as proficient with the computer aspects, so I reviewed my hard copy notes and kept an eye on the security cameras.

Erin was the first one to ask for a meeting. "I'm stuck. I have mapped all the financial trails we have. They're definitely off. Now, proving the congressmen actually knew what was going on is a different matter.

GRU has offshore financing, they launder the money with real estate deals, send the profits through U.S. banks to offshore banks, and then on to a holding company called International Trading and Holdings, ITH. About as generic a name as you can get. Which to me is suspicious. Most of these companies want flash and splash. The holding company held the money behind the offer to the Chinese shell company, to purchase 3DMedia through an eastern European shell company based in St. Petersburg. I matched the deposits in and out of the shell companies through the Maltese bank. Keeping it all in the family offered less outside oversight.

"I can't find much on the holding company. I'm thinking they are the money pot. The congressmen are on the boards of GRU and 3DMedia, tying them to ITH. Both have received significant contributions to their campaign war chests, from the PAC, which is funded in part by GRU. Robert smelled a rat."

I tapped the desk. "You can lay all this out, and prove it?"

Erin sighed before replying. "I can lay it out. Proof is something else. We need to dig into the congressmen's finances from their end—tax returns, etc. Also, we need to investigate GRU to back track the source of the funds I'm sure originated with the holding company. The PAC finances are also tied to the holding company. The connection and the proof are there. I just need to find them. Robert saw enough to be suspicious."

"Okay, we know what we need to get you going," I said. "Next Marie, what do we have?"

"Nothing as complicated as Erin's stuff, but I

might need her help. I have compiled as many deals as I can find for GRU. They only deal in commercial properties. I have a printout of the properties, purchase prices, dates, sale prices, and repurchase prices on some properties, Erin can look at it later. The obvious thing is that most of the sales were for a much higher price than expected after looking at the comps, and the purchases were usually for less than market value—knock down deals. Individually, they just look like good deals. The inconsistencies are noticeable only when you look at them as a block.

"Most properties are held for a year or two, and when they're sold, some are sold back to GRU at a much lower price than was originally paid. It's all clean money, taxes paid, and all kosher etc. GRU gets a high price on the sale, and on the back end when GRU purchases the property back at a big discount."

Sophie commented. "Clean and clever, but not clever enough. Robert found some of the financial routes, but it cost him his life. We will be more careful. Marie, give Erin everything you have on the transactions and sources, names, everything. She will map it out so a blind man could see it."

Erin nodded in agreement.

"The congressmen's private lives are my target, Sophie said. "We need to connect them directly to everything. The regular PAC campaign contributions to both congressmen via GRU and ITH are probably illegal. We need the smoking money."

All good work. That left me with nothing to do but watch the security monitors while the three women worked away on their own tasks. By mid-afternoon, I was going fuzzy-eyed looking at nothing. Walking around the apartment helped, and the view of the Bay was awesome. Lost in thought, I was looking out the window when Sophie called to me.

"What, sorry I was miles away."

"Obviously. Fiend has some interesting stuff. He's been looking into the congressmen and sent me a file on each. He did a dive on both, back to their parents. Nothing in either family background to raise any red flags. College and business careers were all kosher. Nothing in their early political careers. They met on a committee and obviously found some common ground. From the notes Fiend made, it looks like they are finance driven not ideological. Although they have played that card when it suits them."

I asked, "Anything concrete that proves they are corrupt."

"Not yet. Tons of background, and Fiend even supplied their voting record. That might help link the votes to bills or projects that would benefit the holding company, etc. Fiend supplied social security numbers for them and immediate family members, along with info to bank and investment numbers. That should be more than enough for me to get digging, especially with the promise of more to come."

That was good news.

Erin and Marie continued working on mapping out the big picture and printing it all out. They'd let Sophie know when they were done so she could save an electronic copy to a safe place. Still nothing much for me, except to make sure we were all safe.

The building was quiet during the day, few comings and goings, all residents, or deliveries for residents. No requests for McCarrigan's apartment. No calls. I had the feeling it was the calm before the storm. We were a target. They now knew who we were, but we didn't know who 'they' were. Only "they" were as dangerous to us, as we appeared to be to them.

Reinforcements were needed, not the physical kind we'd used before. The opposition would have access to military or ex-military trained personnel. We couldn't compete with that. We had to be smarter and get the physical pieces off the board, and the first piece to go would have to be Steven, he was their piece on the ground in San Francisco. Getting rid of him would cause some confusion and take time and effort to replace.

Needing to run an idea past Sophie, I risked interrupting her. "Sophie, I have a question?"

"What? I'm busy."

"Yes. dear, but I need your brains."

"It better be good."

"How can we remove Steven without knowing who or where he's located. Would there be any way of doing it with an internet campaign of some sort? Could we broadcast a wanted notice? We have his photo from the car rental place and one from Oso."

"Hmm…not a bad idea. We couldn't do it alone, not with our limited time and workload. This would need cluster to get the momentum going and a secure one at that. I'll get the photos over to Fiend. He'll know how to get it to the media and other darker places, too. Steven is about to be outed. Good idea, Mas."

The rest of the day our noses were buried in computers, but with nothing of interest, my eyes felt like they were glued to watching nothing happening screens until McCarrigan arrived back just after 6:00

p.m. followed by Oso escorting Tara right to the door a little after six.

He and I bumped fists and smiled. Nothing to report, Oso left saying he would be back early tomorrow. We were all tired. Marie took Erin back to her place, and Sophie and I went home.

On the way, Sophie quietly asked if I was up for a play date. The sound of her voice asking the question was all I needed to hear. She sounded tired and stressed, with an under lying tone of concern.

I answered, "Of course, as you wish."

"No, Mas. As in...*we* wish...this time."

"Sophie, I agree we both need to ease the tension. My only question is do you want to play at home or go out?" My cock started to fill the cage.

"Home will be fine. This is for us," she said with a long sigh.

I wasn't sure what Sophie had in mind. Did she want me as Ms. Circe or as Sophie? Whatever it was, I wanted it too.

Chapter Twenty

We were quiet the rest of the way home and held hands as we walked up to the front door. As we entered, Sophie turned to me. "Mas, please secure our home and strip naked, then wait here in the hall and wait for my call."

"As you wish."

"Thank you. Wait on your knees, thinking of what service I might like or request, just to get the juices going."

Huh, like I need to get the juices going. My cock filled the cage. Checking that the house was secure and locked up tight, I followed her instructions. Undressed, folded my clothes neatly, and stacked them. No need to add a punishment to whatever Ms. Circe had in mind for me because I'd left my clothes in an untidy pile.

Kneeling with my thoughts whirling, she was deliberately making me wait, raising my anticipation and anxiety. Such sweet torture. I heard her moving about. Her heels clicked on the hardwood floor, then the sound stopped—nothing as she moved to a rug. Knowing exactly where she was didn't help my excitement. I still didn't know what she was doing.

She called my name from the living room, and I went to her, kneeling in front of her. She was a vision in blue, a long dark blue satin robe covered her from neck to ankle. I could make out the outlines of underwear, a bra, and the line of a garter belt, but nothing else.

As always, just seeing her aroused me. My breathing went shallow and rapid.

She dropped a stiff leather collar and a set of ankle cuffs joined by a chain, between my spread knees. "Mas, please attach and lock these items, then prepare some dinner for me."

I attached the ankle cuffs, locking them on. The collar was new and stiff. I buckled it and slipped the lock in and clicked it shut. Now in proper submissive mode, it never ceased to surprise me how the act of putting on a collar triggered me mentally into my submissive mode.

"Will leftovers from last night be acceptable?"

"Yes, Mas, as long as it's treated creatively...but after you have poured me a glass of wine. Dismissed."

Retreating to the kitchen, I poured, then delivered the wine. Next, I made dinner. Quickly gathering the leftovers, I concocted a savory hash, jacked up with Cajun spices for heat. It was a good-sized portion, and I piled it on a plate for her to eat as much as she wanted, hoping I would get whatever she discarded.

"Ms. Circe, dinner is served."

Putting the plate in front of her, with cutlery to one side, I was about to kneel when she said, "Thank you. A refill on the wine, first, then you may kneel close to my left side."

After delivering the wine refill, I sank to my knees as instructed. Ms. Circe began to eat, slowly savoring each morsel.

"Excellent dish, Mas. Now, open wide."

Looking up at her, I saw she was smiling and had a fork full of food ready to feed to me. Opening my mouth as much as I could with the stiff collar restricting me, I accepted her offer. The temperature was just right. The flavors mixed together in a complex fusion, with the heat hitting at the end. This was a good hash. She returned to the plate continuing to eat, occasionally feeding me a mouth full at her whim.

The fork tapped the plate as she said, "Wonderful job on the meal, and a good portion, although too much for me. I will assist you with finishing it."

The aroma of the food still rose from the cooling plate, and the collar made it difficult for me to eat. I took the food off the offered fork, chewing and swallowing almost in one. Hearing Circe chuckling at my predicament increased my discomfort and arousal. My relationship with Ms. Circe was so much deeper and more complete than anyone I'd been with before.

I'd practically inhaled the last morsel, then licked the plate clean, and sat back on my heels with my hands locked behind me. My face had to be covered in food and sauce. The smile on Ms. Circe's face confirmed my suspicion.

"My, my, what a hungry sub you are, Mas. Hmmm, clean you up or hood you? Tonight, I think hood. Don't run away."

She left me on my knees. I assumed I would be licking her to orgasm. My face would still be in her pussy, not that I minded of course.

Standing in front of me, she said, "Mas, take a good look at your uniform for tonight."

Ms. Circe was holding a set of wrist cuffs joined by a chain, nothing new there. Her putting them on me with my hands behind me, and hearing the locks click closed, sent a thrill to my engorged cock. In one hand she held a black leather hood with a padded removable blindfold to cover the eyes. Two holes, large enough for easy breathing were open where my nostrils would be. The opening for the mouth was open. In her other hand she held a dildo. Not one I had seen before. This one was a black silicone penis on one side with a flange, and the other side was a gag plug.

Our eyes met, and she said, "Just another step on our road together. I love you, Mas, and I love what you freely give to me."

Silently, I watched her push the dildo through the mouth opening of the hood. The gag part was large, and I was not sure I could take it, but I would try. Moving behind me, she unlocked my collar and removed it. Putting the hood in front of me, she placed the tip of the gag into my mouth and started to pull the open back of the hood over my face. The hood smelled of fresh leather. It was intoxicating. As she fitted the hood, it tightened over my face and pulled the gag deeper into my mouth, all the while checking to make sure the nose openings were clear and over my nostrils.

"Mas, this is turning me on. I'm wet already, and I know what is coming." She laughed at her own pun.

With the soft leather molded to my face, seeing nothing, I noted her voice was muffled by the leather shrouding my head. The hood fit perfectly, just under my chin, seating the gag fully into my mouth. Fitted, and clamping my mouth around the invading gag, little by little the hood tightened down the back of my head and onto my neck. Lacking sight, my other senses heightened. The gag and the dildo moved in response to Ms. Circe's ministrations.

Sightless and hearing-impaired, I wondered what

was next. Ms. Circe raised my chin and replaced my collar, forcing my head up. The collar was locked on over the hood. The feeling of helplessness turned me on. I was her responsibility, and I would do whatever she required of me. The only thing I focused on was my engorged dick filling my cage.

The anticipation drove me crazy. I wanted her to start.

After what seemed like an age but could have only been minutes, I felt a tug on my collar. Standing awkwardly, I followed the tension on the collar. Ms. Circe slowly led me around our home, the chain between my ankles restricting my stride. By frequently changing directions, I became disoriented in my own familiar surroundings. We stopped. I flinched as she put a hand on each shoulder and pushed. I lost my balance, and instinctively tried to cry out as I fell backwards.

I landed softly on the bed. Ms. Circe lifted my legs on to the bed and turned me to center me. The chain between my wrist cuffs was long enough for my hands to lay by my sides. Feeling a clip being attached to my left wrist, then similarly one to my right, I was being secured to the bed. The chain between my ankles tightened, pulling my legs together. I could no longer move my legs.

Finally, her hands were on my cage, fondling and teasing me, a beginning, but no release. Nothing. No sound. No movement. I was alone within my thoughts and imagination. Swiftly she mounted the bed, straddling my chest. She put something fragrant on the dildo. The dildo gag moved in my mouth as she worked, and I inhaled the intoxicating fragrance of the lube.

She touched my nipples, playing with them until they hardened under her manipulations, and then...she clamped! One, then the other. I felt the pinch of the clover clamps and groaned at the pressure and the cold sensation when the chain dropped on my chest. She moved up my body positioning a knee at either side of my head. I felt her as she moved. Less pressure, then a weight descended on my face. She'd impaled herself on the dildo sticking out from the hood and gag. I bit down on the gag to stabilize it and waited for her to start her ride.

Motionless, she was experiencing the fullness of the dong inside her. Slowly, she began to move, gently back and forth, and then side to side. She rose on the impaling dildo, increasing her motion. I felt her weight move. She leaned forward, bracing herself on the headboard. The gag moved in synchronization with her as she played with her own body, teasing herself, making the experience last as long as she wanted, drawing out the pleasure for herself and to tease me further.

In my darkened space with stunted senses, my fantasy thoughts went to visualizing her in the throes of ecstasy, imagining how Ms. Circe looked as she rode me to her nirvana. This was my service to her. It was what she wanted, and I was the medium for her pleasure, freely given and taken. Muffled sounds penetrated through the hood, along with a slowing of motion on the dildo.

She'd achieved the release she wanted. Resting in place, I wondered if she would try for a second orgasm. Yes or no, I would have no choice in the matter, and that stirred my hardened cock, maintaining my erection.

Part of the pleasure and frustration of my chastity cage was that I could have as many erections as I wanted, but without Ms. Circe's permission, I was unable to do anything about any of them.

She rose off the dong, and the bed moved. The clamps, when removed, left my nipples burning, and then she was gone, and I was left bound and helpless until she released me.

I figured she was taking a shower, and also letting me enjoy the feeling of satisfying her and being under her control. My mind went there. It was satisfying.

Then a random thought strayed into my consciousness. She needed to release me and have a conversation. I waited nervously, which was unusual for me. I usually enjoyed the feeling of being bound and the experience of waiting for release. This was different.

Sensing her return slightly before the collar lock clicked open, I eagerly anticipated this release. After the hood was removed, I worked my mouth and jaw to loosen the stiffness from holding the gag.

"Please, release me as soon as possible," I quietly urged her. I'd never asked for that before.

"Of course. What's wrong?"

"I'll tell you when we can sit and chat."

I removed my restraints, and Sophie assisted me. This time she unlocked the cuffs, something usually left for me to do.

"Sophie, I don't want to spoil the night, but we've been very foolish. I suddenly realized what a big risk we just took. We should know better."

She heard me and understood what I meant immediately. Her expression of concern was etched on her face. "Oh God, I didn't think. I am so sorry, Mas."

"I didn't think, either. No harm no foul. But if we'd been assaulted by Steven or whoever, we'd have been in a pile of shit. We would have been gift wrapped for them—or at least I'd have been, and I couldn't have protected you. We can't afford to take them lightly."

"Mas, you're right. No more play until this is sorted."

"I thought you would get it. Anyway, that was a first for me. Did you enjoy it?"

She laughed and relaxed. The tension eased from around her eyes. "Yes, I did. I like having you at my mercy. The power exchange is intoxicating. Next time, I may do things a little differently. Food for thought, until we are free to play again."

Freed of my bonds and concern, I cleaned and then put everything back in its assigned place. Continuing with my train of thought regarding our safety, I put the shotgun next to my bed and my pistol on the bedside table. When Sophie saw what I had done, she put her pistol on her bedside table, too.

More relaxed now, I could still smell the leather of the hood and the fragrance of the lube on the way to the shower. Both dissipated with the soap and water in the shower, and I was back as Mas the detective.

Sophie was already asleep when I returned to the bedroom, but I knew sleep wouldn't come easily for me, tonight. I considered every "what could have happened" scenario. But eventually sleep took me. My rest was fitful at best. I couldn't help thinking we'd dodged a bullet, literally. Lesson learned. We wouldn't put ourselves in that position again.

Chapter Twenty-One

Lack of sleep made me cranky, and that added to my frustration because I hadn't progressed any further with my review of the case. Sophie, looking relaxed but thoughtful, brought me a cup of coffee.

"A penny for those thoughts?" I asked.

"Not worth that, at the moment. I've been churning over what we have so far, and what I need to do. So get up, and let's get on with it."

Feeling like crap, I followed Sophie's lead and made ready to go to McCarrigan's. Marie and Erin had beaten us there and started on their tasks. Sophie let out a big "Yes!" as soon as she opened her computer.

We all looked up, and Sophie smiled. "Fiend has come through with some connections. We hadn't gotten around to checking out the families of the congressmen. He did a dive into the wives and their families."

We crowded around her. Graphs and text flooded the screens. It linked both congressmen to funny money and illegal activity, even if only by the joint offshore accounts they held with their wives. The money came into the wives' businesses and then funneled out to the joint offshore accounts.

Broken down...James River's wife, Amanda Rivers operated two Art Galleries, Rivers and Co. One in San Francisco, the other in Washington, D. C. Both places were flush with people ready to pay big bucks for *art*, and the big dollar numbers would not raise red flags. Art was being bought and sold on the same principle of GRU's real estate deals. I wondered what the churn on the artwork they'd sold would be.

Hunter Pollard's wife, Deborah Sands-Pollard was connected to old money and used those connections to build a lifestyle and a decorating-consulting company with offices also in Los Angeles and Washington, D.C. Her business, with no tangible assets, had lots of cash flow. Consultants can charge whatever the market will bear.

Sophie gasped. "This is great stuff. Now I need to get into the personal and business accounts of both families. Fiend will help. He believes there's so much Russian money here that it's powering our political system. Erin, plot out everything we have so far so it's idiot-proof. Make sure whatever you use is flexible enough to add to and adjust as we get more information."

Erin looked excited. "No problem. I can use one of the templates from my PhD research. It will be perfect for this."

Sophie was in full, digital warrior mode. She had a definite plan, and now we knew what to look for and where. She would be working crazy hours, and I hoped McCarrigan would be able to put up with her. I loved her…and sometimes she drove *me* crazy.

I pointed at each one of them. "When you get this layout thing done, I need to see it ASAP. I need to understand the details as much as I can. Right now, it's all big picture."

Erin gave me a thumbs up. "You got it. When it's broken down, it's quite simple. The sneaky shenanigans in the details are what make it look complicated."

With that done, the women started on their tasks, leaving me to do nothing but think. Steven was still on the loose. We bought some time by closing the office, diverting the little snail mail we received, and moving to McCarrigan's. But none of that was a permanent fix. Steven had access to resources we didn't, and I was sure he was still on our trail. Even if we neutralized Steven, they would just replace him.

I thought *"maybe, better the enemy we knew..."* at least until we were ready to go after the two congressmen and everyone else we could find. We had to be paranoid. They *were* out to get us!

The remainder of the day, I monitored the security screens. Bored out of my mind, I stuck to it because I didn't want any surprises. Everyone made progress, and Erin said she would show me what she was doing tomorrow, step by step, as she loaded it all into her template.

At the end of the day, everyone was fried. We all agreed the information we had was deadly. Sophie and I asked if either of them wanted out.

"It's too late for that," Marie said, and threw a hissy fit. "I'm in."

"I can't get out," Erin said. "I know too much about Clegg's work, and I want to get the bastards who killed him."

Understood. That was easy. Perhaps not smart, but the commitment was there.

We had a quick decompression session, and then went our separate ways. Erin went with Marie, and Sophie and I stayed to wait for McCarrigan and Tara to get home. We tidied up a bit, not that we made that much of a mess. Most of what was being done was digital, so mess was comprised of used coffee cups in the sink, plus bags from the take-out lunches we'd had delivered. Mostly just trash.

McCarrigan and Tara arrived together, laughing.

McCarrigan seemed surprised that we were still there. "Thought you would be gone by now. Any problems?"

Sophie answered, "No we wanted to update you on our progress."

I added, "We still feel that Tara is in some jeopardy. Steven knows about our involvement but not about what we've done. I'm worried that we can expect some sort of reprisal, probably against us all."

"There's something you aren't telling us." McCarrigan said. "Come clean. We're all over twenty-one."

Before I could say anything, Sophie jumped in, "Okay, if this is as big as we think it is, we're all in jeopardy."

Tara's expression grew serious. "How serious do you think it is?"

I took that question. "Anyone who has touched this information is in danger. We know it goes all the way to D.C. We're talking about millions and millions of dollars being laundered and used to pay off our already corrupt political system. So permanently removing any and all of us who knows anything about this operation has to be an integral part of their plan,"

Sophie added, "We are telling you this as a precaution."

Tara spoke with a quaver in her voice, "I just do deals, put people together, and facilitate."

"Wrong deal, wrong time, and place," I said softly, shaking my head. "It's not your fault, but we've all got targets on our backs. We have to get out of this," I said, staring at McCarrigan. "There's no back door on this one. We have to see this through to the end."

He nodded in ascent. "What can we do?"

"Keep your schedule as normal as possible. We added a few more cameras to this floor as a precaution. For now, we don't think they'll go after you. They'll come for us first. You'll be part of the tidy up...collateral damage."

McCarrigan put his arm around Tara. "Tell us what you have so far. I want to hear it all from you and make up my own mind about the danger level to us."

I looked at Sophie, and she shrugged "Sophie will explain it much better than I can."

Sophie spent the next thirty plus minutes laying it out for the two of them. They nodded in places and asked questions.

At the end, McCarrigan said, "Shit what a mess. If even half of what you said is true, we are in trouble. I intend us to survive. Whatever you need, if I haven't got it, I'll get it. But we'll want updates."

Sophie and I simultaneously said, "Fair enough."

I added, "This is political and dirty. We can handle the dirty, but we'll need you to use all your political connections in the California and Federal arenas. Those connections will be necessary when we get to that point."

McCarrigan scrubbed his hand down his face. "Sure. But remember they're political. Their kind won't touch anything that could cast a shadow on them—nothing that could damage them in any way. Having said that…if we can slant the outcome positively for them or in their favor, you can count them in."

"The only people I trust right now are our team, you, and Tara. Everything has to be kept tight. We'll have a meeting here tomorrow evening. We should have more information by then. Marie and Erin are aware of the danger and have been updated. They both know too much to back out now, and they know it."

Tara looked over to McCarrigan. The look on his face was stern and serious. He nodded in agreement with his arm around Tara.

We said our goodbyes and left them to their evening. On the way down to our car, I suggested, "What do you think about checking out Simon's place?"

Sophie nodded in agreement. "Good idea."

Even while maintaining our hypervigilant awareness, we saw nothing to raise suspicions, and the drive over to Simon's place was uneventful. Parking a few spots up from the house, we saw the next-door neighbor coming out. He waived and said, "We almost called the police last night. The party was very noisy, but it went quiet, so we didn't bother. You aren't going to have another tonight, are you?"

I said, "No party tonight…promise."

"Okay. Then, have a good night."

"Yeah, you, too."

Cautiously we approached the front door. Sophie had her weapon out. I had one hand on mine, and the front door keys in the other. Going in first, I stepped over a few pieces of mail and glanced around. The place was a mess.

Switching on the lights, confirmed it'd been

properly tossed. All the furniture had been moved, and all the drawers and cabinets searched. The people who did this were definitely not careful. This was more vindictive than thorough. There'd been nothing to find, so they took it out on the house. This was more proof, as if we needed it, that we were on Steven's and his boss's shit list. We had used the house as a deflection, and it had worked.

Kenzo picked up on the first ring. "What do you need?"

"What makes you think we need anything?"

"You called me, didn't you?" He said it with lightness in his voice.

"Well, smartass, you're correct. You might want to get a forensic team over to Simon's place. It's been tossed. Probably won't get much, but one of them may have been sloppy and left prints or DNA. Ya never know when you'll get lucky. We won't be here, the neighbor said there was a party here last night but didn't report the disturbance cause the noise stopped."

Sophie asked for the phone, I handed it over. "Kenzo, it's Sophie. You'll want to really look up RICO law and money laundering." She handed the phone back to me.

"Mas?"

"Yeah, I'm back."

"Point taken, and I'll follow up on Simon's place. I'll use the excuse that it's still a crime scene. Take care."

"Done, and thanks."

Finished with our excitement for the evening, I hoped, we decided to go home via the office and check to see if the boarded-up office had received any

259

attention. Sophie suggested we install a camera or two to observe any nighttime activity since the building was generally too busy during the day for anything untoward to happen. Night was another matter.

Another clever idea I should have thought of. "Do you want to do it," I asked, "or get someone else to handle it?

"Someone else...in case we're being tailed or observed. If a third party does it, it's safer all-round."

"Agreed. Can you take care of it tomorrow?"

"Yes, I have someone who can take care of it."

With that taken care of we made our way to the office, cautiously entering before going up to our floor. Silence, not a sound, we walked to our boarded-up door, the notice we put up was still there. The screws holding the board in place hadn't been touched. That was good news.

"Let's get out of here," I whispered.

Sophie nodded, and we left, quietly heading home.

Later as Sophie prepared for bed, I checked all the doors and windows, bracing a chair under the front door handle. It wouldn't stop a determined entry, but it would give us time. Both of us had our weapons out on our bedside tables.

Nevertheless, sleep came quickly, and morning arrived too soon.

Chapter Twenty-Two

I woke up ready to go. My sleep had been better than I expected. Sophie's, not so much. The strain of long hours of stress began to show on her face. I started coffee and breakfast then took a quick shower. I was ready for the day, and Sophie picked up speed with coffee and was ready for breakfast. As we ate, her phone dinged with a new message. She looked at it, then grabbed the phone and opened the message.

A smile formed on her lips. "It's from Fiend. He found some account numbers we can use to get into the family accounts of Pollard and Rivers. This is a good start."

"How so?"

"Banking systems are too well encrypted to hack directly. Hackers usually get in through human error. Leaving passwords around, duplicating them over several accounts, all sorts of dumb things people do to save time. Or they just get lazy."

"Or like Tara, opening an e-mail she shouldn't have?"

"Yes, that too. I'm sure the wives' business accounts will be the weak spots, here. I'd put money on them doing personal stuff on their work computers. At least I hope so. It will make life so much easier for us. One thing leads to another, and then eventually the jackpot…maybe."

I felt a little lighter this morning. This was a good start to the day.

After breakfast, we headed to McCarrigan's apartment...our new office. Security was getting used to seeing us, and acknowledged us, but still checked our ID's before allowing us through to the elevators. We liked that they took nothing for granted.

Marie and Erin were already in the apartment and working on their individual tasks. Sophie settled in and started looking into the info Fiend had supplied. I went back to my observation of the monitors. Nothing stirred in the hallway, but the reception area was getting busier with residents leaving for the workday.

Thankfully, Sophie interrupted me, saying we would have cameras in the hallway of our office by noon. "Remote wireless feeds, and I'll show you how to monitor them. We probably should get you a couple more monitors, too. I'll have them delivered here ASAP."

"Great, and I'll need to get my eyes tested after staring at these screens for much longer."

Sophie patted my shoulder. "You need a pair of computer glasses. I'll get them. That'll help."

"You're kidding...right?"

"No. I wear them, haven't you noticed."

"Well yeah, I just thought you needed them for the computer."

"I will get you sorted out. Don't worry."

With my eye dilemma settled, we each went back to work. Coffee was on constant brew, and I turned into the office barista, refilling as needed. That was a pleasure. It gave my eyes a brief respite. I didn't know how anyone could watch screens all day without going blind or crazy.

The morning shift ended with lunch being delivered to reception downstairs. Marie went down to collect it and returned. We chatted about nothing much as we ate. I think we were all preoccupied.

The last remnants from lunch disappeared in the trash, when we received a notification about an electronics delivery. Reception needed a signature for the delivery.

"Your new monitors," Sophie said, and I smiled. My eyes felt better already. We went down. She signed, and I carried the two boxes back to our office.

Taking no time at all, Sophie had the new monitors plugged in, and up and running. My laptop screen had reception cameras. One of the new monitors picked up the elevator and hallway cameras we installed, and the last one was blank.

Sophie pointed to the empty screen. "As soon as I get the notification that the cameras are up in our office building, I'll get this one linked to the feed. It shouldn't be long."

Having two monitors actually made it easier to follow what was going on. By moving my eyes from one to the other, it was easier to see—especially with the new glasses. I couldn't see the difference, but Sophie swore they cut down on the irritable, blue light coming from the monitors.

Still nothing was happening except what I saw on the reception cameras, where the only action were the comings and goings of the people, and the deliveries— all logged in. The shifts changed, and each security team seemed competent and thorough—impressive for a residential building. Then I considered the residents who lived here. They had to be wealthy to afford an apartment here, so money was not an obstacle for getting the privacy and security they wanted.

Mid-afternoon, Sophie said she'd been notified that the cameras were installed and ready to be activated. She played with my laptop, and the third monitor burst into life. After a few minutes, I determined there wasn't much happening there either. While it would possibly bore me to death, it meant we were not being assaulted.

Sophie explained she would turn on the motion activation functions later at night. There was no point initiating them while the offices were open for business.

By the end of the day, I began to wish something would happen. The four of us sat and debriefed. Marie updated us on the business of our company. Bills did not wait. She was concise and explained that everything was running smoothly. Sophie was itching to go, but Erin started her report with enthusiasm. She had a printout for each of us with the money trails she found and plotted—including GRU, ITH, the PAC, plus the U.S. banks involved. She admitted there were still gaps, but she said she hoped Sophie could fill those in.

As if on cue, Sophie started and went on for the next thirty minutes explaining what Fiend had sent and what she had discovered, using that information. It fitted in with the work that Clegg and Erin had done. Some gaps were filled, some were still open.

Sophie had been right about the wives being the Achilles heel. She reported having accessed both wives' business accounts, and through that access had gotten into the personal accounts. They were now open books to her, and she was copying as much information as she could for Erin to analyze. She also gained access to the offshore accounts but hadn't really investigated them, yet.

Curiosity got the better of me, and I asked, "So did they leave passwords hanging about?"

Smiling slyly, Sophie responded, "Kinda. Amanda Rives had a file with all her passwords listed, and yes, I copied it. We could have so much fun with that—cancel her cable TV, mess with her schedule so she thinks she is going crazy, order fifty pizzas—the list is endless."

The look on my face set her off. "Jesus, Mas, I was kidding. After this is all over maybe, but this is business first and last. Promise. Anyway, it looks promising. A quick scan of the accounts…lots of cash income."

I asked Erin how quickly she could analyze the data Sophie had copied.

"Quickly. I'm done tracking to date. Maybe this will fill in some of the blanks…I'll get right on it."

As we wrapped up, McCarrigan walked in, immediately asking about any progress.

Before anyone else could say anything, I said, "Yes, some. We have more to work on, but it's looking good, and we'll update you when we have something solid. We're just wrapping up now."

He did a quick scan of his apartment, noticed the two new monitors, and just shook his head. He went to get a drink, offering us all to partake. As one, we declined, and I said we'd leave him to his home.

Packing up our laptops, we left together. On the way down, Sophie said she would send Erin the data for her to work on. I knew the information would be with Erin as soon as possible, and Sophie would go back to investigating the offshore accounts. If Sophie bothered coming to bed tonight, it would be late, and I was useless with this aspect of the case. For me, it would be a solo night, dinner, a beer, and TV before crashing.

Being right isn't always a good thing. I rolled over, awake early, and noticed her side of the bed was undisturbed. It didn't take long to find her. She was slumped over on her laptop, asleep. Quietly, I started our day. I put the coffee on and took a quick shower. Knowing better than to startle her, I began making more noise as I moved around our home.

Stirring slowly, coming to, she looked disheveled and gorgeous. I kissed her lightly on the top of her head and put a mug of coffee by her side.

I made out a muffled sound from Sophie like, "Thank you…what time is it."

"Early. Any idea what time you crashed?"

"Not sure. Late. I feel like…shit."

"Go take a shower. Breakfast will be ready when you're done."

She grumbled another subdued *thank you* and shuffled off to shower.

Really, I wanted to ask if the effort had been worth it, but she'd tell me when she was ready.

I barely managed to get breakfast on the table by the time she came back. Dressed only in a satin robe, she looked delicious. That did no favors for my captured cock, but I enjoyed the visuals and imagined what was to come after this case was settled.

"I feel almost human. I am getting too old for this crap. All-nighters weren't so bad in college, but now they suck. Before you ask…it was worth it. I'll spill when we're all together."

Smiling to myself, I liked how I was getting to know her, and she me. I liked it…our personal intimacy. Sophie was now energized, and I could tell she'd found something worth the effort she put into the previous night.

Beating Marie and Erin to the apartment, we put on the coffee and started up our laptops and the monitors. The first job for me was to check and see if the cameras placed at our office had recorded anything.

Marie and Erin arrived, with Erin looking tired. I guess she did an all-nighter as well. Pouring coffee for everyone, I joined them at the dining room table, and waited for Sophie to start. Surprisingly, she asked, "Erin, did you find anything useful? Go first if you did."

"Yes, I discovered we are correct. The congressmen are in it up to their necks, distanced by running a huge amount of cash through the wives' businesses. I will need to do more analysis on those accounts, separating the corrupt transactions from the honest ones, but the info is there. The PAC money is dirty. That I can prove. It comes from Maltese banks and maybe Russia. Most of that money goes through the real estate company. We have dates and amounts. It's a matter of linking everything up. The husbands' accounts are kept separate from the wives, even their personal accounts are in their own individual names…nothing joint."

I asked, "How long do you think it will take to sort this all out so it will stand up in court?"

"Days? Not sure. Clegg could have done it faster. He had tons more experience." She looked if she was about to cry.

"Don't sell yourself short," I said. "You worked with him. He trusted you and mentored you. He wouldn't do that with just anyone, would he? Be as fast and thorough as you can. The time will take care of itself."

She smiled, a wan smile, but a smile nevertheless, and stared into her coffee mug.

We were all silent until Sophie spoke, "Cheer up, both couples have joint accounts in the Caymans, Malta, and in Eastern Europe, and not surprisingly, they all have Maltese passports. The passport thing is from Fiend. He's still poking around. The accounts are very well-funded. I pulled a history of deposits and withdrawals. It looks like it's their rainy-day retirement funds. Most of the deposits are from the wives' businesses, but are held in both their names, for both couples. Erin will have to do the numbers on the illegal transactions which fund these accounts. Between the U.S. banking and the offshore banks, we can tie dirty money to the congressmen and their wives, plus GRU. I'm not sure if the PAC is aware of where the money comes from, but it's still dirty. The holding company is neatly tied-in for funding the PAC. We got them all. Now we lay it out. Fiend is looking into obtaining their tax returns."

This was huge and…dangerous. When we proved they were dirty, it would be a big story, and we still had Steven to consider. Fiend had concocted and launched a plan to flush him out. I hoped it worked. With that update, we all returned to our tasks.

I was stuck reviewing the previous night's recording from the remote motion sensor cameras in our office building. One or two people entered their offices late. I recognized them. Fast forwarding, they both left after a short time. No issue.

2:35 a.m., two men carried in a bag and a short step ladder. They stayed in the shadows. Looking around, they stopped in front of our door and examined the covering. One opened the bag, pulled out a battery powered drill, and the other kept watch. The man with the drill removed the screws around the frame securing the board in place. Without sound, it was like watching an old silent movie. Even without sound, I could see they worked efficiently. Standing on the steps, one guy removed the last screws.

The second man slid the board to one side, then knelt in front of the door and worked on the locks. We had good locks, but nothing was immune to a good lock pick, and this guy knew what he was doing. As soon as the door opened, he went in to disable the alarm, and two minutes later he waived the second man in, and carried in all their equipment, shutting the door behind them.

The recording stopped. My screen burst into life again. The time stamp was thirty-three minutes later. Exiting the office, the men replaced the board and left the same way they entered.

I called out. "Sophie, come and look." She came over and viewed the video.

"What do you think they were after?"

"My guess would be anything related to Clegg and the 3DMedia deal, and anything else that looked good to them."

"How long were they in there?"

"Thirty-three minutes...why?"

"Just thinking it wouldn't take that long to search our place. My office computer is still on and running."

"Would you know if someone was fiddling with

it?"

"Yes, but I haven't used it since we moved here. I connected remotely to Fiends. His is bigger and more powerful than the one I built, and all the data I need is stored on the cloud."

"So?"

"If they took my hard drives they are in for a surprise. If they piggy backed on to it, it doesn't matter. I'm not using it. Depends on if they want us to know they were there or not."

"Please explain so I can understand."

She laughed which caused Erin and Marie to look up.

"Mas, if they took my hard drives and try to access them, I built in traps so if anyone plays with it, everything on it goes poof. If they piggy backed on to it, still zilch. They may not want us to know they have been in there, yet. What I would have done is what they've done, but I would also leave a surprise."

"What sort of surprise?"

"A remotely triggered device that would destroy the computer, and probably most of the office, just to be sure nothing survived."

"That makes sense. Us not knowing they were there, and the back pocket bang. What do you want to do about it?"

"Nothing, leave everything as it is."

"We can't do that. If they've planted a device and set it off, it could impact everyone in the building. We'll have to get in and check. If we do it during the day, it's less likely anyone will be watching, but there's too much coming and going."

"Why not do it the same time they did. No one

would expect that...would they?"

"Fair point. One thing for sure, you will have to come with me to check out your computer. You okay with that?"

"Yes, but what if there is an IED?"

"We will have someone with us who knows his way around that stuff."

"I'm busy pulling data. Let me know when you have it all sorted."

"No problem."

We would need the same tool set as the interlopers used. Portable drill, steps, but we wouldn't need to pick the lock. Hoping there wasn't an IED, but expecting one, my first call was to Oso. He knew people with a lot of varied skill sets. One of whom was Manuel Hernandez, a former Army demolition expert, and owner of a demolition and deconstruction company on the Peninsula. The call was answered on the first ring.

"Hola Mas, good to hear from you. What's up?"

"You still in touch with Manuel?"

"Sure, he's a relative—a cousin's cousin like."

"Maybe an infestation problem, and we want to cover all the bases. Think he would be up for a late-night visit to our office? Pays cash, and he will need his tool kit."

"Let me get back to ya. I'll be really quick. If he's in, I am coming, too."

"Thanks, Oso, you don't need to, but I won't stop you."

He hung up, and I went back to looking at the different screens. Reception was busy, and security handled everything easily. It was a normal day. The cameras in the elevators showed mostly the same people I had seen over the last few days, and the ones on our floor. Nothing.

With the intrusion into our abandoned office, Steven had to be preparing for an assault on us. By now, he'd figured out where we were. Maybe I would keep Oso around as well. If Steven's team was big enough, he would try taking us separately. Although taking all of us at once was a bigger risk. Numbers wise, it was lower risk, in that we were all in one place. They would infiltrate the building from the service entrance. They wouldn't want to confront security, just bypass them. They'd be posing as service men, delivery men, utility personnel, etc.

My phone rang, a local number I didn't recognize. I answered, "Hola, Mr. Hammett?"

"Yes, speaking."

"Oso said you needed to talk with me about an infestation problem."

"Yes, it's not confirmed, but a distinct possibility."

"Better to prevent than cure. My rates are a grand for the call out, and a scale up to four more, depending on difficulty. You good with that?"

"No problem, meet us at our office at 1:00 a.m. Oso knows where it is and wants to tag along. He can drive you that way. It's easier."

"No problem, Mr. Hammett. *Adios.*"

He hung up, and we were set. Interrupting Sophie, I quickly explained what was going on, and then I went back to staring at really fucking, boring screens. Our only break was for lunch, which we all ate at our workspaces. However, boring my job was, it was critical we weren't surprised by anyone. So…I watched the screens.

Finally, the day ended, and we went our separate ways. Filling in Sophie with more details of tonight's operation, she was on board. We agreed, with the late night to come, we would garb a quick dinner and take a timed nap.

The alarm went off like a siren, jerking me awake. Sophie was already up, dressed as I would be, all in black. Getting up, I had a welcomed coffee and cleaned both our weapons. They were cleaned after the last target practice, but it didn't hurt to clean them again. Sophie was quiet, pacing in anticipation, which was not like her.

"What's up Sophie? This isn't like you?"

"Tired. Nervous. I've worked in the shadows for so long, the real world is a strange place where real people get hurt. I guess I'm not as far along as I thought."

"You don't have to come tonight."

"Mas, that's not the issue. I don't want to lose you, and it scares me that I could. They will kill us if they need to."

"Hey, we're working on that, and tonight is part of that. We're close to proving a case against them...right?"

"Yes, a couple more days should do it. Erin has done most of the collating of data, and she's good. Probably not much more to find. How are we going to drop the hammer on them?"

"Not sure yet, but I would like it to be on multiple fronts. Time to go. Are you ready?"

"Yes."

We left with me carrying the bag of tools, and Sophie carrying the short steps. Parking near the office at this time of night was easy. We would have the office open and ready for Manuel and Oso. The screws holding the board over our door came out quickly. As soon as I moved the board, Sophie used her keys and had the door open in seconds. Entering, we did not use the lights, only flashlights. It was odd coming into our own office like burglars. At the first sound, we shut the flashlights off and waited, weapons drawn.

Oso called out, "*Hola*, Mas, it's me 'n Manuel."

"Come on in. We only just opened up."

Both the men were dressed for clandestine work. Oso's size made him a black mass against the light coming in from the street. He introduced Manuel, and I handed him an envelope containing one thousand dollars.

He nodded in acceptance and asked, "You just let me be for a while, till I make sure what we are dealing with eh? *Bueno*?"

"Sure." We waited by the entrance. I could see his flashlight move around the office, creating shadows. What seemed like an age, later, but could only have been a few minutes, he called us into the area where Sophie and I usually worked. We saw a small package attached to her computer.

"You have an infestation, a nasty one. There's enough C4 to take out this office, an' lots more. Over-kill. With remote detonation or preprogramed for a specific time. What you wanna do."

"Is it safe?

Laughing, he said, "Safe enough for now. If the phone rings, run like fuck cause it gonna blow."

"Got it. Can you disarm it, and leave it in place?"

"Sure. This is a simple one, effective but simple. Give me a few minutes."

We waited, and as promised, Manuel called us back into the office. "All safe, but you musta really pissed off some important *jefes*, they're using DoD supplies."

Sophie asked, "They could be stolen from the military, right?"

"Nah. That shit is kept locked up really tight. Could get you a tank before I could get my hands on DoD stuff like this."

Joining in, I asked, "You think someone official approved this?"

"I was in the U.S. Army, not the Salvation Army. Course someone okayed it. Had to be official to get his hands on this stuff. Anyways, it's safe. If a call comes in to set it off, it will fry the phone and seem like it's gone boom."

Sophie asked, "Is it all right to check out the computer?"

"Sure."

Sophie quickly inspected the computer and all her peripherals, looked over at me and said, "They were smart. They have piggy backed onto my computer. Anything I do on this thing, they will see. I'm a sneaky bitch. Fuck them, I'm pissed. We need to get this closed down and fast before anyone else gets hurt."

Sophie was mad, angry at what had happened and was happening. She was already on her phone furiously tapping away…send. Ping an almost instant reply.

She said, "Fiend's little program on Steven is getting legs, a life of its own. Let's go home."

Manuel packed up his tools, and as he was leaving said, "Two more G's. That's it for this infestation. Give it to Oso. *Adios*."

As they left, I asked if Oso would hang with us in McCarrigan's place after dropping Tara at her office.

He shrugged. "Sure."

That was more relieving than I expected. With them gone, the silence became oppressive. Sophie took one last look around, we locked up, and set the alarm. Screwing the board back in place, it looked as it did before. After putting the tools back in the SUV, we went home without incident. Crashing as we hit the bed, neither of us bothered to undress.

Chapter Twenty-Three

It took a while to surface after I woke up. I felt as if I was in a fog, like the ones that envelopes the Golden Gate Bridge so frequently, damp and oppressive. We'd taken care of the IED. We were aware of the computer interference. Sophie had pre-emptied that one. We would need to be more careful than ever. I didn't get that ominous feeling very often, but when I did, there were usually unpleasant results.

Sophie stared at my face. "What's wrong?"

"Just worrying, that's all. Nothing concrete."

"Yeah, well it worries me when you worry. It usually means something nasty's going to happen."

"We need to make sure we have all our weapons near us at all times. I will take some more shotgun ammo with us as well."

"Jesus, Mas. You really think that's necessary?"

"Yes, and we need to plan how to tactically use McCarrigan's apartment to its best advantage. How we're set up isn't bad, but we can do better."

"Okay. I'll drive, and we can pick up breakfast."

Already thinking about the apartment, I absentmindedly said, "Sure."

Sophie had quickly picked up a lot of San Franciscan driving habits, but she drove well, feeding her need to control. She parked in a visitor spot in the garage. That triggered another thought. We went through security as usual and up to the apartment. Both McCarrigan and Tara were preparing to leave at the same time.

Oso was dressed in his suit and waiting for Tara. "*Hola,* Mas. Miss Sophie. Just picking up Miss Tara and dropping her off at the office, then I come back, no time."

"That's good, Oso," I replied, absently.

I'd been mulling over what Steven's options were. Assuming he knew where we were located, the office sabotage was just part of the bigger plan. How would I go about eliminating us as a threat? Taking us out in two couples would be easier, numbers wise, but risky if it didn't work, or if we had time to warn the others. Taking us all at once made more sense, all of us working together in one location. In a secure location, a frontal assault wouldn't work, not with the security guards at reception.

What were the building's weak spots? The service entrance had less security, and fewer observation cameras. Come in dressed as maintenance or in delivery uniforms. Arrive in one or more vans at the same time. Use fake work sheets or make a fake delivery using the service elevator to access the floor. Thankfully, we put in the extra cameras. They would provide extra time to warn us. Add a diversion at the front desk to distract them from watching the monitors.

We were talking about six or seven to take the apartment with the element of surprise. Another two people max for a distracting diversion.

This was all supposition, but it made the most sense. I was relieved Oso stayed to back us up, while we waited for Marie and Erin to show up. They were later than usual, making me reconsider my thesis. Could I have been wrong? Were they were going after us in couples?

I breathed a sigh of relief when the women arrived, complaining about how the traffic was backed-up, but after those few scary moments, we should be prepared no matter what. First, I gave directions to rearrange the entrance hall. McCarrigan could complain when he got home.

Next the living room. We turned it into an obstacle course. It wouldn't affect us, but it would slow down any advance team. The kitchen's open plan with a view into the dining and living areas needed work. We moved the dining furniture around, creating more obstacles to break up the open, easy access to the area.

The breakfast island in the kitchen had stools. The sink and dishwasher were built ins, bordered on either side with full cabinets—not completely bullet proof, but sturdy enough. I hoped we wouldn't need it for cover. The bedrooms were off on the other side of the living area—a master and two smaller bedrooms were separated by a bathroom.

With only one entrance into the apartment, we would be trapped. My plan was for the four of us to work in the dining area. If we were attacked, we had to survive the onslaught until reinforcements arrived. The best place for Sophie and me was the kitchen. I planned to station Oso in the bedroom next to the Master. His field of fire would be across the living area and some of the entrance way.

We would move Erin and Marie in with Oso. Sophie and I would use the breakfast bar for cover. Our field of fire would be the dining and living areas, at a ninety-degree angle to Oso's. That way any assault team would get caught in a crossfire. They would have to come at us head on and have someone in an attacking position from their side.

Plus, we'd have surprise on our side.

Everyone got down to work, focused on their individual tasks, and I went square eyed looking at the camera feeds. With nothing to report by lunch time, the afternoon dragged on with little conversation, and most of that was between Sophie and Erin. Marie was in her own world keeping everything running. The day finally ended with Oso going to pick up Tara, who was not pleased with the rearranged apartment. She just shrugged her shoulders and went into the master bedroom. I heard the shower start and it ran for quite a while. As we finished packing up our stuff, McCarrigan came in, and looked around with a frown. "What the hell."

Before he could say anything further, I jumped in, "It's a defensive measure. Nothing broken. I promise we'll put everything back as it was when we leave, and that should be soon.

Mollified, he asked, "How soon will you be finished? Have you got what you need?"

"Pretty much," Sophie responded. It's a matter of processing the data and putting it in sensible order. It will be a complete package, and whoever gets it, will be able to run with it quickly."

McCarrigan ran a hand down his face. "I want Tara in the clear, and safe."

"We all do. You are our clients," I answered. "Have you thought of any State politicians you would trust?"

"Huh? I never completely trust a politician. I have a couple or so in mind who would listen to me in private."

"We'll need them in order to push this to a federal level. Would they do that?"

He laughed out loud. "As I told you, if it would score them points, they would invade hell. So yes, they would run with it."

"Good, you may want to drop them some hints now. See you tomorrow."

He was still chuckling to himself as we left. Marie and Erin went home in a cab called by security, and Sophie and I in my SUV. It looked like another quiet night of take out and apprehension. Sophie was on her laptop when a hissing *yes* left her lips.

"Steven has been outed. The files Fiend put up on the internet have been getting a lot of hits. I mean a whole lot, and from all over the country—I mean from everywhere. Many are centered in DC, the northeast, and here. Oh boy, I would not want to be Steven. His bosses are going to be pissed."

"Which makes him even more dangerous. If he doesn't act soon, it will be too late. How close are you and Erin from completing the whole enterprise?"

"A full day, maybe two. After that, it will be just organizing it."

"If it's too slick, it will look suspicious. Can you make it a bit scruffy around the edges, so whoever gets this, has to do some work?"

"Sure, once we have it sorted out, I can do that."

We kissed and got ready for bed. I was restless. Laying there listening to her even breathing was a meditation, eventually I fell asleep.

Waking before the alarm, I was worried. Something was not right. We foiled the attack on our office, but then there'd been nothing against us at McCarrigan's. Steven or someone had to make a move against us, soon. Before Sophie woke, I started breakfast, pottering about, thinking about how high this went. It had to be way up the chain with what had come down to Kenzo and his investigations.

Once breakfast in the warmer, I heard the shower running. Taking two cups of coffee into the bathroom, I put Sophie's on the side, and sat watching her shower. The sound of the water and seeing her soaping herself was a sensual vision—a great start to the day.

After breakfast and clean up, we left for our temporary office. Marie was following up with the GRU real estate data. Erin said she was finalizing the flow charts and graphic money trails for the principals of GRU, 3DMedia, ITH and the PAC, and anyone associated with them.

Sophie went to work after a brief consultation with Erin, and I sat looking at the boring monitors. As usual, nothing. I wasn't complaining—it was good news, but that ominous feeling wouldn't leave me.

Oso came back after dropping Tara at her office where she planned to be for the day. The morning dragged by, and I organized a delivery lunch. Oso collected that from the security desk. Then after lunch was finished, we chatted about what gaps Erin and Sophie had filled in. There was proof the two congressmen's wives were involved, in up to their expensive necks, using their individual businesses to launder money. It was really coming together.

My idea of going back to work, was back to

watching nothing. Then it wasn't. "Shit."

Everyone looked up.

I growled, "Get moving. Marie, Erin with Oso. We got company."

Moving quickly, Oso herded Marie and Erin into the bedroom, leaving the door ajar as we planned. I heard him rack the shotgun while Sophie and I pulled out our weapons with the spare magazines and hunkered down behind the breakfast bar.

I could still see the monitor over the top of our position. Eight men were making their way up the service elevator, and I was betting they were coming for us.

"Sophie call Kenzo," I said. "Tell him where we are, and the situation. We need a SWAT team ASAP."

"Got it."

I could see her calling from the corner of my eye, as I checked the invaders' progress on their way along the corridor.

I called out, "As soon as you hear the door, go cover your ears and eyes, they will probably use flash bangs to disorient us."

Hoping the SWAT team was on their way, I looked over to Sophie for a sign. "SWAT are on their way. This is real, isn't it?"

"As real as it gets. Breathe. Remember your training. I love you."

The color drained from Sophie's face, and her hands trembled only slightly. I had faith in her ability. Then the next thing I heard was the apartment door splinter. I put my hands over my ears and shut my eyes as tight as I could.

The noise was loud in the confined space. I heard

shouting.

"Get down—stay down—get down—stay down."

The men rushed into the apartment, stopped, surprised to be met by no one. They cleared the two rooms off the corridor, shouting, "Clear. Clear."

That's when I shouted, "Drop your weapons. We have you covered. SWAT is on their way."

Everyone turned, looking in the direction of my voice. The invaders were spread around the room as we'd planned.

Silence. Then a voice from near the entrance corridor spoke. "I don't think you're in a position to give any orders, Mr. Hammett. We outnumber you and outgun you. Surrender your weapon and come out, hands on head. Ms. Chandler, you too."

After seeing them in the elevator, they were all wearing tactical clothing, and only carrying side arms. I'd seen no assault weapons. I hoped they had on body armor. Taking a chance, I looked around the edge of our hiding place and took a shot at the closest man.

Hit center mass, he went down cursing.

Ah yes, thankfully body armor. I didn't want to kill anyone, even in self-defense, unless I had to.

The voice said, "That was not a good idea, Hammett."

"Just a warning, Steven. You've put your men in jeopardy again. If you try to take us, we will respond."

"Come on, Hammett. Do the math. Two against seven—not good odds."

"What makes you think it's only two." That info caught him by surprise. Even if we hadn't called the police, he was running out of time. Smashing in the door and using a flashbang had to have provoked the entire building. Security would be calling the police as well.

I whispered to Sophie, "Go for center mass, just like you were taught. They're wearing body armor."

She nodded in understanding.

"Last chance, Hammett"

"Hey Steven, how did your bosses like your picture all over the internet?"

"That was you? I owe you a 'fuck you' for that as well." He turned to his men. "Take them alive if possible, if not—terminate."

I shouted, "Now."

Sophie reached around her end of the bar as I did at my side, picking our targets. The advancing team had no cover and an obstacle course to maneuver through. They started to shoot at us to cover their advance just as the boom of Oso's shotgun went off. The advance team, taken by surprise, turned in Oso's direction. Two of the attackers had been hit by the shotgun load. Sustaining only minor damage, they were still on their feet. I took a quick look, noting the opportunity to take out the man closest to me. I pulled the trigger and put a quick shot in his ass. He went down.

Boom another shotgun blast went off, adding additional minor damage to another invader.

Sophie and I shot back.

Two men went down with shots to the chest. They staggered and moved toward the entrance corridor. Caught in a crossfire, the attackers knew the better part of valor meant getting the fuck out of the kill zone.

More shots were fired. Windows hit, cracked, but they didn't shatter.

Those left uninjured, took the man I shot in the ass.

His blood stained the rug on the way out. As they retreated, moving out of the apartment under covering fire, one invader turned toward the bedroom and raised his weapon. I shot him in the leg, and he went down. The man in front of him immediately helped him out.

I hoped they'd all be trapped in the service entrance.

The shotgun had put a number of holes in the wall, and I began counting the cost of paying for repairs and redecorating McCarrigan's place. Still, we were unharmed, and I'd call that a win.

"Oso, stay where you are. We'll check if it's secure, okay. Then we'll wait for the police."

The apartment was a mess, but safe. No one left behind, and no dead bodies—although several would be sore, and two or more would need medical attention. We'd been lucky. If they'd been armed with assault weapons, we'd be dead. Steven underestimated us, again. I hoped there wouldn't be a next time.

"Oso, bring out Marie and Erin. Everything's okay."

They came out looking shaken and pale. Marie had taken the shotgun from Oso and put it on the counter beside my weapon. We heard running in the corridor.

"Sophie, put your weapon on the counter and your hands up"

"What? Okay." She put hers next to mine and stood beside me with her hands up.

The men in black entered, commanding us to kneel with our fingers linked behind our heads. We complied. The SWAT officer surveyed the room and asked if anyone needed medical attention. No one did. Kenzo walked in behind another SWAT officer, and we were allowed to stand.

With a hint of a smile, Kenzo said, "Another fine mess you've gotten me into, Mas."

"Trust me, Kenzo, I don't want to be in this sort of mess any more than you do. But I'm in it and will see it finished. By the way, it's bigger than we first thought. Did you get any of the perps?"

"Not yet."

"What do you mean, not yet? There were seven armed men plus the leader. Several were bleeding, in need of medical attention. A few others were very sore."

"Very good, Mas. No dead bodies?"

"We were lucky. Steven ordered us taken or killed. Why haven't you cornered the perps?"

Kenzo said, "Working on containing them. Looks like you were expecting something, the way this place is set up. The crossfire was good thinking. Who had the shotgun?"

Before I could say anything, Marie said, "That was me, and my shoulder is complaining."

Good one Marie. That kept Oso out of trouble. I mouthed a "thank you" to her, and she smiled.

Kenzo continued, "We'll need statements from everyone, and I'm sure you have licenses for all the weapons?"

Sophie spoke up, "Yes, they are all legal, mine is the sub compact. Mas's the full size and the shotgun that Marie used."

Kenzo nodded. "Just covering all the bases. We'll give you receipts for them and after we've tested them, they'll be returned to you. Seems like a case of self-defense. Would you like protective custody?"

"No chance." Sophie and I spoke at the same time.

Kenzo said, "Mas, think about it. Do you even know who these people you've pissed off are?"

"In general terms *yes*, specifically *no*. But we are close to winding this thing up, and it's going to blow up here, Sacramento, and in DC. That much, I can tell you."

Quietly, Kenzo asked, "Do you still need me to hold the packet you left me?"

"Yes. You'll be getting an updated version. If something happens to us, run with it. You will also get assistance from Collen, the journalist. You know her, right?" Kenzo nodded, and I added, "And a professor from Berkeley, Diana Garcia Alvarez."

He looked surprised. We had better clear up here. CSU will be going over everything, there looks to be enough shell casings to keep them busy for a while, don't suppose you recognized anyone or can give descriptions?"

"They were all wearing face coverings, tactical gear, gloves, etc. Unless you can pull prints off the casings there won't be much to go on. They probably arrived in work vans, with coveralls over the tactical gear. Any usable CCTV in the loading dock?

"Someone will be going over it." Kenzo left to do whatever he needed to do.

Oso was quiet, keeping an eye on Erin and Marie. We all made statements. Erin had hidden in the bedroom and had little to offer. Marie backed up my description of the assault team, occasionally rubbing her shoulder to back up her story of using the shotgun. Oso played the 'no *hable* English' card and rambled on in Spanish, much to the annoyance of the detective taking his statement.

We were winding down when McCarrigan rushed in bullying his way past the officer at the door, claiming rightly, it was his place. He saw the carnage and exclaimed, "What the hell happened? Is everyone alright?

Not what I expected. I expected him to be mad about his wrecked home.

"Yeah, we are good, and lucky. The police are going to get Tara and make sure she is okay. Looks like the perps got away. Barely. They were organized and had their escape route well planned."

He looked around. "Did they get what they were after?"

Sophie answered, "No. If they couldn't take us easily, they were going to kill us."

The shock set in, and she started to shake. I was surprised she held it together so well for so long. I went to her and held her, stroking her hair, and telling her how brave she had been.

McCarrigan went over to the drinks cabinet and poured several large doses of bourbon into cut glass tumblers, handing them to each of us. Oso downed his in one and smacked his lips in appreciation, holding his glass out for more, the rest of us sipped the amber liquid. Not a big fan of bourbon, I liked this one. It was smooth, and probably out of my price range. Then I remembered I was going to be a millionaire. I chuckled and everyone looked at me.

"Sorry, just a funny thought. Glad to be alive, and McCarrigan, I'm sorry about your apartment."

McCarrigan looked around and shrugged. "It's about time I redecorated. Besides, I am sure Tara will take that in hand."

We all looked at him in surprise. He smiled and continued, "Well seeing that you are camped out in my home, and almost friends, you can be the second to know I proposed to Tara last night, and she accepted. Mas, I suppose I should thank you for suggesting Tara move in."

Well, shit a brick, that was something I didn't see coming.

We all congratulated him as the police worked around us. Eventually the police units picked up and cleared out, but we were allowed to retain our computers. McCarrigan arranged for a temporary secure door, and we all left him to it.

As we were leaving, Tara arrived looking shaken. "I am so glad you're all okay. Will you be safe?"

I gave her a wink. "We'll be fine. We're sorry about the mess."

Tara gave me a warm smile. "Don't worry. Kevin can afford it. You'll keep us up-dated on your progress."

That told me she was still worried about what had happened to her—an expected, normal reaction.

"Sure, no problem. You'll need to know the resolution so you can move on. Don't be surprised if it's bigger than you imagined."

Chapter Twenty-Four

Putting an end to the conversation, we left, collected my SUV, and started for home. Oso jammed in behind Sophie, Maria sat on him, and Erin sat beside him.

As we drove home, I considered what would make me feel safer. I turned to Oso. "Do you know anyone who could provide us with a couple of weapons on short notice?"

"Si, maybe. What do you need?"

"A shot gun and a couple of nine millimeters. Good ones, not street crap."

"Sure, I know someone who knows someone. Anyone gotta a phone I can use? I'm sitting on mine." That raised a laugh, and it was a good release of tension.

Oso made the call and arranged to have someone meet us at the house in two hours. Marie called in a dinner order for delivery. Erin had been quiet for most of the ride, so when she spoke, we listened. "Will we ever be safe again?"

"Yes. Once we have this investigation completed, and all the dirt is out there, visible to the public, we'll be safe." Sophie sighed. "It's the only way. Turn the light on and expose them for what they are."

She was right. We kept to our own thoughts until we arrived at our house, then Sophie showed Erin the spare bedroom and told her she could stay for the duration. Sophie parked herself in the dining room and made room for Erin who plugged in and started to work. I checked the house and found nothing suspicious.

Dinner arrived, and we sat around the dining table and ate like normal people. The food filled a hole. Normality. It was needed. Intermittent conversation focused on the tasks at hand. Oso agreed he'd continue escorting Ms. Tara, and he would leave when his weapons contact completed his visit.

As promised, the arms man arrived on time with a long bag and a suitcase. We went into the spare bedroom, where he laid out his wares on the bed. He was silent and let me do the looking. First thing I inspected were the shotguns. Two Remington's and a Mossberg. All three had seen use, probably a lot. But they were clean and looked after. The Mossberg felt like the better quality of the three. Putting it to one side, I started inspecting the pistols.

Eight semi-automatics and one compact, a Beretta. I picked it for Sophie, due to its size. It was bigger than the CZ subcompact she was used to, but better than any full size. It looked clean, I disassembled the slide and barrel. There were no signs of excessive wear. It had a smooth action, and a decent trigger pull. Still, with its serial numbers intact, I could track its history if I wanted to.

Next for me, I rejected the two Glock's. I'd tried a Glock before and didn't like the hand grip. The two S&Ws were too worn and beat up. They felt like they'd been around the streets too long—clean but tired—and the serial numbers had been removed. That left two

Berettas, an H&K, and a CZ. Didn't like the feel of the trigger on the H&K. That was out. One Beretta felt off, not smooth, but the other was in contention. That left the CZ75, it felt good in my hand, clean and smooth. Settled. Now to negotiate the price, I figured that was going to take longer than it took to make my choices.

Francisco was a shrewd man. I didn't know what Oso had told him, but he wanted the business. The three weapons would make his day for sure and being illegal would not come cheap.

The cost didn't worry me. Steven and his crew did, and they were still out there. In order to evade the police who'd converged on the building, their escape route had been well-planned.

Back to business. Haggling, back and forward, offer and counteroffer. Oso quietly watched us in silence. Finally, we agreed on a price. Counting my emergency fund cash from my hand into his, Francisco smiled as the pile grew. It was a lot more than it would have been if we'd bought them new from a dealer. We didn't have the luxury of time, nor could we afford to wait around unarmed. This would have to do. As a former inspector, I never imagined I'd be doing an illegal gun purchase. Still, it was better to be prepared, illegal and alive, than legal and dead.

Oso bummed a ride from Francisco and left with a promise to look after Ms. Tara. Next? How to sort out what we were going to do to complete this investigation. Who and when? We already knew where.

Marie called Chung, explained she was all right, and told him to pack some clothes, she was going to be staying with us for a few days. Erin chimed in asking if Chung would pick up some things for her, too, if she could arrange it with her apartment share. Chung, of course, said he would. Once all calls and arrangements were made, we waited.

Chung arrived with bags in hand and dropped them to properly hug Marie. Taking me aside, he asked, "Mas, you promise to take care of her, right?"

"On my word. We are hoping this will be over very soon."

"Okay, I'll hold you to your promise."

"We need her as much as you do," I said it with a smile I didn't feel inside.

It had all started with McCarrigan's call—one I hadn't wanted to take. I should have listened to my gut. *Too, late now.* Chung left, and we all attended to tasks.

Sophie and Erin went back to reviewing and collating the data. Sophie sent an e-mail to Fiend for updates. Marie took care of the house and made up the beds before getting back to her real estate tasks. Me, I took the weapons apart and gave them a thorough cleaning, pleased with my choices. All three were good, serviceable weapons that I hoped we wouldn't need.

I left Sophie's beside her computer, loaded and within reach. Lacking a proper holster, I tucked mine into the back waistband of my jeans, not an ideal spot, but it was on my person. The shotgun? I carried it with me at all times.

Alone with my thoughts, the congressmen were at the top of the pile, perhaps isolated from some of the illegalities, but not totally divorced from them. The wives? They were deeply involved.

Risking annoying Sophie, I asked her how much digging she did on the congressmen's wives?

"What?"

I repeated the question.

"Not finished yet, why?" she asked.

"The congressmen are too slippery and insulated, we need to get at the wives to prove the corrupt connection. Both the wives' businesses are cash heavy. Would you investigate the transactions and sales? You said they are laundering money through them, skimming, and stashing the money in the offshore jointly held accounts. There has to be something off with those businesses. What do you think?"

"I think you're smart, and I'll get on it. Erin is loading everything we have into her template and making it understandable to anyone. Now leave me alone."

"Gladly, dear."

She blew me a kiss.

My next task was to call McCarrigan, and he answered on the first ring. "Anything new?"

"Not really. The police are still chasing the perps, but that isn't why I called."

"You need something." It was a statement not a question.

"Yes, your knowledge and a telephone call."

"What do you need?"

"I nced a call placed to the SEC to block or delay the sale of 3DMedia. Can you make an anonymous call with enough info to make the SEC at least check into the merger, takeover, or whatever you call it?"

"That's it? This I can do. It's a piece of cake. First thing tomorrow, I'll call the east coast. Since they're three hours ahead, they can relay the info to the SF office. It'll be waiting for them."

"It has to be anonymous. Got that right?"

"Trust me, Mas. You do your thing, and I can take care of this."

Done and done. I still had a feeling we were missing something. We were protected, at least physically for now. The girls were finishing up their end of the business. McCarrigan would do his thing tomorrow. Which left me with nothing to do except think.

Not a good prospect.

Eventually we all crashed. First, Marie and Erin. Erin in the spare room, and Marie curled up on the couch. Sophie kept plugging away at her computer, frustrated at having only one monitor to work with. Bleary eyed, I checked all the doors and windows, then I crashed before she did. I fell asleep, fully clothed, on top of the covers.

Something disturbed my sleeping mind. I jumped off the bed, wide awake. Everything was quiet. Then I heard the sounds coming from the kitchen—normal sounds of people starting a new day. The fragrance of coffee began to drift through the house. Slowly, I moved through the house. I looked into the spare bedroom. Erin was still out, her red hair spread all over the pillow. It looked like the pillow was on fire. Sophie was slumped over her computer and still out. Marie saw me coming and put her finger to her lips.

Quietly she said, "Coffee is on, and breakfast will be delivered in about ten to fifteen minutes."

"What time is it?"

"Seven-ish, I tried to be quiet, but with the lay out of your place, it's hard to be really quiet."

"Don't worry about it, and thanks for making the coffee."

"Huh, what makes you think it's for you? I drink coffee, too."

"Well, thank you anyway."

"Do we wake them or leave them?"

"Leave them for a while, they both need the rest. It looks like Sophie tried another all-nighter. I hope it was worth it."

With the coffee ready, Marie and I took our cups out on the back deck, sitting quietly and embracing the early morning sunshine. When there is no marine layer, it makes you thankful to be alive in San Francisco.

Breakfast arrived as we were finishing our coffee. Marie and I took ours back out on the deck with our coffee mugs refilled. The feeling that we'd be finishing our part of whatever this was, made me more relaxed. I wasn't sure why, but it felt right, and I was confident.

Erin came out on the deck with a mug of coffee. She looked tired and disheveled, and she'd wrapped herself in one of my robes. She looked good in it. Her nipples hard and pointing through the silk, one leg parting the opening, and going seemingly on forever. *Shit, Mas pull yourself together this is business.* Back to reality with a bump.

Sophie opened the door and spit out, "What the fuck, why didn't you wake me. I need coffee, and then we have a lot to go over. Mas you hit it. The wives are the 'in' we needed. Let's move people."

Sophie emphatically shut the door. Marie and Erin looked at me.

I shrugged and said, "Can't help it, I love her. You two get on with your day, I'll get coffee for the slave driver."

They both laughed, and we all went back into the

house. Sophie was in the shower. I left her coffee on the side. I checked my e-mail…nothing of note. A text came in. Oso had picked up "Ms. Tara" and all was fine. McCarrigan called, and I asked. "Hi, how did it go?"

"Piece of cake. From the attitude and things left unsaid, I think the SEC was already looking into the deal. At least, that was the impression I got. My call added fuel to the fire and gave them details only someone close to the deal would know."

"What details?"

"Nothing that could lead back to you or Tara. Enough details about the origin source of the funds, and the dubious nature of the bank it was coming through."

"Fair enough. Thanks for getting it done."

"Hey, it's to my benefit as well."

Guess a leopard doesn't change its spots. He was looking out for Tara and by extension himself. Sophie was done with her shower and waiting for me to finish my call. She had eaten quickly and inhaled at least two coffees.

She started her briefing. "We have everything we need, and we are building it into a good case of domestic corruption, and foreigners messing with us domestically. Last night was a long one."

We sat silently waiting for Sophie to continue. "The two wives' business dealings are integral to all of this. Amanda Rivers runs two art galleries and sells paintings by medium to upper-level artists for good money, and some by artists who don't exist. At least, none that I could find. A fake sale puts the money through their books, and it comes out clean. Mas, I would like you to look into the invisible artists anyway."

I nodded.

"Next is Deborah Prescott-Pollard, a design consultant, and she can charge whatever she wants, especially if the clients don't exist. She has some kosher clients, but nowhere near the number that would generate her cash flow. Fake client consultant fees processed through her business comes in and clean money goes out.

"We obtained a lot of data, and the result is that we got foreign money meddling in our government, a PAC funded by a foreign money with funds laundered via the realty company, the holding company, and the two wives' businesses. Congressmen and families being supported by illegal funds and fraud, and personally doing money laundering themselves. Not discounting the offshore accounts—this is more than enough to cause a shit storm, even in DC."

Sophie stopped and looked at us. When she explained it all like that, no wonder someone wanted Clegg's information. And he hadn't gotten as far as we had, just enough to get himself killed. Well, if we pulled this off, it would be a good ending for what Clegg had started.

All this made me wonder how many other politicians were dirty. Probably quite a few, and dirtier. They just hadn't been caught, yet.

Sophie wound up with our tasks and asked me, "Do you think it would be safe to go back to the office? It's just easier to process this data on three screens. If we stick at it, we can probably pull all this together, including the new info, really fast."

"Don't know, let me check the cameras and see if

they've picked up anything suspicious. With what's happened, I am not sure anywhere is completely safe. We've been incredibly lucky, and we can't bank on staying lucky forever. Let me think about it."

"Please, Mas. If there's anyway, we would finish faster."

"Okay, I'll figure something out."

"You're the best. I love you." She kissed me, long and deep.

"Go play with your computer."

Having said I would figure something out, now I had to come through. More coffee was needed. I sat thinking. The office was not the greatest position to defend, but if a sufficient deterrent were in place, maybe it could work. Calling Kenzo, I put an ask to him. He said he'd think about it. Next, I made a call to Big Boots. He was amenable to my request, and said he'd get back to me.

Chapter Twenty-Five

Now to wait for the return calls and hope they were what I needed. Meanwhile, I called Mack, the handy man, and arranged for him meet me at the office to remove the door covering. It would be nice and more comfortable to return to our own space.

Sophie and Erin were neck deep in data, so I told Marie to take care of them and the house, until I returned. "Hopefully, we're moving back into our office."

"Don't worry, mother hen, I will cover everything here. Take your time."

I had faith in Marie, but I was also concerned that Steven was still out there, and we had to move fast, giving him few or no chances to get at us. Moving again would throw him. If he were planning anything at the house, he would now have to regroup. That would take time. However little time, it was still time, and his bosses wouldn't tolerate many more failures, if any.

Mack was waiting for me and quickly removed the covering off the office door. It was a strange feeling entering the office again. Everything looked as it should, with no signs of anyone being there since we left. We'd left little things as tells, and nothing had been moved. Marie answered on the first ring, when I called. No stress code, so all was right.

"Everything here is good. Let Sophie and Erin

know we will probably be moving back here later today."

"Got it, Mas. I think Sophie's buddy has come through with some more information. Sophie and Erin have been talking up a storm and seem really excited about how it's all coming together."

"Good, I won't be happy until we can hand all this off to the local and Federal authorities."

"Mas, I have never heard you talk like this before."

"Never had anything like this before. Wrong call at the wrong time. Now we have to finish our part and move on. I'll see you later. Thanks for being there."

"Be careful, Mas."

"I always am."

"Bullshit." And she hung up on me. Probably shouldn't have said what I did. It slipped out, and showed I was worried about the final outcome. If we could make it until we had the complete package delivered to the appropriate desks, we should be alright. It was a big if.

My phone went off. Big Boots getting back to me.

"Mas, you're on. I have enough folks signing on to cover you for the next three days around the clock. Will that do?"

"Yes, that'll be perfect. Please pass my thanks along to them. Let me know what I'll owe in paid hours."

He laughed. "Don't worry about payment right now. We'll settle up when you get a chance. No rush. We know where you live and work." He paused for effect. "And more importantly, where you play."

That was a big relief. I felt my anxiety level drop from panic to just below, *oh shit*. My phone went off.

Not a number I recognized, but I hoped it was about what I arranged with Big Boots. It was.

"Mas?"

"Yes."

"Just got off the phone with BB, he said I should call you and let you know we are about five minutes out from your house. Let them know there will be two of us watching."

"Perfect. I will let them know and thanks." Click the line went dead.

I called Marie telling her, "There are two off duty police officers on their way to watch the house until we can move into the office. You may not see them—just know they're there."

"Mas, no problem. You sound more relaxed than before. I was starting to worry."

"Probably because I was. We have reinforcements and more protection. See you soon." As I hung up, my phone went off again—another number I didn't recognize.

"Mas Hammett?"

"Yes."

"We are covering the entrance to your office building. Big B said you needed your back watched for a couple o' three days. No problem. Nothing suspicious so far. Use this number if you are going anywhere, we'll follow you, and leave someone here to cover."

"Thank you. It's appreciated."

"Part time jobs are always welcome, especially for former officers who pay cash."

I laughed. "My pleasure. Cash is not a problem, if you're worth it."

He laughed and hung up. Big Boots had come

through. Now I felt we could pull this off. Calling back the last number, I said I was going out, giving them a timeline, where I was parked, and the address where I was headed. All I got in response was, "Copy that."

Good enough. I locked up the office and returned home. I saw one of the watchers, not the other. I surmised he was around the back. Calling out to Marie as I approached the door, she opened it and quickly shut it behind me. Sophie and Erin were silently concentrating on the screens in front of them. I needed to disturb them.

"Sophie, Erin, we are on the move, again. Back to the office. We have extra security. Pack up. We need to do it now."

Sophie looked up first, asking, "What move, where?"

"We are going back to the office."

"I thought you said it wasn't secure?"

"We have a security upgrade."

"Mas, you came through. Give me a minute to save this, and we can go." She turned to Erin. "Everything okay, with you?"

"Yes, just need to save this, and I'm ready."

Marie packed everything else we needed—clothes, snacks, and the shot gun. I collected the ammunition for both the shot gun and our pistols, then we were ready to go in fifteen minutes. All of us climbed into my SUV, and we headed back to the office. Tailed by the watchers from the house, and the ones who had followed me from the office, I felt secure.

Nothing seemed suspicious at the office, so I opened up and checked it out. The women piled in after me, and instantly the energy level went up. Being back in familiar surroundings seemed to ease the tension, tension that had been palpable since we'd left for McCarrigan's apartment.

Sophie and Erin plugged in and began checking that everything was up and running as it should be. Marie organized a food delivery and called Chung to let him know where we were, and then Erin's apartment share, keeping her in the loop.

With everyone else busy with their tasks, I sat and thought about where we could go with this. Kenzo was the first stop. Him, I trusted, and he would be able to get the information to the correct folks in the San Francisco Police department. We needed to spread the goods, to make sure nothing got swept under any rugs. Colleen, the journalist would be the next to get the information, with at least enough to whet her curiosity and get her on the trail toward uncovering the rest— plus anything else we would feed her. The FBI, the DoJ, and the IRS would also get a packet.

Dinner arrived, and I gave a good tip to the delivery man who looked a little shaken, probably for being scrutinized by some heavy looking men at the entrance. We sat as a team and brought each other up to date on our specific tasks. Sophie had the most to offer as she was packaging everything.

"We got them all. Erin has processed all the financials, money laundering, tax evasion, campaign fund irregularities, and that's just the congressmen. Their wives are also in deep—money laundering, tax evasion, and fraud. The realty company is in for money laundering, and campaign irregularities. The PAC for campaign fund irregularities, and the management will be in for an uncomfortable time. The Holding company as well if the principals can be identified. Not our problem."

Erin chimed in, "Sophie is brilliant! I just stitched together the financials, statements, and the other documents she supplied, in addition to the material Robert had discovered." Her voice broke as she mentioned Robert Clegg. "Marie came up with a lot of GRU real estate material which I linked to the money laundering and campaign funding. People can be very clever and very careful, but they always leave a trail, however faint. Some of these were almost invisible, but not quite."

Sophie jumped back in, "Fiend helped out big time with some of the info on the wives, and by checking into the Maltese bank, although not much there. As I said, it's too difficult to break into bank systems, unless you have a lot of time and people power, and even then, it's usually an 'ooops' by an employee. Anyway, we can lay it all out, backed up by proof or where to get it."

I had to ask, "Yeah, but how did you get your proof-evidence? Will it hold up in court?"

Sophie answered that quickly, "Mas, stop thinking like a policeman. That is not our problem. What we have provided is a starting point. We lay it all out, give it to the right people, and they use grand juries, subpoenas, and the full weight of the law, the DOJ, the IRS, and whoever else wants in on this one. When you build a house of cards, you only need one to fall, and the rest go down."

"You make it sound so easy."

"It's not. I guarantee this one will get messy before it gets settled. I'm good as long as we are out of it."

Erin said, "I've been thinking, if the IRS get

involved, we could even get a reward, a percentage of the funds recovered that should have gone to the government."

Quietly, I thought, *screw the money*, I wanted us out of jeopardy. Although…if a reward came our way, I wasn't going to turn it down. "Let's not count our chickens, until we're sure we are safe."

That was a downer, and it showed on their faces. "Hey, we…meaning you, have a lot to do and do it right. Then we can celebrate, and we will."

"Mas is right, we have a lot to do," Sophie said. "I figure we'll be done with our part by end of day tomorrow at the latest. Then what we do with it is up to you Mas. That's your area."

"I've been thinking about that, and I have some ideas. Get me the final files on thumb drives. If you can slice and dice the info, I will be spreading the wealth. Give everything criminal to Kenzo, and SFPD, then give enough to get our local journalist interested, and some CA politicians. The whole thing goes to the FBI, DoJ, and the IRS."

Marie said, "Mas, I hope you know what you're doing?"

I laughed. "So do I."

With that, Sophie and Erin went back to computing stuff, Marie and I tidied up, and prepared the rough sleeping arrangements. I planned on staying awake as long as possible. Even with the watcher's, I wasn't going to take chances. My last call of the day was to McCarrigan.

"Hi Mas, and you need?" Even with that opening there was a lightness in his voice.

"Hi to you, too. How quickly can you get in touch

with your political friends?"

"Some quickly, others when it suits them."

"Are they reliable?"

"Christ, Mas, they're politicians, of course they aren't reliable. If it benefits them, you know they'll move mountains. Will this benefit them?"

"Probably, especially if they know there'll probably be two CA seats available in DC."

"Shit, is it really that big?"

"Yes, this is just between us for now, but we'll get interesting info to you soon, probably tomorrow, maybe late."

"Who I send it to depends on what the info is, and no promises that anything will happen."

"Oh, something will happen, I guarantee it." I hung up with a smile. Now the boring stuff. I would try to stay awake as long as possible. The office door was locked, and a chair put under the handle. Marie and I moved her desk directly in front of door, so if someone did get in, they still had an obstacle to get around. Not much, but better than nothing when seconds can mean surviving.

Marie finished what she was doing and then curled up on the sofa, going out like a light. Sophie and Erin were doing their thing. I watched Sophie for a while. I couldn't get over how good it felt to be with her. She definitely had been worth the wait.

Erin was next to drop, "I am almost done and want to be fresh to finish it off with no mistakes."

As she rolled out a sleeping bag on the floor, I said, "Good idea."

She crawled inside and as she turned away from me, asked, "This is going to get the ones who killed

Robert, isn't it?

"The ones who allowed it to happen? Yes. Two are already dead, the others who were there, probably not. The ones who actually ordered the action, top of the chain, probably."

"Thank you." She rolled away from me, and I could see her shoulders move, she was crying.

I hoped I was right, and those responsible for this shitstorm would pay, one way or another.

The office was quiet. The only sounds were the sound of Sophie's fingers tapping away on her keyboard. The sound was slightly hypnotic. I had to distract myself. I used my phone to track news items. Nothing exciting—the usual bad news and more bad news. Why couldn't the media put out at least one happy story every day? There had to be good stuff happening somewhere.

Waking with a start, my phone was going off like a siren. Shit, I had fallen asleep. Groggy, I tried to focus as I answered. Whatever time of night it was, it wasn't going to be good news. I was right, it was Kenzo.

"Mas, are you guys alright?"

"Yes-why?"

"We just found more bodies on the bridge. Same exact place as the first two." That brought me up short.

"How many, and do you know who?"

"Two Caucasians, naked and not castrated this time, just badly mutilated, no teeth, or fingertips, and faces bashed in. It will be DNA or nothing."

"Anything else?"

"One had a leg wound, looks like he bled out. The other had no visible injuries, just dead."

"Check his ass." I said, "I shot two at

McCarrigan's place, one in the leg, the other in the ass."

"Nada on the second body. Like I said nothing to indicate manner of death."

"Then it may be Steven. He failed with Robert Clegg, and twice with us. Three and done?"

"Maybe. Any way you would recognize him?"

"No, not really. The only time I saw his face was in the vehicle rental photo. You said the faces were bashed in."

"Yes, beaten beyond recognition."

"Kenzo, you will soon be receiving a flash drive. You will need to make copies and decide where to disperse them. It's criminally and politically explosive."

"Same as before?"

"Yeah, and a lot more. You will need to figure out who you trust."

"Fuck, Mas. Why do you do this to me?"

"Because we love and trust you. Besides, you didn't do too badly in the last crisis."

"True, but I'm not sure my blood pressure can cope with much more of you guys."

"This thing is going to come into the open real soon."

"Okay, let me know what you need doing and when. I'll see if I can assist."

"All we can ask, but it will tie up some loose ends for you, body wise."

He hung up without saying anything else. Marie stirred, rolling over without waking. Erin was in a deep sleep. I was surprised that Sophie hadn't woken up. I'm not a quiet person. Looking over I saw she had crashed at her desk. I took a cushion from one of the chairs and slid it carefully under her head. No point in me trying to sleep after that conversation, I looked at the clock. 6:07 a.m., too early for anything.

Quietly as I could, I started the coffee. The sun was coming up. It was going to be another perfect San Francisco day. Leaving the office, I locked up behind me and went to find the watchers. They were alert as soon as they heard my footsteps on the tile floor. Nodding at me in acknowledgement. I asked, "Would you like coffee."

They both said yes. One came with me the other stayed at his post.

Making my way to Liguria bakery, which opened to the public at seven, I went around the back, knocking on the back door.

One of the workers answered and asked, "What you need, Mas.

"Some good focaccias."

He laughed and got out his order pad.

Rattling off my order I said, "One each of mushroom, black olive, rosemary and garlic, and Jalapeno and cheese."

"You feeding an army today?"

"No, just a few friends."

He disappeared, returned with four wrapped packages saying, "Settle up later, gotta get going. Chao, Mas."

Around the corner, I picked up three coffees and made my way back to the office. The watcher assisted by carrying the coffees. We sat on the bench near the entrance, each took a coffee. One added sugar, the other took it straight black, I had fixed mine with cream and sugar at the cafe.

We sat in silence for a minute. I had to ask, "Anything unusual?

Both answered *nothing* at once. I didn't know either of them, but the taller continued, "Best money for doing nothing I ever got. Cheers." He raised his coffee cup.

I responded likewise. "Come on up and get something to eat."

The same man answered, "Thanks for the coffee. We'll come up after our relief gets here, alright?"

"Yup, that's fine. Just make sure you announce yourselves." They smiled and said they would announce themselves loudly.

Knocking on the door loud enough to wake the dead, I put my key in the lock and the door swung open.

"Where the hell have you been?" Sophie exploded on me.

Holding up the breakfast packages, I smiled and said, "You were all out cold, and I didn't want to wake you. I love you, too." Then kissed her on each cheek.

"I was worried about you. Mas, you can't just disappear like that without telling anyone, not now."

"Okay, just don't holler at me when I wake you."

She smiled coyly. "Thanks for putting a cushion under my head."

"My pleasure." Marie and Erin were also awake. They were all appreciating the coffee and began tucking into the spread of focaccia. Mumbled thanks, and a chorus of "this is amazing" were the only words I heard until we were all sated.

The watchers announced themselves loudly, saying the relief crew had arrived. I invited them to partake of the remains of the four focaccias, and they thanked me.

Sophie was back at her computer when I went to her. "What time did you crash?"

"Not sure. Late. It was worth it. I should have everything completed by lunch time or afternoon at the latest. Then I'll parse it out like you asked, and mark who gets what on each flash drive."

"Thanks. When this is all over, we all take a vacation. I don't like you doing so many hours and then crashing. It's not good, health wise."

"Thanks for caring, Mas. I love you. That's why I hollered at you earlier."

"I know. I forgive you. You needed the sleep."

"Well then, leave me alone, and I'll finish sooner."

"Done."

Marie was doing whatever office managers do, and Erin just sat staring at the floor. She was tired—a mixture of grief, stress, and the long hours had taken its toll.

Sitting down next to her, I said, "This will be all wrapped up soon. What are you going to do then? Finish your PhD?"

"What? Sorry, I was miles away. I don't know. Haven't thought about it to be honest. Robert was more than a mentor. He was a friend. We clicked. Although we never played together, we were close, and we were always there for each other. He showed me how to embrace my kink side. Until I met him, I always thought there was something wrong with me. He made me realize it was just a facet of me, not the whole me. Something that made me, me. He was a strange man, but kind. Have they told you about his idiosyncratic habits, like his coffee mug?"

"Yes, we heard about that and others as well."

She laughed. "Unless you knew him, you have no idea. He only wore lace up shoes, which he cleaned after every time he wore them. Only white shirts when he was working, and never white when he wasn't. He was harmless, very smart, interesting, and eccentric. I will miss him. She started to cry. I held her, knowing how she felt. I still missed Simon. Sometimes life sucks, but the living continue living and make the best of it. This was becoming maudlin. I needed to concentrate on the current problem.

I had to call Colleen. I promised her a heads-up scoop. It never hurt to cultivate a good journalist. Still too early to call her directly, I called her office number and left a cryptic message, knowing I would get a call as soon as she got the message. Chuckling to myself and betting Colleen would be bugging me for a meeting today. A meeting I would be happy to take, after Sophie had finished her part.

The day progressed. Erin assisted Sophie as needed. Nothing happened. It was quiet, too quiet. Even if one of the bodies on the bridge was Steven, it didn't mean there weren't others interested in us, and these others, we didn't know at all.

The morning dragged on, then the watchers reported in on a suspicious van driving around. My heart rate went up. The van looked like a surveillance vehicle, which it was. It turned out to be Kenzo, who was also keeping an eye on us. My heart rate dropped, thankful for the official back up.

Colleen called just before lunch. "Mas, I just picked up your message. Can we meet?"

"Starting hours are nice." Knowing that would push her buttons.

"Fuck you, Mas. I didn't get in until very late...and no I wasn't partying. You have something for me, right?"

"Right."

"Well, when can we meet?"

"Later today, and this will be hot off the press. You are getting an upfront look, as promised. The same place as before, same process. When you have reviewed it, we can talk. Have you looked at the stuff I left with you before?"

"No, damn it. I gave you my word, so I haven't. I've been tempted. It's burning a hole in my safe. Is this connected?"

"Yes, but that's nothing compared to what you will get today. You won't regret your patience, promise."

"I trust you, Mas. If I didn't, we wouldn't be talking."

"Colleen, that is a two-way street."

"Agreed. Looking forward to seeing you."

"I know you are." Second string in place. Lunch was a delivery.

"Done!" Sophie exclaimed, "We are as done as can be, without over complicating it. Fiend had some last-minute data on the wives' businesses and the offshore bank accounts. We merged it with all the other data. I am no lawyer, but I'd say they are all in deep shit.

"I assume that is a legal term. You've already split it up?" I said, "Damn you guys are good."

Testily, she responded, "Of course. Erin did that as I handed stuff off to her. I kept the master for Fiend, just in case. Kenzo gets the criminal stuff here in SF and the RICO stuff to pass on to whomever he wants. We, that means you, will be sending one to the SF FBI office, for fraud with the spouses' businesses in CA and the money laundering aspect with GRU and ITH. Next one to the FBI DC office for the same as well as the contributions to the PAC, fraud by the wives in DC. Finally, we bring in the IRS for tax evasion and the offshore accounts, and the DoJ for the congressmen. The professor gets most of the file and campaign stuff. Think that's it.

"Great, and good thinking on Fiend."

"I know," Sophie said.

Erin asked, "Are you two always like this?"

Before we could say anything, Marie answered, "Yes, they are, and often worse."

Sophie and I looked at each other, smiled, and blew each other a kiss. I picked up all the thumb drives noting which was which and loaded them into padded envelopes. I included our business cards and a note in each one. We were sure all the "theys" would want to talk to us about a lot of things, especially regarding where we "obtained" the information. Those would be difficult conversations for another time.

This time, I had no problem going directly to Kenzo at his office. I still had mixed feelings about going into police headquarters. Kenzo sent an assistant down to bring me to his office. She was silent and efficient, leaving me at Kenzo's door. He waved me in and said with a smile. "Good to see you, Mas. What am I about to get into?"

"Nice greeting. Here is your portion of the shit pile, we have split it up, so you can concentrate on the dead bodies and other criminal activities in SF, you will probably be tripping over the Feds, too. They get their part this afternoon. Know anyone I should contact?"

"What aspect are you dumping on them?"

"Money laundering and foreign interference in political campaigns for starters."

"Most of the guys I know are more aligned with what we do here. There's one person. She can be difficult, but a bulldog once she gets into something. I'll call ahead."

"No, no thanks, just give me the name, I'll drop it off. If she wants to meet later, fine."

"Okay. Patricia Cozzi. It's pronounced, 'Cot-zi'. Don't say I didn't warn you." He laughed and opened the envelope.

I left him to his review. My next call was Colleen. She answered on the first ring.

"Hi, Mas. I was getting worried."

"Had some deliveries to make. Still on for a meet?"

"Is the Pope Catholic. Ready when you are."

"Fair enough. Meet you in about an hour, same place as last time. Grab a coffee if I'm late."

"Got it. See ya."

She hung up. I could get to the FBI building and still be on time to meet her, but it would be tight with traffic. Still San Francisco is better than LA for any number of reasons. My prejudice was showing.

The trip to the FBI building was as bad as I expected. Taking a chance, I parked illegally. Writing Patricia's name on the envelope while at a red light. I ran it in to the reception area, handing it off to an officer rather than going through the metal detectors and waiting in line. He looked at the name and address, he nodded and put the envelope through the x-ray machine. If we didn't hear from Patricia in a couple of days, we would mail her a signature required copy.

Colleen walked into the Westfield Mall as I arrived. Timing couldn't have been better. We walked to the elevators, positioned ourselves at the back, and rode up two floors, waiting for people to exit. Dropping the envelope into her open bag, I got off at the next floor. She stayed.

The drive back to the office was slow. Our team's plan was in play, and we'd done all we could. The waiting would be a pain, but I didn't think it would be a long wait.

Marie had taken charge of the thumb drives to be mailed to the DC FBI office, the IRS, and DoJ all with proof of delivery. Fiend had supplied names to direct the delivery of the envelopes. How he got the names, I didn't want to know. As I walked into the office, my phone went off. Colleen.

"Hi, what's up?"

"Are you kidding me? This is explosive…if it's true."

"Putting you on speaker. It's all true, and we haven't given you everything. You are going to have to chase this one all the way to DC. Kept my promise. You are the only journalist we've contacted. Don't wait, the national vultures will soon be picking at this carcass when they find it."

"Thanks, Mas. I owe you one, and I pay my debts."

Minutes later, Kenzo called, "We must be popular, just got off a call from a journalist."

"I wonder how they got on it so quickly."

"Mas, don't be an asshole. I know you've spread the wealth on this one, to protect yourselves. Just calling to say you really stirred up a hornet's nest. This has already gone up the chain, and something will be done about the killings, including Mr. Clegg. Thanks to you on that one, it's too big to hide. I'll keep you informed as I can."

"No problem, we appreciate it."

Sophie asked, "Have you called McCarrigan yet?"

"Shit, with all the running around I'd forgotten that piece. I'll do it now."

His admin picked up and put me through without asking any questions.

"It's safe to talk."

"Just give your politicians a heads up. They will probably be happy about the info you give them, and the two seats coming vacant. Finally, who would you use for legal representation in our situation?"

"My first choice of attorney would be Spencer Brooks. I'll drop the right words in the right ears. Thanks, Mas."

"Sounds expensive."

"Yes, he is, and worth every cent. I'll call and warn him to expect your contact. Here's his number. When the dust settles, we need to celebrate."

"Yeah, all this shit started with a phone call I didn't want to take in the first place. You're picking up the tab for this celebration."

"Happy to do it."

Looking over to Sophie and Erin, they looked serious. I asked, "What."

They both broke out into smiles, and Marie, came in with a bottle of champagne and four glasses already poured.

Sophie lifted her glass and said, "To us."

We all chorused, "To us."

Erin asked, "What's next."

"We wait," I answered, "and we'll be pulled in for questioning by the SFPD, the FBI, the IRS, and any number of departments with lots of initials. We are getting legal representation, and that includes you, Erin. McCarrigan recommended him. We haven't done too much that's in fact illegal that they can actually pin on us. I am sure most will be overlooked. The results are too good to fuck up."

Sophie chimed in. "Until all this becomes public, it would be a good idea to keep our heads down and stay vigilant."

With the information being spread around, we felt it would be safe to return to our house, and we'd take Erin with us. Marie went home to Chung.

Chapter Twenty-Six

When I surfaced, there were several texts on my phone. I smiled to myself, sure that Sophie's phone would be in the same condition. Well, we asked for it, now we had it. As I put on the coffee, I hollered for Sophie to look at her phone.

I heard a loud groan, and then… "What have we done?"

The information was released and out of our hands. We should be safe if the authorities didn't fuck it up.

The coffee was ready, as Erin walked into the kitchen. "What's all the fuss was about?"

"Check your phone."

She did and sighed.

The first text on my phone was from Patricia Cozzi of the FBI, requesting that my associates and I come in for an interview that day.

I wasn't playing that game. Texting back, I offered, "Today isn't convenient, perhaps tomorrow?" That should get her attention.

I left a message for Spencer Brooks, who I hoped would be representing us, and hoped he was as good as McCarrigan claimed.

Inhaling the fragrance of breakfast cooking, I saw Sophie and Erin working together, and I was distracted by the sight of Sophie in a long T-shirt, her tits free and pointed, jiggling as she moved. Erin was similarly dressed—if you can call it that—with the addition of semi-sheer pants, her full tits moving easily under her tight T-shirt. This was an enjoyable visual, which of course, went straight to my groin and filled my cage.

Now it was my turn to groan. They were both unaware of the effect they were having on me. I left to get dressed and hoped the effect would wear off. Physically, I can wear the chastity cage for long periods. It's the mental frustration that gets to me. Which is exactly the point.

Sophie called out, "Breakfast's ready."

As we ate, I had a thought and said, "How about we take a day off and go to the beach?"

Sophie said, "Great idea, can we go to Half Moon Bay?"

"Wouldn't you rather go to San Gregorio?"

Sophie looked at Erin and asked, "How do you feel about clothing optional beaches?"

"I've never done it."

"First time for everything. Let's get going." Sophie sprang into action, getting the necessities for our day trip. I called Marie to see if she wanted to go with us. She did, so I told her we'd pick her up.

Sophie was ready to go in no time. We piled into my SUV and picked up Marie. This early, we made good time crossing the city and headed down Route 1.

The beach was almost deserted, just one dog walker, and she left soon after we arrived. Making our way to the south end, we found some small wind breaks built from driftwood. This was going to be torture for me, and it was my idea. *Dumbass*.

Sophie was the first to strip down nude, completely open and self-assured. I laid out the towels. Marie, who had been dressing more provocatively since putting her Chung in a chastity cage, went topless. This was the first time I had seen her without clothes. She looked good—darker skinned than Sophie—aureoles were darker still, standing out against the surrounding skin. Wow, she had a great body, no wonder she had started showing it off.

Erin was more circumspect in undressing, facing away from me until she was also nude. Sophie turned her, so she could put sunscreen on Erin's back. That caught Erin by surprise. Too late to cover up, she dropped her arms to her sides. Letting Sophie apply a generous amount of sunscreen. Damn she was tall, and she had a great figure. Her tits were in proportion for her height, and she was the opposite of Marie, pale skin almost translucent, a shaved pussy, and those legs. This was not as erotic as I had expected, but the sight of the three women was an awesome vision, and yes, I filled my cage.

Sophie asked, "Will someone do my back."

"My pleasure," I volunteered, and she laughed. Squeezing the sunscreen onto her, I slowly massaged it into her beautiful body, working my way down to her perfect apple ass cheeks, making sure I did not miss any area. Finally, I had her covered and she was ready to luxuriate in the warming sun. We lay in a line—me, next Sophie, then Erin, and Marie last. The sound of the ocean was soothing. Feeling the tension melt from me, I drifted off.

I wondered where Sophie and I would end up. Wherever it was, as long as we were together, I was good with it.

Conversation was sporadic and light. We ate the

hastily put together lunch and drank only water. As needed, we reapplied sunscreen on ourselves and each other. It was a lazy day that eventually had to end.

As we dressed, the self-consciousness returned to Marie and Erin. They seemed shy dressing in front of others. That surprised me with Erin, knowing she was a bisexual switch, and that she had played in public before. Perhaps her BDSM persona was her outlet, just as it was mine.

The drive back to the city was leisurely. We dropped off Marie and went back to our house to get Erin's things then took her back to her apartment.

A great day all in all. Was it the calm before the storm? More than likely.

The next morning, I woke to an insistent ringing phone. I looked. The FBI. Not a bunch I wanted to piss off completely, just irritate enough to let them know we would not be push overs. The call went as I expected. Pleasantries and then the veiled threats, which I laughed off, saying we would be visiting the San Francisco office soon, along with legal representation.

After a leisurely breakfast, I called Spencer Brooks. He'd left a message the previous day, but too late for me to call him back. He picked up on first ring.

"Good morning, Mr. Hammett. To answer your question, my associates and I…will be delighted to represent you and your colleagues. We need to have a chat before any of the unpleasantness starts. Please come to my office ASAP. The folks you will be dealing with won't wait. They will subpoena or arrest you unless we are prepared."

"Not a problem, Mr. Brooks. We will be with you shortly. Sophie Chandler and I will arrive together. Erin

Moray, Marie Lee will arrive separately."

"Excellent. I look forward to meeting you all."

"Ditto, Mr. Brooks."

Hollering out to Sophie, "We have an appointment." I called Marie and Erin to tell them to meet us at Mr. Brooks office and texted the address.

The trip over to the attorney was quiet, since we didn't know what to expect, and neither of us really trusted attorneys for multiple and varied reasons. Marie was already there, and Erin arrived soon after we were shown into a conference room as big as our entire office. Coffee was offered and accepted by all.

Mr. Brooks was not what I expected. He was approximately mid-fifties, in really decent shape, mentally and physically. He and his number two asked a lot of good questions, while a PA recorded the conversation and took notes. The meeting went well and consumed most of the morning. At the end we were all exhausted.

Mr. Brooks said he would take care of the FBI for today, but to expect to meet with them very soon, with him or an associate in attendance. explained that the process was going to take weeks, if not months to sort out. We should expect interviews and interrogations. He and his firm would be with us every step of the way.

We lunched at Kathleen Branigans Irish bar and grill, where we all agreed that we felt better knowing we had legal representation. We ate the hearty Irish fare and washed it down with Guinness and Harp.

Back in the office, we were archiving the data we had accumulated when Kenzo walked in, quickly shutting the door behind him. "I am not here and never have been."

"Great, the invisible man's here, again."

"Mas, I'm serious. Whoever you pissed off has clout. There's pressure to can parts of the investigation. I heard a rumor there are going to be articles to discredit you guys and poison the well for everyone. Can your tame journalist run interference for you?"

"We can ask. I don't want to influence her."

"It's not about influence, it's about covering your collective asses."

"Got it, Kenzo, thanks."

"See you around guys. Take care." Kenzo left us with more to think about. More thankful than ever we had Spencer Brooks in our corner.

Colleen answered on the first ring. I explained what could possibly be happening, and asked if she could do anything pre-emptive to protect us?

"Take it as done."

We had great press from her, and some of the national papers picked up on the story. Nice one, Colleen.

The next couple of weeks were as bad as Spencer said they would be. Robert Clegg, because he was the start of everything, was an FBI and IRS issue. They could fight for jurisdiction between themselves on that one.

The FBI had interviewed us separately—always with Spencer or one of his associates present. They advised us, and we all followed their advice, often to the dismay of the FBI agents conducting the interview. The agents were good, very thorough, and not really looking to go after us. They wanted to make sure the data and information we had given them was accurate, where it came from, and how it was acquired. They needed to know they could rely on it, to get convictions on the charges they were going to be bringing against multiple individuals and businesses. Of course, they didn't tell us who any of the interested parties were. They were also pissed that the media had somehow gotten a hold of the story.

It seemed the IRS didn't care where the info came from, as long as it was accurate. Sophie and Erin were drilled on that data. Erin was the point person on this one, the IRS agents were impressed with her depth of knowledge, and how the data was processed, arranged, and presented. They were looking into multiple charges against multiple individuals. One of the agents, as an aside, did mention there was usually a reward on anything the IRS recovered. That was the least of our worries.

The San Francisco Police Department would be the easiest to deal with. They were local, not federal. The murders and bodies on the bridge became a local crime, which could be neatly wrapped up, and buried as Kenzo had said it would be. So long as there was a saleable resolution, they would be happy. Neither the FBI nor IRS wanted to touch those murders. It would just muddy the waters for each of their cases. The pressure on the SFPD seemed to evaporate as more information was released to the media, from official and unofficial sources.

Mr. Spencer Brooks was worth every penny. He protected us from the authorities and ourselves. We had told him everything, which was covered under attorney client privilege. He seemed surprised we had survived. He made sure the different authorities had what they needed from us, and that we were protected from any prosecution or further scrutiny, and he got it in writing. We kept Fiend completely out of it, which he greatly appreciated.

Toward the end of our depositions with the various entities, events took an interesting, but not surprising turn. Before the two congressmen were named and indicted, Hunter Pollard and his wife, Deborah disappeared. They took off in a private plane and just vanished.

I wondered how, as they didn't have access to their secret stash of financing. Those accounts had been frozen. Sophie suggested they must have had more accounts we didn't find. If Sophie and Fiend hadn't found them, they were well hidden, probably involving Deborah's' family.

James Rivers and his wife were killed in a car accident. The accident was being investigated, but on first appearances looked like a tragic accident, although it was on a road James knew well. Accidents happen. Coincidence? Don't believe in them. I mentioned that to Kenzo. It would be a clever idea to suggest to the local police department investigating the accident, to do a thorough job. He said the FBI would investigate it because a congressman was involved. If anything turned up to suggest it wasn't an accident, it would be buried. No one wants to hear that a congressman was murdered, especially if he was as dirty as he seemed to be.

The Golden Realty Union principles were charged with fraud and money laundering, shutting that channel down. The PAC who supported the congressmen was dissolved after paying huge fines, and the primary officers were charged. Another channel for laundering political funds closed.

Anyone, who hoped the story would fade and go away, was sadly mistaken. Colleen kept digging and publishing, extending the story way beyond the normal news life cycle. Finally, out from under federal scrutiny, we let McCarrigan know it was celebration time. He organized a spa weekend in Napa Valley, fully paid by him. Everything.

Cynically, I suggested, "He'll use this as a business write off."

Sophie clapped. "I don't care. It's a cool way to celebrate."

McCarrigan sent out invitations to all and included a plus one if desired. Oso was included, but he turned the invite down, saying he didn't feel comfortable with the idea of him in a spa. McCarrigan sent him a check for what it would have cost him. The nice gesture surprised me. Marie brought Chung along, and I noticed a key on a thin chain around her neck. I smiled to myself. Neither Erin, nor Kristen wanted to bring anyone. Erin was now able to grieve for Robert, and Kristen had recently broken off a relationship and wanted alone time. That Friday all eight of us piled into a limo and were off. Lunch was Champagne and small luxury bites.

The spa was nestled into a hillside and surrounded by vineyards. Each suite was an oasis. Just what we needed. Both Sophie and I, for once, felt at ease. We dropped our belongings, stripped, and climbed into the hot tub. The hot water and jets were just what the doctor ordered. Sophie sat opposite me, relaxed, and we just smiled at each other. No conversation was necessary as we soaked for what seemed like hours.

Later, pruned fingers and other parts said enough. We used the outdoor shower to freshen up, put on the fluffy robes, and returned to the main room, to open the chilled bottle of Champagne.

Popping the cork, Sophie poured. "We made it. When Tara and I were taken. I was afraid I would never see you again. That scared me more than the pain." Her lip trembled.

We held each other for a long time, then she broke away from me. "I need more Champagne." I agreed.

The rest of the afternoon, we spent lounging in the room, cuddling, snoozing, and doing nothing. A call brought us out of our reverie. McCarrigan called to tell us the dinner plans. Getting ready, I noticed a certain key dangling from Sophie's neck. Maybe, I would get lucky, maybe not. Not knowing was part of the pleasure.

Gathering in the bar, we had drinks. Everyone was relaxed, and the atmosphere easy. Friends meeting for a weekend. Not strictly true with McCarrigan and Tara along. Surprisingly, Tara addressed that issue immediately.

"As most of you know, I did not like Mas or his associates. Our first interactions really colored my view. However, with recent events, I have had to revise my opinion, and thank you all for what you have done. This is a celebration. Let's eat."

McCarrigan added, "You all have my thanks, as well. Your actions will not be forgotten. If any of you ever need anything from me, just ask. If it's doable, it's done."

Well, that was a turn up for the books. An apology of sorts was the best we could expect from Tara. The offer from McCarrigan, that was an open-ended offer, one I hoped I'd never have to cash in.

We ate dinner and the conversation was light. Marie and Sophie picked on me, telling off-colored incidents at my expense. I didn't mind at all. McCarrigan—a good storyteller—was quite funny when he was relaxed. Tara was the most reserved but joined in the fun at the appropriate times. Chung, Erin, and Kristen were included in all the conversations, and Kristen did tell a couple of tales out of school regarding Tara, who took them good naturedly. The dinner was a long, slow affair, enjoyable, and no one was in a rush for it to end. After dinner and drinks around a log fire, we all eventually drifted apart.

Sophie, as soon as we reached our suite, said, "I have something for us."

"And that is?"

As she twirled the key on the chain around. Yes…that key. My eyes widened in anticipation. Sophie continued, "It's not what you're thinking. I considered a kink weekend, then thought better of it. I want this weekend to be us, a normal couple—well, as normal as we get. I'll never forget how good and supportive you were after we sorted out my sister's murder. I liked the feeling of the two of us. I wasn't used to it, and I've grown to love it. You make me a better me, Mas."

"I love all the Sophie's. You make me a better me—two sides of the same coin."

We said nothing else and undressed each other slowly, as if it was the first time. In bed, we explored each other's bodies, marveling at the intimacy we shared. After finally climaxing together, we fell asleep tangled in each other's limbs.

A deep dreamless sleep, a first in a long time, ended when I came around, wondering where I was. Disoriented, I saw Sophie sitting, naked, looking out over the vineyards that stretched into the distance. I watched her silently, certain I'd never tire of looking at her. A sixth sense made her turn and look at me.

She smiled. "Good morning sleepy head. You looked so peaceful I didn't want to disturb you."

"You should have woken me."

"No, we need this weekend. I have booked us massages, but not until later. Coffee?"

"Hmm, sounds good."

She brought me a mug and kissed me lightly on my forehead. The coffee was good, and I felt ready to face the day. We breakfasted on our own and enjoyed each other's company. We had the massages. My body had been in shock, so the massage therapist released so many knots in my back and shoulders that it felt first-rate afterward. I made a mental note that we should have massages on a regular basis when we returned home.

In spite of doing nothing but relaxing, the day passed quickly for us. We all met again for drinks and dinner ready to enjoy another great evening. This time, we were all even more relaxed than the previous evening. We chatted as equals, as if we'd been friends forever. Getting to know Tara and McCarrigan in a social setting was enlightening. Both of them were smart and made a good couple. We made an interesting group.

The weekend passed too quickly, and Sunday afternoon arrived like an unexpected bill. Everyone seemed happy but subdued, and the ride back to San Francisco was mostly in silence. The silence seemed to get heavier as each person left the limo. Soon it was just Sophie and I left with McCarrigan and Tara.

As we stopped at our home and stepped away from the car, McCarrigan said slowly and sincerely, "Thank you both. I meant what I said on Friday. If you ever need anything, just ask."

I answered, "Understood, and thank you."

Sophie added, "And if you need us, don't hesitate."

McCarrigan smiled his professional arrogant smile and signaled the driver to go.

We watched the limo disappear, and then we both started to speak at the same time. I said, "You go first."

"I like him, but he can be such an asshole."

"Exactly what I was thinking. Let's get inside."

With a laugh Sophie said, "Good idea. I need to lock my property up."

Back to reality with a bump, and I wouldn't change it for the world. I had that in Sophie.

Chapter Twenty-Seven

Monday arrived, and I wasn't ready for it. Wide awake, my captured cock filled the chastity cage. The pleasure of frustration, and the frustration of pleasure.

I got up, careful not to wake Sophie, made coffee, and wondered what Hammett, Chandler, and Associates had in store as we moved forward.

Now we had time to address the processing of the new partnership and begin bringing the offshore funds legally into the business to disperse from here. Marie and Chung would be able to buy their own home. I made a note to give them my realtor's name and number.

"Why didn't you wake me?" Sophie's words made me jump, startled that she'd could creep up on me that way.

"Because Mondays suck, and the longer you sleep, the less there is of Monday."

"Why thank you, kind sir, but we need to sort out the office stuff."

"I was just thinking the same thing. Would Erin do the tax stuff?"

"I don't know if she'd want to. We can ask. I'll do it. I have some other things to discuss with her, anyway."

"Such as?"

"Oh, this and that, nothing to worry about." That

worried me, what the hell did Sophie have in mind now. Whatever it was, I would find out in due time.

When we arrived at the office, as usual, Marie was already there, making a dent in the paperwork. Sophie called Erin while I called the law office we used for the partnership changes. According to them, we were good to go.

Sophie wiggled her fingers at me, and I moved in closer, to hear what she said.

"Erin will be happy to look at our accounts and check the tax implications of bringing in the offshore dollars."

"Great. That takes a load off my mind."

Most of the day, we kept busy with routine comings and goings. Later, Sophie, Marie, and I visited the law office and picked up the documents. Before the daily grind ground to a halt, Marie had a bunch of checks for me to sign, and then by the time I finished it was late afternoon.

I sat back in my chair and stretched. "We should celebrate...how about a Happy Hour Tipple."

No one turned down the suggestion and we all drank too much, but by the next morning, a smiling Marie greeted us, again and we got back on track—headaches and all.

Busy with the day-to-day stuff of running the office, our days melted into one another, and the days turned to weeks with no repercussions on us regarding the scandal that had broken in San Francisco, Sacramento, and Washington, DC. It was fun to watch the various authorities parse out the information to the media, while the political talking heads tried to explain and wriggle the information into something in their favor. The fact that one of the implicated politicians disappeared and the other died under mysterious circumstances didn't seem to surprise anyone.

Sophie used our *back door* into the SFPD to check the status of the investigation regarding the bodies on the bridge and Robert Clegg. Robert's death was written off as a robbery gone wrong by unknown perpetrators—which in a way, it was. The case around the first set of Chinese bodies was closed as a gang-related killing, and the second set went down as a copycat killing. The second two men were identified as ex-military, and the police reports noted their DNA had been flagged by certain Federal agencies, heretofore unforthcoming. If I were a betting man, my money would be on Steven being one of them, but we'd likely never know for sure.

A news item caught Sophie's eye, and she pointed it out to me. "Hunter and Deborah Pollard were picked up using Maltese passports while trying to access an account in an Eastern European bank. The extradition process has been started."

"I don't think it'll be easy to get them back to face U.S. justice."

She nodded.

I shook my head. "Not our problem."

Life finally returned to what passed as normal for us. The SFPD returned our weapons with no follow up. We collected our fees from McCarrigan and Tara. She attached a handwritten note, which was a nice touch. Tara kept Oso on as her driver—good steady job was exactly what he needed. All the bills had been settled for us, or by us. Everyone paid.

To both of our delight, the Dominant/submissive

part of our lifestyle resurfaced, and we indulged enthusiastically. Our bodies appreciated the biweekly massages meant to relax and rejuvenate our well-used muscles.

Sophie and I researched chastity cages and agreed on the stainless-steel design similar to the one I already had, but with the integrated lock. That was as good as it got, cage wise.

Sophie had other ideas. Her eyes twinkled when she suggested I get a Prince Albert piercing. "Just think," she said, "when you're healed, I can lock the ring to the end of the cage."

A thrill traveled up my spine. There would be no getting out of that combination without her permission.

Later that week, Erin came by with great news. She'd decided to continue with her PhD and promised she'd consult with us on tax stuff. "And Mas, there's more surprising news. Your company will be getting a percentage of the funds recovered. I don't know what the amount will be yet, but you'll be contacted by the IRS."

I was speechless, until she asked, "How will you deal with it?"

Together, Sophie and I said, "Split it evenly!" That brought out happy laughter from all of us.

"I thought so. I just wanted verification." Erin grinned and bobbed her head in confirmation.

Well, well, so Hammett, Chandler, and Associates would be getting a reward for monies recovered. How about that?

We talked for a while longer setting up future appointments to meet. Marie and Chung were still in the process of house hunting, and with some of the funds now available, their excitement grew.

Life was good, and I intended to enjoy it. Tomorrow isn't promised to any of us.

A word about the author...

Richard Albion lives in Sarasota with his wife (who is the pillar supporting him) two grown children out of the nest, and multiple rescue animals to make the nest better.

He is a European melting pot, exceptional cook, clothing designer, artist, and writer of erotic Fem-Dom fiction. Graduate of both U.K. and U.S. colleges. Retired Sales professional now engaged in working on the artistic side of life. Enjoys travel, volunteering, martial arts. Cannot live too far from the ocean-its genetic.

Richard's novels are contemporary, erotic BDSM, Fem Dom, love stories. The first book series includes "Maid to Serve," "Maid for Service," and "Maid in Service"—track one man's journey into submission and discovery of physical and psychological satisfaction, but most of all love. "Bodies in the Bay" is a mystery/thriller with erotic BDSM overtones. Also available is a gender flip, the "Mistress of 'O'."

"O" is now male. Waiting on Siren, one man's journey into submission. The latest book, Secrets Unveiled, is a mystery/thriller with romance and revenge.

Thank you for purchasing
this publication of The Wild Rose Press, Inc.

For questions or more information
contact us at
info@thewildrosepress.com.

The Wild Rose Press, Inc.
www.thewildrosepress.com